HOUSEWIFE
IN TROUBLE

Alison Penton Harper lives in rural
Northamptonshire with her husband
and two daughters.

Also by Alison Penton Harper

Housewife Down
Housewife Up
Housewife On Top
Housewife In Love

ALISON PENTON HARPER

HOUSEWIFE
IN TROUBLE

PAN BOOKS

First published 2010 by Pan Books
an imprint of Pan Macmillan, a division of Macmillan Publishers Limited
Pan Macmillan, 20 New Wharf Road, London N1 9RR
Basingstoke and Oxford
Associated companies throughout the world
www.panmacmillan.com

ISBN 978-0-330-46156-6

3 5 7 9 8 6 4 2

A CIP catalogue record for this book is available
from the British Library.

Typeset by SetSystems Ltd, Saffron Walden, Essex
Printed in the UK by CPI Mackays, Chatham ME5 8TD

Visit **www.panmacmillan.com** to read more about all our books
and to buy them. You will also find features, author interviews and
news of author events, and you can sign up for e-newsletters
so that you're always first to hear about our new releases.

For Jonathan
(not that he'll ever bloody notice)

Marriage isn't a word – it's a sentence.

King Vidor, caption from his silent film
The Crowd, *1926*

ORIENTATION

Season five in the *Housewife* saga, and for those of you who have no idea what's going on (and let's face it, who does?), here's a quick whistle-stop tour of the situation so far . . .

Julia, my big sister, rudely destroyed my wedding by going into labour four weeks early. Married to David (nice guy, perfect for walking all over).

Sara, Julia's nuclear-powered PA, was catapulted to the dizzying heights of business partner. Married to Dudley (woefully lacking in the penis department).

Leoni, my best friend, failed to sell her children on eBay after receiving no bids. Married to Marcus (praying daily for a premature death).

Sally, my gay neighbour, politely declined Leoni's offer of the tradesman's entrance. Married to Paul (the crumbliest, flakiest man in the world).

So there we have it. A nice little cosy clutch of wedded friends, all busily ignoring the overwhelming statistic suggesting half of them will end up in the divorce courts. It's little wonder I once vowed never to marry again. Trouble is, Rick's really not the kind of bloke who takes no for an answer. As Britney Spears once said – whoops, I did it again.

Chapter One

THE BIG M

IT'S NOT EASY being married. For a start, you're expected to live together, and if there's one thing I know, it's that women really shouldn't be forced to suffer the indignity of sharing their space with a man. Like asking a cobra to shack up with a mongoose, trouble is bound to ensue. Yet, with the benefit of hindsight and one disastrous marriage firmly deposited in the piggybank of experience, I somehow came to the stunning conclusion that it would be a good idea to have another crack at The Big M. After all, you never know. Rick and I might just turn into one of those crusty old couples who pop up on the local news bulletin every now and then, celebrating their double-diamond wedding anniversary, putting the success of their longevity down to salty porridge every morning and plenty of torrid tortoise sex in the afternoons.

Why some of us have that inexplicable urge to super-glue ourselves permanently to one partner is nothing short of bizarre when you really think about it. We all know that the whole thing is probably going to come horribly unravelled at some point, yet we insist on picking up the crusading flag of blind commitment and giving it a shot anyway. I know very well that the day may well come when I want to stab Rick in the eyes with a fork or pour boiling water in his ears while he's asleep. That I will look at him across the breakfast table one morning thinking *I hate you*, and will feel great empathy for that woman who stirred a generous dollop of antifreeze seasoning into her husband's curry on their seventh wedding anniversary. Maybe he'll be looking right back at me thinking exactly the same thing.

It's a gamble, whichever way you weigh it, which is why I have decided that this time things will be different. This time, I will learn from my previous mistakes and determine to put right all those wrongs I fell foul of the last time. In order to break the marriage-from-hell cycle, I have decided to completely reinvent myself, stripping away all those old-fashioned notions I used to hold about marriage being little more than legalized domestic slavery with the odd drunken bunch of petrol station flowers thrown in, and replacing them with a thoroughly modern, positive outlook. I intend to be highly independent, devastatingly interesting, impervious to housework guilt, and a regular stick of dynamite between the sheets (provided I've loosened my moral elastic with a couple of stiff gins beforehand). According to my homespun theory, my husband will be so busy trying to keep up with me that he won't have time to behave like an arsehole, and I will thus have a successful, fulfilling marriage, culminating in a stomach-churning piece on the local news on the eve of our billionth wedding anniversary, him gazing at me lovingly with no teeth, me muttering crazily that I've never seen him before in my life.

Thus, I proudly present to you the new me: Helen Wilton, superwife in the making. Anyway, it seems like a good plan, seeing as we've only been married five minutes.

'MORNIN', BABE!' A champagne cork flew across the bedroom and ricocheted off the wall.

'What's all this?' I hauled myself up from the pillows, bravely unconcerned about the frightful state of my hair. This in itself was something of a breakthrough. Only a week ago, I was still sneaking off to the bathroom before Rick woke up in order to carry out a bit of basic maintenance so that he wouldn't be faced with *Tales from the Crypt* the moment he opened his eyes. A quick run-through with the gas-powered hot-brush secreted under the sink and a swoosh of Listerine later, I would then creep back into bed and pretend to be fast asleep with naturally tousled locks and unfeasibly fresh breath. Unsurprisingly, after a couple of weeks of this perverse behaviour, I was so knackered that I overslept two mornings in a row and woke to greet him in all my gruesome glory. Ask me if Rick noticed. Well, of course he bloody didn't. Men, eh? I don't know why we bother.

'It's our seven-week anniversary,' Rick announced, pouring a couple of flutes and handing one to me. 'Cheers, babe!' Clink, slurp, belch.

'Great.' I stared into my glass, wishing it were a cup of tea instead. I'm sure I'm getting an ulcer. 'So we're going to do this every week, are we?'

So far, we have celebrated countless similarly dubious noteworthy events, each with a flimsier excuse than the last. Quite what he'll do if we actually make it through our first year I really don't know, but I'm thinking something along the lines of the closing ceremony of the Beijing Olympics.

'Yep.' He scooched up on the bed beside me and topped up his glass. 'Like I told you, from here on in I'm gonna spend the rest of my life making you happy.' He pulled a fat cigar from his dressing-gown pocket, stuck it between his teeth and struck a match against the flowerpot on the bedside table.

'I'm already happy,' I smiled, wondering if I'd clocked up sufficient marriage-miles to mention the issue of his smoking in bed yet. 'But my liver's threatening to go to Injury Lawyers4U if I don't let up on the champagne breakfasts.' I watched him suck the yellow flame into his Cohiba, stoking it along with a few heavy pulls before extinguishing the match with a flick of his fingers and dropping it in the ashtray balanced precariously on his fur-lined stomach.

'This is gonna be a major feature of your new life, babe.' He took a long drag and scratched his armpit. 'So you might as well get used to it.'

You mean, like all the hundreds of other things I was going to have to get used to? Like the awful concept of someone else being in the house while I make a special sortie to the furthest bathroom to answer a call of nature, having left every radio and television on in the house to muffle any unladylike sound effects? Like not being able to stretch and yawn like Shergar after festering on the sofa in front of *Bargain Hunt* all morning? I meant what I said earlier about men and women living together. How this little detail could have slipped my mind beggars belief – that I would henceforth be living under the same roof as Rick, sharing the same bed, eating the same food at the same time from the same table. Once we got back from Vegas, having done the undoable deed, the realization of it came upon me like a python dropping out of a tree.

'You all right, babe?' Rick took the glass from my hand and put it aside. I tried not to stare at him, this person who I had promised to spend the rest of my life with, a man with all the subtleties of a brick coming through a plate-glass window.

The wedding in itself should have been fair warning of things to come – queuing up, red-eyed, in a rental car on the Las Vegas Strip, fighting jet lag, waiting our turn at the Tunnel of Love drive-thru wedding chapel behind a pair of Hell's Angels, possibly of the same sex. Although the sign outside had proudly advertised the availability of a quick in-and-out jobbie at forty bucks, Rick had really pushed the boat out and treated us to the full enchilada. Before I'd had time to question whether or not this was an auspicious start to a lifelong partnership, I found myself cruising through the Tunnel of Vows – a cross between an outsized jet wash and a home-constructed carport, with faux Roman columns and a huge mural on the ceiling proclaiming 'I Can't Live Without You', flanked by airbrushed cherubs with eerily Disneyesque faces. As we exchanged the standard promises in front of the man in the bulletproof booth, who might well have been a car park attendant for all I knew, a rhinestoned Elvis impersonator slid out from the shadows and began warbling 'Love Me Tender' as though his life depended on it, curling his lip and finishing off with a couple of forward pelvic thrusts with windmill arms to give us the full effect of his spangly tassels. A few minutes later, we emerged from the other side of the carport as man and wife. Uh-huh-huh.

The pillows rustled and Rick gave me a little nudge, reminding me that he had probably said something, but all I could think about was what he might have looked like in that Elvis outfit. A cold shiver slid down my spine and I suddenly felt terribly self-conscious about my hair.

'You look a bit, well, you know . . .' He twitched his cigar, a ribbon of smoke curling expectantly from its tip. I touched my head apologetically.

'Messy?'

'Nah!' He ruffled his unruly tufts, dropping ash all over the pillows. 'We look fucking great in the morning, and don't you ever let anyone tell you otherwise.'

'It's just so much to get used to,' I said. 'Sometimes I wake up and get that discombobulated feeling for a split second, you know, like when you come round in a hotel room on holiday and you can't remember where you are? It's still a bit weird, us being married. Don't you think?'

'It's gonna be brill.' He put his arm around me and squashed my face uncomfortably into his chest. That man doesn't know his own strength. 'Like you said, this time is gonna be for keeps. I promise never to neglect you or take you for granted, babe. There's nothing on this earth you could do to make me feel any different about you. You can tell me anything. Anything at all.

We'll face whatever life throws at us together, you an' me.' He squeezed his point home, temporarily closing off my windpipe. 'There'll be nothing we don't know about each other.'

'Really?' I mumbled non-committally.

Don't get me wrong, but this didn't sound like an altogether Nobel Prize-winning idea. The whole point of getting married, as far as I was concerned, was that it would be, in effect, a bit like wiping the slate clean. Or like clocking a car, depending on your point of view. No matter what had gone before, it didn't count, so long as you both stuck to the rules from the second you said 'I do'. I like to think of it like that moment on sports day at primary school when you got tied by the ankle to a kid you didn't particularly like at the start of the three-legged race. It was all about finding an acceptable way to rub along together, getting into a rhythm and trying not to come a cropper in the process. Anyway, I had absolutely no intention of spilling my numerous beans to Rick, or anyone else, for that matter. Let sleeping dogs lie, or, come to think of it, never mind the dogs – just lie.

'Absolutely,' he said.

'But don't you think a woman should retain just a little bit of mystery?'

'Mystery? You?' He laughed, letting out a huge, aromatic cloud of class A Cohiba. 'I think it's a bit late for all that, babe!'

'Don't be so bloody rude!' I pulled away from him and reached for my drink. If this conversation kept going the way it was heading, I might as well start dulling the pain now. 'There could be all sorts of surprising things you don't know about me.'

'Oh yeah?' He tried not to look amused. 'Like what, for example?'

'Like none of your business.' I took a few hesitant sips and tried to look all mysterious.

'I thought so.' He effected another long pull on his stogie, chipped it in the ashtray and slid down beneath the covers. The duvet rustled as he thrashed around beneath it. 'You might not realize it, babe, but you've got one of those faces.' Rick emerged from the bed heap, naked but for a smile, and flung his robe to the carpet. 'Let's just say you'd make a rubbish poker player.' He winked at me. 'Give us a kiss, missus.'

'No.'

'Go on.' I felt his hand wandering. 'You know you want to.'

'How could you possibly know what I want?' I slapped his hand away. Bloody cheek. 'Just because we're married doesn't mean you've suddenly become some sort of mind-reader.'

'Yes I have.' He started nuzzling my neck, reached behind his back for the duvet and pulled it over our heads. 'You're my other half, in every way.' His kiss was tender and warm. 'There'll be no secrets between us.'

'Mmm,' I murmured, curling my arms about his neck.

No secrets? Are you kidding? It was a good job he couldn't see the whites of my eyes.

Chapter Two

BE CAREFUL WHAT
YOU WISH FOR

WHILE WE'RE on the subject of life-changing experiences, I had always assumed that my sister and I would go through life keeping each other company in our childlessness. (Quick explanation: she couldn't, I hadn't.) It was a cosy little arrangement in an unspoken sort of way, and by the time my eggs started shrivelling, I felt relatively confident that I had made the right choices. There's more to life than breeding anyway, even though our hormones will do their damnedest to try and convince us otherwise.

11

I remember having gone through a phase when I used to think about having a baby all the time. I suppose it had started at some point in my late twenties, by which time I was living in the purgatory of my first marriage. Whether it was my biological clock tapping on my shoulder or an insane notion that somehow having a baby might improve the hideous situation I had found myself in, I'm not entirely sure. Suffice to say that I never did anything about it. Between you and me, I think I had been plagued by a latent fear that if I went and produced a boy, it might just turn out like its bloody awful father. A real *We Need to Talk About Kevin* moment, if you know what I mean. So I dithered for another year or two, then we stopped having sex altogether because he'd found some other woman's grill to stick his kippers under. So that was pretty much that on the baby front.

I got over it soon enough. No point in crying over spilt milk. Sure, there were some days when I felt a certain yearning, a certain emptiness, but those days became fewer and farther between as the years slid by. Perhaps I'd never really been that maternal in the first place. I have always felt that parenthood was a young person's game anyway, yet, in this topsy-turvy world, who's to say? Sometimes I see couples out and about with a child and I think to myself, *They must be the grandparents, right?*

In a bizarre twist of fate, Julia found herself lying on

a bunk in the Chelsea and Westminster hospital two months ago giving birth at the age of forty-three to an eye-watering nine-pounder. Well. Talk about moving the goalposts. Being a mere slip of a girl at forty and a half, does this mean that I will now be expected to take my sister's lead and follow suit? With a brand-spanking new husband in tow, it's not as though I have the excuse of no fertilizer any more, and, judging by the five children Rick has already spawned, there aren't any quality control issues in that department either.

It may sound silly, but Julia having an unexpected baby has had an alarmingly disturbing effect on me. It's raised all sorts of issues that I thought I had dealt with long ago – you know, the perennial questions about whether or not I'd live to regret my past decisions. Maybe, had I not seen at point-blank range what having a baby can do to a woman's life, I might actually have been tempted to put one of my eggs through its paces. I can't have that many of them left, and the few that remain must be getting pretty close to their use-by date. Since peaking the hill and starting their downward descent, my hormones have remained tight-lipped on the subject, and, despite having been thrust into baby-land courtesy of my new nephew, I can honestly say that I just don't feel the urge to have one myself. I'm too bloody old, for a start, no matter what anyone says. I keep getting flashes of Julia, in her fifties, hanging around outside the gates of the local primary school looking like the witch from the gingerbread house in Hansel and Gretel.

There is no doubt that Julia's pregnancy sent her doolally, and, as for her figure – well, had I not seen the carnage for myself I would never have believed it. We're talking the kind of decimation that makes television presenters say, 'If you're of a nervous disposition, look away now.' There is also the well-reported case of mad Leoni, who used to be relatively normal before she had the twins. That she went on to have a third child was simply unlucky. Had it not been for that fourth Martini and a timely power cut one New Year's Eve, there's no way she would have let Marcus play hide the sausage.

As they say, be careful what you wish for. It's been two whole months since Julia brought her miraculous child into the world, and I've never seen her so miserable.

'Will you look at that?' Julia flung her *Grazia* across her kitchen table at me, seemingly unaware of the two-inch grey-flecked roots peering out from the crown of her untended hair. 'Nicole Kidman, six weeks after giving birth and ten pounds lighter than she was before she got pregnant. Bitch.' She ran her hands mournfully across her bulging tummy, shrouded beneath a pair of tracksuit bottoms that had seen better days a long time ago. Oh, how the mighty have fallen.

'Early doors,' I said to her. 'And Nicole Kidman

probably had an army of dieticians and personal trainers swarming around her before she hit the delivery table.' A piercing wail screeched through the fleet of baby-listening devices set up in every room. Julia visibly wilted. 'It's OK.' I wiped my hands on the tea towel and threw it aside. 'I'll get it.'

Upstairs, Frank Junior was lying indignantly on his back in the bassinet set up beside Julia's bed, squirming angrily, fists clenched, his mouth wide open and wobbling as he filled his lungs again, ready for the next onslaught.

'Sshhh.' I gathered him up, wrapping the blanket around his sturdy little body, snuggling him against my shoulder while I went into my regular pacing motion, up and down the bedroom, pointing to the birds outside the window, murmuring little noises to quell his protests. He seemed to stall for a second, then unleashed an almighty scream right in my ear.

'Sshhh,' bounce, bounce. 'It's OK,' jiggle, jiggle. 'Don't cry, Frankie.'

'*Waaaaaaaaaaaah!*'

It was nearly an hour before he exhausted all the air in the universe and fell asleep again.

'Thanks, Helen.' Julia hadn't budged from the old leather armchair by the fridge; there was an air of emptiness about her. 'I didn't get much sleep last night. He's been grizzly ever since I packed in the feeding.' She brought her hands to her war-torn breasts. 'Christ.

I couldn't take much more of that. You should see the state of my knockers. They might as well have gone through a mangle.'

'They look all right to me.' I smiled. 'Be patient. You'll soon be back to your former glory.'

Julia burst into tears. Again. That was the fourth time since I'd got there this morning. I took a deep breath and switched back into tea-and-sympathy mode, which, I have to say, was becoming increasingly difficult in the face of her violent mood swings. It's hard work trying to console somebody who cannot be consoled. Everybody knows that new mothers can be prone to a bit of post-traumatic stress disorder, or shell shock as it used to be called, but ten weeks down the line I was beginning to wonder if this might not be something more serious. In any case, I was fast running out of platitudes and rapidly beginning to bore myself.

'Hey.' I bobbed down in front of her like an air stewardess, resting my hands on her knees. 'Don't beat yourself up, eh? You can't expect miracles overnight.'

'Huh!' she snivelled with a wry smile, fishing a soggy tissue out of her sleeve.

'It's OK.' Here we go again. 'Your hormones are still all over the place. You've got to give yourself time to recover your strength.' Blah blah blah. 'Cut yourself some slack and stop pushing yourself so hard.' Yawn. 'You've only just had a baby, and now is not the time to start fretting over a mere matter of cosmetics.' I made a pointed effort not to glance at her roots. Or her untidy eyebrows. Or the rainforest ankles poking out from the bottom of her soggy joggers. 'You're a gorgeous, vibrant woman in the prime of your life.' Deep-eyed sincerity, choking back an irresistible urge to yell into her face, *Pull yourself together, woman*. 'And in another couple of months, you'll be wondering what all the fuss was about.'

I know that this is probably a terrible thing to say, but there is a tiny, shameful sliver of me that has enjoyed a certain *Schadenfreude* in the nose-diving of Julia's show-stopping beauty. The fact that Julia looks the way she does (i.e. amazing) and I don't is one of life's little unfair ironies. She's never had to 'come to terms with' her appearance like some of us have. She's never stood in front of the mirror and pulled at her face and flesh, trying to imagine what she would look like if she were taller/slimmer/less hamster-cheeked. She's never gone to the hairdresser and hoped, totally irrationally, that a new hairdo would somehow herald a miraculous transformation. She's never bloody well had to. So forgive me if I sound less sympathetic towards my big sister than I perhaps ought to, but I firmly believe that all women of outstanding natural beauty should be subjected to at least one dose of ugliness in their lives, if only to teach them a little humility.

The telephone started ringing. Julia made no attempt to rise towards it.

'I've got it,' I said (again). 'Hello?' A familiar voice flew down the line. 'Mum?' Julia's head jerked up sharply and she waved her tissue in a firm *no*.

'Helen?' Mum sounded surprised, nay, disappointed that I should have answered the phone.

'Correctamundo.'

'Where's Julia?'

'She's asleep.'

'What? At half past eleven in the morning?'

'Yes, Mum.'

'Is she ill?'

'No, Mum. Just tired. She was up half the night with Frankie.'

'Hmph,' she said. 'Well, that's what happens when you go in for all this feeding-on-demand nonsense. If she had got that baby into a proper routine like I told her to, he'd be sleeping through the night by now and she wouldn't be—' I put the receiver down quietly on the worktop and filled the kettle, switched it on and got the coffee things out of the cupboard, rolling my eyes at Julia, then cut us a couple of rounds of sandwiches, taking my time before finally picking the phone up again, the mother still in full flow '—must be less than half her age, and he's gone and bought a motorbike, of all things. Your father said that he's perfectly entitled to remarry, but you know, she doesn't speak a word of English.'

'Who?' My interest inadvertently piqued, the question was out of my mouth before I could stop myself.

'Have you not been listening to a word I've said?'

'Sorry, Mum. I was momentarily distracted. I thought I heard the baby crying.'

'That's because his mother's asleep in the middle of the morning and thoroughly neglecting him,' she sniffed. 'Is she still feeding him herself?'

'Er . . .' I shrugged at Julia, pointed to the phone, then gave one of my zongers a quick squeeze. Julia shot me a warning glance and nodded. 'Yep. I think so.'

'Because it's very important if she wants to get her shape back. Heaven only knows she'll have her work cut out for her there. My waistline was never the same after Julia arrived. Then you came along.' She sighed protractedly.

'Yes, Mum.' Oh, give it a rest, Mother. Nobody cares any more. 'Shall I get her to give you a ring a bit later?'

'I suppose so. Although she'll no doubt forget. Tell her I've arranged for Mrs Critchley to do the church flowers whenever she's ready for me to come and help out. Your father will drive me and I can stay for as long as she wants me.'

'OK. I'll tell her.'

'As soon as she's got that baby on a bottle, I'll be on my way. Now go and wake her up and tell her to stop shilly-shallying. A child doesn't raise itself, you know.'

'Yes, Mum.'

She hung up.

'Let me guess,' Julia said. 'Dad's finally had enough and decided to hang himself in the garden shed, and she's moaning because he didn't use the right sort of rope.'

'You wish.' I topped up the cafetière. 'She's got her suitcase packed and is planning to invade.'

'What? *Here*?'

'Yep. Repel borders.'

'Oh dear God in heaven.' Julia deflated. 'That's all I bloody need.'

The green lights on the baby listener whirled into a flashing arc, the first snuffles rapidly reaching a red crescendo as Frank Junior loosened up his foghorn lungs and tried to bring the house down.

'I've got it,' I said cheerily, my smile enforced.

'There are some bottles made up in the fridge.' Julia thumbed towards it. 'Just sling one of them in the microwave for twenty seconds and shove it in the noisy end.'

Being a dutiful citizen, I didn't pretend not to have noticed the nuclear explosion in Frankie's nappy like his dad usually does. It's one of their parental bugbears already, as Julia has told me several times over. David doesn't mind dealing with a wet one, but anything else and he suddenly loses all sense of smell and has to dash off to attend to something urgent in the garage. I've seen Julia scowling at him, no doubt plotting some dastardly revenge. Frank Junior put on his usual howling display of indignation while I snapped on the gas mask and dealt with the fallout, then as soon as he was powdered and popped into a fresh nappy, he gurgled happily and gave me a big gummy smile.

'Better?' I tickled his pudgy chin. 'I've got a nice warm bottle of artificial milk ready for you in the kitchen. It's made in a factory by robots. Isn't that amazing?' I eased his chubby little legs into a clean Babygro. 'They get it out of a cow, then do scientific things to it so that it doesn't kill you, then they shove it in a tin can and send it all to Boots!' He looked at me suspiciously. 'What do you think about that?' I blew a raspberry on his tummy while he grabbed a handful of my hair. 'OK, let go of auntie's hair now. Ow, ow, ouch!' He yanked at it happily and kicked one of his legs right into my epiglottis.

'Does his nappy need changing?' Julia stood up wearily.

'Nope. All done.' I took the bottle from her hand. 'You just relax and leave it to me.'

After making a bit of a hash of it at the first few attempts, when I was still too nervous to exercise a firm hand and just stick the thing in his mouth, I now like to think of myself as something of an expert when it comes to feeding time. Tea towel over the shoulder, baby wedged in the lap, and we're away. I snaffled Julia's comfortable chair while her back was turned and proudly demonstrated my part-time parenting skills while she hung around and looked on.

'Funny, isn't it?' she said after a while.

'What?'

'The way life turns out sometimes.' She looked at us oddly, as though trying to assess the whole concept of this new person and his impact on the world she had once known. 'I never really thought about how I would feel after he was born.'

'Ecstatic,' I reminded her. 'This isn't a new handbag, Julia. We can't take it back to Selfridges for a refund if you change your mind.'

'I know.' She poured herself another coffee from the lukewarm pot. 'But it's like I can't remember anything about my life before he arrived, as though none of it was really me. It's the weirdest thing. You know, sometimes I find myself just wandering around the house like a fart in a trance.'

'I thought all women did that.'

'I've got no energy. No enthusiasm for anything. If somebody came up to me right now and threatened to cut my head off, I wouldn't give a toss. I don't even know what I was thinking of.'

'What on earth do you mean?' I tried to keep my voice light and breezy, not wanting to communicate anything of my concern to the babe in arms. They're like tiny little radars, you know. I read about it in a book. Julia didn't answer. Instead she just stood there, pressing the coffee cup to her lips, observing us closely. 'Look,' I said. 'I don't know if you've noticed, Julia, but you've been mighty out of sorts lately. I realize that it's perfectly normal to suffer from a little bout of the baby blues after giving birth, but have you ever thought about whether or not you might be suffering from post-natal depression?' Julia raised an unplucked eyebrow. 'I don't mean to worry you, but it doesn't take a rocket scientist to see that you're not firing on all four.'

'You said it was early days,' she said dryly.

'Yes . . .' I back-pedalled hard, trying another tack. 'But you're not showing any signs of improvement, are you? In fact,' – gulp – 'if anything, I think you might be getting a little bit worse.' Given that Julia is the kind of woman who hates being presented with a problem without at least some suggestion of a solution, I quickly added, 'Maybe you should make an appointment to see your doctor and see what she's got to say about it.'

Instead of telling me to mind my own business, as she usually does, Julia shrugged an open-ended response and said nothing. An awkward silence crept between us for a little while, so I went back to concentrating on the feeding.

'Who do you think he looks like?' she said.

'You,' I replied, on account of Frankie's dark head of hair and deep blue-black eyes. David is as fair as they come, so his genes never really stood much of a chance against Julia's dominant pool.

'Mmm.' She cocked her head at us. 'Maybe. Maybe not. I don't see it myself.'

'I could come along with you, if you want. You know, if that would make it any easier. It's nothing to be embarrassed about. Loads of women get it. It's just a chemical imbalance.'

'Oh,' she said. 'We're back onto that are we?'

'If that's what it is, then you really ought to get some help.' My textbook crash course sprang into effect. 'If it goes untreated, you might just end up in the loony bin eating insects like granddad. Ask Brooke Shields. Better to nip it in the bud.'

'What if I were to tell you that it's definitely not post-natal depression?'

'Well . . .' I started nervously, unconvinced by her steely expression. Frankie let out a series of small, satisfied grumbles, his fingers tinkering with the edge of the bottle. 'Then I suppose I'd have to suggest that you're probably in denial, which is a classic early symptom of most serious forms of emotional illness. You know – "There's nothing wrong with me".' I imitated a depressed person pretending not to be depressed. God knows, after the life I've had, I can give an Oscar-winning performance when it comes to putting on a brave face.

'Oh, I don't know about that.' Julia looked as though she might be about to start bawling again and gritted her teeth against the onslaught. 'Looking back on this last year or so, I'd say there's plenty wrong with me. Maybe if I had bothered to get my head examined before this whole thing started, I wouldn't be in this mess.' She went to the drinks cupboard, took out a bottle of brandy and poured herself a glass. 'Too late to turn the clock back now.' She took an unapologetically large gulp, grimacing as she swallowed, then stared emptily at the table. 'I should have known all along that this would end in tears.'

'Julia?' She seemed not to hear me. 'Listen,' I said, this time more urgently. 'Everything's going to be all right.' The sight of her distress turned my stomach over. She's supposed to be the strong one. You can throw anything at Julia and she won't even flinch. It's me that falls to pieces and chases mice around in my head. 'We'll go to the doctor together this afternoon and get you whatever help you need. Counselling, maybe. Perhaps some short-term antidepressants—'

She cut me off with a small, cold laugh.

'Pills?' She shook her head. 'There ain't no pill in the world to fix this.'

'What?' I said.

She stared into her glass, then threw the remaining brandy down in one go, a small, bitter smile creeping across her face.

'Julia! For heaven's sake, what is it?'

'Forget it.' Julia put the empty glass down on the table and pushed it away. 'It doesn't matter any more.'

Chapter Three

CAUSE FOR ALARM

'DOES HE FART in bed yet?' Leoni had slowed to her usual snail-pace shuffle-shopping speed.

'No,' I said. 'I've been spared that particular delicacy so far.'

'Give it another week, tops. Men will only clench their buttocks for so long, then it's El Niño and you wake up in a World War Two trench filled with mustard gas. Oooh! That's nice!' Leoni wrenched her arm from mine and picked up a wafer-thin, delicately etched champagne flute. 'How about a couple of dozen of these?'

'With you around?' I took it from her and placed it carefully back on the display. 'I think we'd better stick to the plastic picnic cups.'

Despite Rick's insistence that nobody bother with wedding presents for us (boo, spoilsport), we had received the usual array of questionable offerings from friends and acquaintances who felt it would be rude to comply, although why anyone would have thought we needed a matching pair of ceramic greyhounds I really couldn't say. The silver spoons were nice, so I kept those, but as for the rest of the stuff, well, there are only so many Lean, Mean Grilling Machines a girl can use. Thankfully, quite a few of the rejects seemed to have come from the same no-imagination-required department store, so I'd sent them back and picked up a nice fat credit note to squander at my leisure instead.

'What about plates?' Leoni suggested.

'Nope. Rick's got loads.'

'You mean, *we've* got loads.'

There it was again. The Royal We. The constant reminder that I must obliterate the notion of first person singular from my vocabulary.

'Sorry. *We've* got loads.'

'Better.' She linked her arm back through mine. 'You'll soon get the hang of it, you know – *we* only drink semi-skimmed milk, *we* watch *Midsomer Murders*, *we* hate children. Before you know it, you won't even feel sick when you say it. How about a nice set of Le Creuset pans?' She pointed to a stack of pretty pink ones languishing under a promotional discount banner.

'Have you ever tried to lift one of those things up when it's full of vegetables?'

Leoni decided to conduct an experiment right there in the middle of John Lewis, placing one pan inside another then picking it up from the display table. 'Holy shitzenspuds,' she groaned. 'I think I've just given myself a hernia.'

'Exactly. Anyway, I've already got a set of those at home and they've never seen the light of day.' I realized my mistake immediately and flinched inwardly. 'By home,' I explained, 'I mean at the flat. Not home, as in Rick's house.'

'*Our* house.'

'Oh, whatever,' I sighed. 'It's all so bloody final. How do I know I haven't made a horrible mistake?'

'Did he make you sign a prenup?'

'No! Of course he didn't!'

'Then, believe me, you haven't made a mistake.' Leoni stopped at a row of silver Alessi egg timers shaped a bit like chicken heads and picked each one up to give it a quick wind. 'For a start, he's loaded, which means that you're guaranteed a major consolation prize either way. And he's got a big wanger.'

'Leoni!' I glanced around quickly to check she hadn't been overheard, catching the eye of the sales assistant hanging on Leoni's every word.

'What?' she said indignantly. 'Everyone knows it's true. Helga told us at the wedding after she'd had a

28

few voddies. Mind you, it took us a while to work out what she was talking about. What did she call it?' Leoni frowned and trawled her goldfish memory.

'*Moskovskaya,*' I mumbled.

'That's it!' She put her finger on the tip of her nose. 'Moscow sausage!'

'Oh, for God's sake. Is nothing sacred?'

'What you really ought to be asking yourself is how come his cleaning lady's seen his growler.' Leoni gave a final twist to the last of the timers and put it back on the shelf with the others.

'She's Russian. She likes spying on people.'

'I'd have a word with her about that if I were you.'

'No chance. I'm not sick of living yet.'

'True,' she nodded. 'I have nightmares about meeting Helga in a dark alleyway with a poison-tipped umbrella. Anyway, things could be a whole lot worse. You could be married to a twat like Marcus. I keep hoping that the high-cholesterol diet's going to kick in any day and he'll keel over with a fatal heart attack. I'm doing him a king prawn curry tonight, followed by bread and butter pudding with extra blood-clotting cream.'

'You're *cooking*?' My God, this was news indeed. Leoni's the kind of person who burns soup. In the microwave.

'Don't be daft.' She tapped the side of her nose. 'Mum's been to Iceland. If he caught me actually making something from scratch, then he'd *really* be suspicious.'

It's hard to know sometimes whether or not Leoni's joking. Poor Marcus spends most of his time tiptoeing around on eggshells, trying to stay out of the direct line of fire in case Leoni should train her blunderbuss away from the kids for a few seconds and point it at him instead.

'I just don't know,' I sighed. 'Maybe I rushed into all this a bit too quickly. Everything happened so fast. One minute it was just a bit of fun, like trying on a dress you have no intention of buying, and the next . . .' I flapped my arms against my sides in explanation. 'I don't even feel like we had a proper wedding.'

'Oh, come on!' Leoni said. 'It's hardly Rick's fault that Julia decided to go into labour halfway though the ceremony.'

'We should have rearranged it properly instead of running off like that.'

'But you have to admit,' she insisted, 'it was a pretty romantic gesture.'

'Looked a lot better on paper,' I said regretfully. 'The reality of it was far less glamorous, I can tell you. It just didn't seem right, getting hitched in a car wash, no family, no friends. We haven't even got a bloody wedding photo.'

'Don't worry about it, pickle. Just remember – if it all goes tits up, you can jump on a plane to Tijuana, grab a quickie divorce and trouser half his bank account. It's hardly a big chin-scratcher, is it?'

'Thanks,' I said. 'But right now I'd rather concentrate on trying not to feel like an intruder in Rick's house.' Leoni glared at me. 'Sorry. *Our* house.' We moved along to the frying pans. 'It's just so bloody creepy, especially when I'm there on my own, like nothing is mine and I don't really belong.'

'Still?' She frowned. 'You really ought to tackle that, Helen. It's not normal. Why don't you get the decorators in and do something really radical? I'm sure Rick won't mind.' She instantly warmed to her idea. 'In fact, I could give you a hand if you like!' Oh God, no. Leoni turns into Idi Amin the moment colour swatches are mentioned, and I'm just not emotionally strong enough to get involved in another one of her white-knuckled home improvement projects right now. 'We could go through loads of catalogues and put together a fantastic new look!' she enthused. 'By the time we've finished, neither of you will recognize the place.'

'That's what I'm afraid of.' I prodded her gently.

'I'm serious.' She swatted my hand away. 'That's what people used to do in the Victorian times. They used to strip the house that was to become the marital home and have it done up from top to bottom in the latest fashionable style to celebrate the marriage and welcome the bride. Like giving them a fresh start in a brand new home.'

'Is that so?' I have no idea where Leoni gets her information from, but she's full of fascinating factoids which are usually correct. Certainly her pub-quiz mentality was enough to net her a very respectable twenty grand when she surprised us all and appeared on *Who Wants to be A Millionaire?* a few months ago, hence today's rather pricey Miu-Miu slingbacks. True to form, she refused to share a penny of it with her family, pinging her teeth in Marcus's direction when he suggested they could do with a new boiler and a loft conversion, and announcing her intention to spend the whole lot on shoes and nail varnish. Way to go, girl.

'Obviously we're only talking about the wealthier classes who could afford it.' Leoni continued the mini-history lesson with her usual authority. 'Poor people had to make do with an extra swig of gin while the new wife had all her teeth pulled out so that the husband would never have to face a dentist's bill.'

'No!'

'Yep,' she said. 'It's just another version of the same old story of the woman getting the arse-end of the deal.' I made a mental note to book myself in for a check-up. It's been a while and I'm sure one of my fillings is loose. 'But you're not exactly lumpen proletariat cannon fodder, so I suggest you take a lead from the Victorians and get the painters in.'

'I can't do that!' To tamper with Rick's magazine-perfect interior would be nothing short of deliberate vandalism. 'Have you any idea how much that wall-paper up the stairwell cost?'

'Don't care,' she said. 'Rip it all out and start again. Let's face it, when you get divorced he'll have to give you the house anyway, so you might as well do it up the way you want it now. At least then you'll be able to put your feet up on your own choice of sofa and feel like you're actually at home.'

'Thanks for the offer. I'll bear it in mind.' Deep down, I knew that she may well have a point, but sometimes it's so much easier just to sit back and do nothing. 'I know it sounds ridiculous,' I said, as though I'd only just thought of it, 'but I think I'm feeling homesick.'

'Tell me about it.' Leoni picked up a shining stain-less-steel lid from one of the pans and checked her reflection in it, baring her teeth. 'I'm bloody sick of my home too.'

'I know I shouldn't wallow in the past, but I loved my flat,' I said forlornly, suddenly yearning for my old home. Waving goodbye to my erstwhile sanctuary had been the biggest sacrifice of all. Home is where the heart is, and I couldn't help but feel that I had left at least a part of mine in the now empty apartment overlooking the leafy Kensington square. The forfeit had included the instant loss of my upstairs neighbours, Sally and Paul, who had somehow brought me back to life just when I thought it was Game Over. The thought of living without them was almost as frightening as the thought of living out the rest of my days with Rick, the wrench of our parting having been every bit as traumatic as a chick being heave-hoed out of the nest by a cuckoo. I opened my handbag, pretending to look for a tissue, secretly feeling for the set of keys that remained tucked in the side pocket like a security blanket. 'I can't bear the thought of someone else living there. It feels like sacrilege.'

'You're not selling it, are you?' The pan lid dropped from Leoni's hands, crashing into the display with an unceremonious clang. Her reaction was understandable, considering she'd extracted a promise from me some time ago, after one too many mojitos, to bequeath it to her in my will, then made me write it down and sign it on the spot, with the barman and waitress acting as witnesses. 'I thought you'd decided to keep it just in case? I know I bloody well would. But then again, I married Twatman.'

'I am,' I said. 'But Rick wants me to rent it out. He said the place will only deteriorate if it's left empty.'

'Bullshit!' Leoni bucked her head aggressively. 'He's just worried that you'll go running off to your convenient little safety net whenever the going gets tough.'

'Precisely,' I said. 'I keep getting these sudden panic attacks and thinking, *What the hell have I done?*'

'Yep,' she said. 'Sounds about right. I had that very same thing the moment Marcus shoved this ring on my finger.' She flicked me the bird. 'I should have ripped it off before the vicar declared us man and mug and told him to stick it where the sun don't shine.'

'You love him really.' I smiled.

'Are you out of your mind? I hate his guts. The only reason we've stayed married this long is because I want him to be as miserable as I am. Once those bloody kids have left home, I'll divorce him so fast his teeth will rattle. Just you wait. You won't see me for dust.'

'I don't know how he puts up with you.'

'He's got no choice. For better or worse, remember?'

'That cuts both ways, Leoni.'

'No it bloody well doesn't. I've given birth to his kids. So unless he's prepared to swallow a bowling ball and crap it out the other end, three times, he's never going to know the true meaning of the phrase "for worse".'

'Talking of which, Julia mentioned that she's barely heard a peep from you since bringing little Frankie home. You really ought to pop in on her, you know. She could do with the moral support.'

'Sod off,' Leoni snarled. 'With a bloody baby in the house? No thank you. Been there, done that, got the puke stained T-shirt. She'll expect me to coo over him and change his nappy and all that kind of stuff. Why is it that just because I'm a woman I'm expected to go all gaga when faced with someone else's sprog? Urgh.' She shuddered. 'I hate babies.'

'Well, you don't hate Julia, and she's been feeling

really down these last few weeks. It's the very least you could do.'

'Huh,' Leoni said. 'She ain't seen nothing yet. And I suppose David's being a completely useless cretin?'

'That's a little harsh.' I attempted to defend him, regardless of the accuracy of Leoni's diagnosis. 'It's a big period of adjustment for both of them.'

'I'm right, aren't I?' She allowed herself a smug, self-congratulatory smile. 'I'm always right. Marcus was about as much use as a condom machine in a convent. But that's men for you. They're nothing more than selfish, self-centred, puffed-up sperm donors. He should count himself lucky that I haven't walked out on the lot of them.'

'Lately,' I muttered.

'That's not "walking out",' she said, no doubt refer-ring to the numerous occasions she had packed a bag (with bottles) and turned up on somebody's doorstep (usually mine). 'That's called "teaching him a lesson". I always go back, eventually. God knows I deserve a bloody Victoria Cross, all the shit I've had to put up with over the years.'

I ground to a halt next to the espresso machines.

'Rick wants us to be best friends.' The moment it was out of my mouth, I could see the extent of the trouble it spelled.

'What?' Leoni pulled one of her faces at me.

'You know.' I picked up a battery-operated milk

frother that I hadn't the slightest interest in and gave it a quick buzz. 'He wants us to share everything and not have any secrets from each other.'

'Yeah.' A vulgar snort burst from Leoni's nose as she tried not to laugh. 'Like that's *really* going to work.'

'So it's not just me then?' Oh, thank God. I'd hardly slept a wink the last two nights. Having been out of the loop, as it were, since the early nineties, I wondered if the basic ground rules for marriage hadn't gone and changed since my first spin on the merry-go-round. 'Thank God for that.' My relief was almost palpable. It was situation normal: do not, under any circumstances, confuse the role of 'husband' with that of 'friend'. It's like picking up the wrong coat at the end of a party, and we all know where that can lead, don't we? I smiled my appreciation of Leoni's unimpeachable wisdom. 'I thought I'd totally lost touch with reality for a moment there.'

'Listen, honey. All this joined-at-the-hip stuff is a load of old bollocks. Now that you're married, you have to learn to lie like a senior politician. Start off with the small stuff, you know, like how much you spent on a pair of shoes.' She thought about it for a moment, glancing down guiltily at the pointy-toed, mock-croc Miu Mius gracing her feet. 'Hang on a mo. That can be a bit tricky. Maybe save that for stage two. What I'm saying is, take your time and hone your skills on a few innocent micro-fibs until it feels like second nature.

Then gradually take it up a notch or two over the course of a couple of months until you're able to lie through your teeth without flinching.' I found myself nodding in tacit agreement. 'My life is none of Marcus's bloody business, and if he thinks I'm going to share my deepest, darkest thoughts with him, he can sod right off.'

'That's kind of what I thought.'

'Men only say that they want us to share everything with them because they're scared shitless that we might be doing something they don't like. It's not because they're even vaguely interested in our lives, it's because they can't stand not knowing what we're up to. Or worse still, what we might *like* to be up to.' She glanced around the department, her eyes settling on a battle-weary man, irritably standing by while his high-main-tenance Prada-clad wife weighed up the merits of a Teflon-coated electric wok. He had one of those shall-I-shan't-I looks on his face, his hand hovering above a copper-bottomed pan that would have done the job quite nicely. 'Then there's the deeper paranoia about what we're really thinking,' Leoni added. 'That's the stuff that really bakes their noodles. Believe me, Helen, they're not to be trusted. Not for one second. Anything you tell them will be neatly catalogued in their twisted, insecure little minds and used as ammunition against you the minute a row kicks off.'

There was no doubting that what she said had a

certain ring of truism about it. In the past, I'd been on the receiving end of that kind of heavy artillery several times myself, cowering under a tin hat while grenades were hurled at my known weak spots by a husband who wished me dead on a daily basis.

'So we're agreed,' I recapped. 'Keep any disclosures on a strictly need-to-know basis and preserve the mystery.'

'Mystery, schmistery.' Leoni shuffled along to the Tupperware display and gave it a cursory glance. 'The only mystery in my case is how come I haven't had Marcus assassinated yet.'

'Thanks, Leoni. It's good to talk.'

At that very moment, fifteen egg timers went off a few yards behind us. Somebody shouted, '*Fire!*', throwing the department into chaos, and my shoulders hunched involuntarily at the tinkling crash of expensive glass. Leoni sniggered to herself evilly.

'No worries,' she said. 'Besides, you know what they say about marriage: the first decade is the hardest.'

Chapter Four

BAD ENERGY

'Yes? Can I help you?'

Answering the front door, I found a fresh-faced young woman dressed in a rather fabulous bottle-green shot-silk trouser suit, with a blazing mound of red hair pinned into unruly surrender on top of her head by a pair of ornamental chopsticks. Wow. I had no idea who she was, only that she looked bloody sensational. Youthful, fashionable, full of confidence. I wished I looked like that. In fact, at that moment, I wished I could be her. She looked like she had a really interesting life. I took another eyeful of the stunning trouser suit. Maybe I could sneak a photograph of her and have it copied. It was exactly the kind of thing I had in mind for the New Me.

'Mrs Wilton?' she asked.

'Yes?' I replied after a moment's hesitation. *Mrs Wilton.* No matter how many times I heard it, it just sounded stranger and stranger. Mrs Wilton. Mrs Wilted Spinach and Stilton.

'I'm Lily.' She was already peering over my shoulder, trying to sneak a good look inside the house. 'We spoke on the phone?' The penny dropped.

'Of course.' I motioned at her to come in, feeling downright dowdy in her glamorous presence. 'I've been expecting you,' I said, leading her through to the sitting room, wishing I'd worn something a little zingier this morning. My cream linen-mix high-street trousers crept along shamefully beside her. 'I'm afraid I haven't a clue what all this is about. I read an article in a magazine last week and found your advertisement in the back. It seemed like as good a place to start as any.'

'Don't worry. You're in safe hands,' she assured me with a bright smile. 'I've been doing this for a long time.' At her age? I doubted that very much.

She plonked herself down quite comfortably in one of the three enormous mink-brown suede sofas, opened her outsized handbag and pulled out a big yellow pad.

'There are a few things we need to run through first,' she said, clicking her ballpoint repeatedly. She looked me up and down a bit, then gave me a sympathetic smile. 'Why don't you sit down and I'll tell you how this is going to work?' I found myself thanking her for inviting me to take a seat in my own home, confirming my suspicion that this appointment was way overdue. 'Comfy?'

'Yes thank you.'

'Good.' She clicked her pen again and poised it over her pad. 'What's your star sign?'

'I beg your pardon?'

'Your star sign? You know . . . Shelley von Strunckel? Moons rising in second houses? I need to know your personal zodiac elements before we can get started.'

'Pisces.'

'Oh!' She made a couple of notes. 'That's good. Water people are the best ones to work with. It's the fire signs you have to watch out for. Tricky characters. The minute you start making suggestions, they get all defensive. It's very frustrating. I'm thinking of blacklisting the lot of them. What year were you born?'

'What?' Oh, please don't ask me that. Now that we're hurtling through the third millennium at the speed of light, anything with a swinging Sixties date tag sounds positively ancient. I reluctantly mumbled my vintage. She consulted a small printed list of tabulations.

'You're a sheep!' she announced with the sort of glee that meant she was glad it wasn't her. Oh, how very alluring. A fat, lanolin-soaked farmyard animal with enormous brown-stained teeth and no brains, useful for only one thing: pot roasting. Thanks a bunch. I smiled at her tightly. 'Now,' she said. 'You say that you just can't seem to get settled here?'

'That's right,' I replied, feeling a bit stupid. It hadn't sounded quite so daft when we had spoken on the telephone, but then again I'd seen off a couple of glasses of fermented grape juice at the time and it had seemed like a perfectly sane idea. It's amazing how persuasive some of these knit-your-own-yoghurt articles can be when you're lying on the sofa after one too many, searching for an answer to life's dilemmas in the pages of *Heat* magazine. Now that she was sitting here in front of me with her brisk yellow pad and inquisitive eyes, I wondered what on earth I must have been thinking of. What a sucker. I'm the proverbial Eskimo you can sell snow to.

'When did you move in?' She glanced around the room and took a few deep breaths. 'It doesn't feel like a new home. It feels like . . .' She rolled her shoulders around a few times, soaking up the ambience, wrinkling her nose at the ceiling. 'It feels like everything's well and truly bedded in.'

'It was my husband's house for quite some time before we got married,' I explained. 'So I suppose you could say that it's me who's new, rather than the house.'

'Mmm,' she said. 'That's interesting. Must be quite a strong character if you haven't managed to make much of an auric impact on the place.'

'He is,' I admitted.

'Only, it's usually the woman who has her metaphysical paw print stamped all over a home. Have you made any changes since you've been here?'

'No.'

'New curtains? Furniture? A bit of redecorating maybe?'

'Afraid not.'

'What, *nothing*?' She blinked at me. Now that she came to mention it, it did seem a bit inadequate on my part, but it's not that easy to make the leap from paid domestic help to Lady of the House. I suppose that, had I first arrived here as Rick's girlfriend rather than his professional housewife, I might have felt less inhibited about introducing the odd home-made swag here and there. The fact that every room was technically perfect just as it was didn't help. If it ain't broke, don't fix it.

'I thought about changing the blinds in the kitchen,' I offered hesitantly. 'Only I've been a bit busy.' Pathetic.

'I see. Are there any parts of the house in particular that make you feel uncomfortable?'

'Not really,' I shrugged, not having given it much thought. A mouse began twitching in my head. 'Actually, come to think of it, I've never liked this room much. It kind of gives me the creeps. And the big bathroom on the second floor.' I shuddered. 'I don't know what's going on in there.' I somehow managed to stop myself getting carried away and putting forward a spontaneous theory hinged on the notion that someone might have been axed to death in the sitting room, then dragged upstairs and dissolved in a tub of acid. It's an old house, so chances are that it's seen its fair share of skulduggery.

'And what does your husband do?'

'Do?' I felt my brow rumple. 'You mean, for a living?'

'Yes.' She smiled.

'Well, er, he, erm . . .' It suddenly occurred to me that I didn't really have the foggiest what Rick got up to in that office of his. For all I knew, he might sit around in a suit all day, making paper planes and stringing paper clips together. I sat there, stumped, trying to cobble together a reasonable response that wouldn't sound quite as feeble as not having bothered to change the kitchen blinds. 'He's a businessman.'

'What kind of business?'

Good question.

'Er . . .' I wondered if she'd notice if I just made something up. 'He's, erm . . .' My nerves started hurling indiscriminate suggestions towards my mouth. 'Well . . .' rodeo rider – 'to tell the truth . . .' arms dealer – 'he's something to do with . . .' pheasant plucker – 'commodities, I think.' That'll do.

'Oh! I won't pretend to know what that means.' She dived back into her bag and took out a leather pouch, from which she produced an ornate instrument made from smooth, red wood with a delicate brass inlay. The whole thing was about the size of a side plate, etched with unintelligible markings and inset with a load of funny-looking dials.

'Have you ever seen one of these before?' Lily asked. I shook my head in ignorance. 'It's a Lo Pan compass. I'll be using it to find out exactly what's going on here.' She then drew from her bag a red square base for it to sit on. 'This represents the earth and allows the compass to be aligned against the walls, and these inner dials represent heaven.'

'Uh-huh.' I tried to look fascinated while wondering how to slip into the conversation the small matter of where she had got her suit.

'Each dial is segregated into various divisions, all of which represent something: earthly elements, mythological Chinese mountains, dragons, seasons, lunar positions.'

'Excellent,' I said, not having absorbed a word.

'What we need to do is to protect your house from harmful influences and to maximize the flow of chi.'

'Chee? I think I've heard of that.'

'Not chee. *Chi*.' She corrected me with a rise of her hand, chirruping the word with an oriental accent, narrowing her eyes. 'It means energy.'

'You mean like yin and yang?' I tried to join in.

'Not really.' Her smile was patient, if a little condescending. 'It's more about invisible magnetic lines and balance, rather than the actual forces themselves.'

'Of course.' I cleared my throat.

'Do you mind if I take a look around on my own?' She stood up. 'I find it much easier to get a feel for the flow of chi when it isn't interrupted by someone else's aura.' I briefly eyed her capacious bag, wondering for a split second if this wasn't just some enormous scam to gain entry to the house and burgle me blind. She shrugged off her jacket and dropped it to the sofa, revealing an equally fabulous white silk shirt with super-deep cuffs. 'OK if I leave my things here?'

'Sure,' I said, feeling like a fat slug beside her waspish waistline. She took up the Ping Pong compass and seemed keen for me to leave the room. 'I'll be in the kitchen,' I offered obediently, and left her to it.

Twenty minutes later, the suspense was almost killing me. Whatever she was doing up there, she was being mighty quiet about it. I flicked through a couple of magazines, both of which were decidedly thin on the ground in the celebrity gossip department, apart from the usual smattering of sad, staged paparazzi shots featuring Z-list micro-celebs going about their daily business of trying to be photographed while pretending to be annoyed about it. It was clearly a slow week for scandal. Even Kerry Katona had run out of things to say about herself. I gave up on the magazines and cast my eyes around the room in search of something else to occupy my twitching hands. More coffee? Perhaps not. My nerves were already skittish this morning, and another double-shot latte would probably result in a full-blown attack of the heebie-jeebies.

The mound of red hair peered around the kitchen door. 'What a fantastic house!' she gushed. 'That bathroom off the master bedroom is a real doozie! You could do lengths in a tub like that!'

'Thanks,' I said. 'We're hoping to sail a yacht round it some day. Coffee?'

'If it's coming out of that thing – ' she pointed at the Gaggia – 'then yes please.'

'How do you like it?'

'Frothy, man.' She dropped her voice into a perfect impression of the Cresta Fizzical advertisement from the Seventies. I gave her a look of surprised amusement and loaded up the machine.

'You're much too young to remember that!'

'I'm forty-nine,' she said.

'You're *what*?' I span round and stared at her. I mean really stared. She half closed her eyes and gave me a small, knowing smile of the sort that said she knew where the bodies were hidden. 'No!' I said incredulously. 'That's impossible. You're nine years older than *me*?' It was like a stinging slap landing on my cheek. Her skin was flawless. Her hair shone like the coat of an Irish setter perched on the Best in Show podium at Crufts. I felt my mouth hang open while I put the silver beast through its paces, desperate to ask if she'd had any work done. And, if so, what, where, and, most importantly, by whom? My God, if I could buy a slice of that, I think I'd gladly sell my soul to the devil.

'It's all in the genes.' She accepted the cup from me. 'And of course the balance of my personal energies.'

'I'm speechless,' I said, bursting with admiration. 'Excuse me for gawping at you like this. Forty-*nine*? Are you absolutely sure?'

'I have a miraculous Chinese herbalist,' she confided with a whisper. 'He makes special anti-ageing remedies. They taste foul – ' her face pulled into a grimace – 'but you can't argue with the results.'

'And where's he based?' I tried to sound casual in my query, resisting the urge to search feverishly for a pencil and paper.

'He lives in a little village in Xinjiang Province.'

'Oh.' Damn. I stirred a little sugar into my cup and tried to act nonchalant.

'You should ship it over in bulk. You'd make a fortune! I'd certainly take a couple of bottles off your hands.' Hint, hint.

'If I had a pound for every time someone had asked me,' she said with a small laugh. 'But I'm afraid it doesn't work like that. Everybody's different, you see. The formula is made to match my own personal energies and elements. It wouldn't be any good to anyone else.' She dipped her finger into the milky froth and put it on her tongue. 'Some of these herbs are extremely potent and could even be fatal in the wrong hands.'

'Oh.' Like I care. Just hand the stuff over, lady, and I'll take my chances.

'Now. Let's get down to business, shall we?' She put her cup down. 'Feng shui is all about finding the best way to align the space you live in so that the good energy, chi, can flow freely like water.' I nodded politely, although I had completely lost interest in the house, fixated as I was on her youthful bloom. 'But unless you want to start knocking the walls about, which I'm guessing is doubtful, there's only so much we can do, so I'm going to recommend moving a few things around and bringing in certain objects that ought to make a difference.'

'Like what?'

'I'll send you my report in a few days. But first, I want you to get rid of any clutter and to throw away anything that's broken.'

'Done,' I said, making a mental note to sling out the hideous vase Rick's lemon-sucking secretary, Angela, had given us as a barbed wedding present. I keep meaning to bury the hatchet with the woman, preferably in her head.

'You'll need to move the bed to face east, and the television in there will have to go.'

'The television?' Oh no. Not the telly. How am I supposed to enjoy the weekend without kicking off with a couple of hours lying around in front of *Saturday Kitchen*, working up a monstrous appetite in time for lunch?

'Definitely,' she said. 'You can't have any distractions in that department, if you know what I'm saying.' She gave me a sly nod. 'And you have to get rid of that dark wallpaper. There is far too much masculine energy in this house. It's awfully oppressive. No wonder you feel like a fish out of water.' I pictured myself flapping about in the hands of an enthusiastic angler before having my head bashed in on a rock. 'Is there anything in this house left over from his previous relationships? You know, old love letters, furniture bought with other people, odd little trinkets dotted around?'

'Er . . .' I looked at her blankly. 'I'm afraid I wouldn't know.'

'I see.' A small frown passed across her wrinkle-free face. She picked up her coffee cup with a flourish of female conspiracy. 'Then may I suggest you find out?'

Chapter Five

SLEUTH

IT'S NO GOOD hiding from problems and hoping they'll just go away of their own accord. Lily Lo-Pan Compass was right. There was only one thing for it: to take the bull by the horns and tackle the issue head-on. This was my home too, now, and I had every right to make it my own, even if that meant resorting to subterfuge. After dusting Rick out of the door first thing with a brief, wifely kiss, I straightened up my resolve and reasoned that any woman worth her salt would have done what I was about to embark upon months ago.

I'm not a natural snooper. If there's one thing I know, it's that if you go looking for trouble, you're bound to find it. I have never once gone through Rick's house (sorry, *our* house) and sifted through his stuff. For one thing, it's a pretty big place and I really didn't know where to start, although, come to think of it, the locked filing cabinet in his study might be a logical point of entry. I thought about it for a while before deciding that trying to jemmy it open with a chisel would probably turn out to be something of a non-starter. I've never been much cop with woodwork and might well have ended up chopping my own fingers off by mistake. No. I'd have to bide my time until I found a suitable opportunity to sneak the key out of his briefcase and have it copied at the cobblers up the road. With the house empty, I spurned my guilty conscience and put the chain on the front door, lest he should come home unexpectedly and find me excavating his past lives, then headed upstairs.

When taking on any serious project, I like to have some kind of rough game plan to follow. In this case, I had contrived to put myself in the position of the person I was about to investigate. Now, if I were Rick, where would I hide all those juicy little things that I didn't want anyone else to find? The answer came to me as quick as a flash: top cupboards of the wardrobe, hidden away in a couple of decoy shoe boxes pushed right to the back, just like I used to do. Being of diminutive height, it was all I could manage to reach the knobs and pull the little doors open, never mind actually see what was in there.

Before long, I had made discovery number one: Rick didn't own a stepladder. At least, if he did, I couldn't bloody find it. Risking life and limb, I went for the health and safety hangable offence of standing on a chair instead, and found myself eye to eye with the usual jumble of half-forgotten detritus. A discarded selection of hideous jumpers, a fishing hat (*fishing?*), an old VHS video camera with some tapes, and a handful of magazines that you wouldn't want your mother to see. I turned a blind eye to those and reasoned that, judging by the dusty dates and silicone-free models, they had been there for ages and he'd probably forgotten all about them. At least it wasn't evidence of a regular subscription to *Transvestites Weekly*. I pushed the jumpers out of the way, revealing a wide, shallow, white cardboard box. Ah-ha. I gave it a tentative shove. It was heavy. Heavier than it looked. I slid it towards me and let it drop into my arms. Mmm. What have we here? Carefully stepping off the chair, I wiped the dust from the top of the box, settled it on the bed and lifted the lid. Beneath the rustle of the top layer of tissue paper, the soft scent of leather binding rose to greet my nosiness. My heart skipped a beat. It was a wedding album. *Put it back*, I heard my head say.

The bride wore white, a Fleetwood Mac dress, all Gypsy Rose and daisy chains. Her doe eyes gazed out at me. A willow of a girl who might be swept away by a strong breeze, wild eyebrows, early twenties maybe, with long brown hair woven through with ribbons. Sitting beneath a tree, vaguely holding a bunch of wild flowers, her bare feet stretched out carelessly on the uncut grass before her. She was beautiful, like a summer of love, and her smile said it all. It was invincible, full of the vitality of youth, the promise of endless possibilities. As I examined her guileless face, a slow realization came upon me, halting my pulse, thickening the blood in my veins. Rick's first wife was a sky-scraping blonde with legs up to her armpits and a mouth like an industrial letterbox – that much I knew from the picture he used to keep in the study, taken just before she had packed up their two children some time around the mid-Eighties and emigrated to Australia with her replacement husband in tow. I'd recognize her face anywhere – the triumphant expression she wore, designed to portray just the right amount of vitriol while simultaneously obliging him with a final snapshot of his soon-to-be-estranged kids. Rick's second wife, the Brazil Nut, hailed from Rio and had skin of a similar shade to a rosewood dining table. I'd met her once briefly, and she bore no resemblance whatsoever to the girl in the picture. So who the bloody hell was this?

Gawping at the forbidden photograph, I looked at her observing me, as if she knew, and turned the page. Her again, this time caught unawares, hair flying, head tilted back, laughing with reckless abandon at something delicious the camera hadn't quite caught. I turned the page over and felt like I had swallowed a boulder. There they were, she and Rick, strolling hand in hand beneath the dappled shade of an arbour, heavy with the yellow blossom of mid-May laburnum, a cigarette dangling loosely from his lips, flared trousers, wide collar, hair down to his shoulders. He was slimmer than he is now. Much slimmer. And, shockingly, unrecognizably good-looking in a cheeky kind of way. I couldn't have torn my eyes from him if my life had depended on it. His gaze was bright and untroubled, lifted in that moment to challenge the camera as though suddenly amused by its presence. He was in love and didn't care who knew it.

Staring down at the picture, stunned by this stolen glimpse into a life that I knew nothing about, I tried to correlate the boyish image in the photograph with the snoring rhinoceros I'd woken up next to this morning. The thought of it knocked the wind from me. It was as though I'd never seen him before. I felt sick, my hands clammy as they shakily replaced the tissue paper.

Instead of sticking to my original plan and moving along to see what surprises the next wardrobe held, I retreated sunkenly to the kitchen and poured myself a large glass of wine from the fridge. You stupid, stupid woman. Did you really think that a man like Rick could have reached the grand old age of fifty-three without collecting a stack of baggage? God only knows what else you'd find if you really went for it. So what if he's got a few skeletons stashed away in the closets? Haven't we all? This was supposed to be a fresh start for both of us. Now look what you've gone and done. Shame, shame, shame on you.

It was as though I had deliberately set out to debunk Rick the Man without realizing the consequences of what I was doing, like passing him through an airport security X-ray machine, only to find that he had a pair of ovaries. I'd accidentally altered my perception of him entirely in one fell swoop. Suddenly, he wasn't the same any more. Now, he was just some bloke I didn't know at all.

I couldn't get the images out of my head. Rick, the shameless lothario, flitting from flower to flower. An endless string of infatuated women stretching from here to Timbuktu. Illicit afternoon rendezvous in swanky hotels in St Germain with hot and cold running chambermaids. Steaming croissants in the mornings. The Eiffel Tower surging upwards to the sky. Oh, for heaven's sake, enough! It was my own bloody fault for sticking my nose in his privates. I stared at the wine glass in my hand, which was suddenly inexplicably empty, and went for the big refill. Now what? Sit here and get rat-arsed on my own? Yes. Why not? And a fat lot of good that will do you, won't it? Then you'll have to explain to Rick how come he's got home to find you comatose on the kitchen floor stinking of Pinot Grigio. Now pull yourself together and do something constructive instead of digging yourself into a morose pit of depression. Julia's doing quite enough of that for both of us.

Hauling myself up by the boot straps, there was nothing for it but to retreat into a safe bubble of domestic displacement activity. I pulled a few bowls out of the cupboards, flexed my biggest balloon whisk and set about putting together one of my legendary almond cakes, as though I could bake my way out of the guilt. Just as I was about to pound the living daylights out of a bag of blanched nuts, there came a deafening crash before the front door slammed, sending a rippling shockwave through the house.

'Goot monging!' Helga yelled from the hallway.

'Morning, Helga!' I bellowed back. We have the fine art of international relations down to a tee. The rolling pin slowed in my hands. Hang on a minute. Didn't I put the . . . ?

Helga came scampering into the kitchen, dropping her Tesco bag-for-life on the floor and throwing what remained of the security chain on the table. 'I sorry,' she said, shrugging at it. 'I think is stuck, so I go, WHOOMPH!' she shouted, doing a passable mime of running at the door with her shoulder.

'Never mind,' I sighed, looking at the splintered wood around the broken bolt and shuddering at the damage she must have inflicted on the door frame. 'It can't have been a very good one anyway. You didn't hurt yourself, did you?'

'Ah,' she nodded, chewing her lip, a sure sign that she hadn't understood a word. We've been working on her command of the English language for quite some time now. Although it has come on in leaps and bounds in relative terms, one has to bear in mind that Helga probably wasn't the sharpest tool in the box at school, if indeed she ever went, which is doubtful. She scowled at the ingredients laid out on the counter. 'You make brid?'

'No. Cake.'

'Ah.'

'You know cake, Helga?' I picked up the cake tin and showed it to her, pretending to turn it out and cut an invisible slice.

'Aaah!' she cried as the linguistic fog lifted. 'Cack!'

'Yep. Although we usually say caaaaaa-ke.' Helga took a deep breath and gave it her best shot.

'Caaaaaaa-ck.'

'Perfect.'

'Goot. I like cack. Now I work.' She slapped her chest. 'I go clin Reek study. Then I make bids. *Da*?'

'Thanks, Helga. I'm afraid he's gone and dropped cigar ash all over the carpet again.'

*

A GUILTY CONSCIENCE is a real killer. I drowned out the whispering voices in my head by pretending to listen to the radio while whipping a cup of caster sugar in with the softened butter, concentrating hard on the pattern forming in the bowl while the mice took hold. *How could he have kept that from you?* I clenched my teeth and thrashed away. *Maybe he's a serial bridegroom and there's a whole stack of secret wedding albums hidden around the house, which is more than you've bloody well got, eh?* I measured a careful teaspoon of almond essence into the sugar paste. *Why don't you go and have a grope around in the other wardrobes, hmm? There might be all sorts of stuff in there. He'll never know.* I cracked the eggs into a separate bowl, reached for a clean whisk and gave them a bit of what-for. *Nobody knows the man they marry. You of all people should know that. You've got to live with someone for at least ten years before you get any reliable inkling of what they're really like.* I loosened the sugar paste with a couple of spoonfuls of the beaten egg, and began to work it in, my heart pounding in my chest.

'Boo!' Rick sprang out from behind the kitchen door, scaring the living bejeezers out of me.

'Aaarrrrrrgggggh!' The whisk leapt from my hand and clattered to the floor. 'Rick!' Colour flooded my cheeks, the corruption of my Sherlock Holmes morning written all over my face.

'Surprised?' he beamed.

'Yes!' I screeched, the boulder in my stomach threatening to explode and burst through my apron.

'You all right, babe? You seem a bit jumpy?'

'Jumpy?' Ha-ha! 'Me?' For heaven's sake. You're sounding hysterical. Just hold it together. No sudden moves.

'What's with the front door?' he said, dumping his briefcase on the table.

'Helga decided to test the security chain this morning.' I did my best to sound ordinary, forcing my voice out of its stranglehold. Rick slunk up behind me and slid an arm around my waist, pressing up against me, planting a kiss on the back of my head. Guilty adrenaline pounded mercilessly through my veins.

'Where is she?'

'In the study, sucking cigar ash out of your carpet with a straw.'

'I can feel your heart beating,' he whispered in my ear, reaching out to stick a finger in the cake mix. I'm not bloody surprised. Give it another couple of minutes and you might just witness a full-blown coronary. 'Shall we give Helga the afternoon off and make a mess of the bedroom?'

The bedroom. Oh dear God. My insides lurched. What if I hadn't covered my tracks properly? I tried to run quickly over every small detail of the shakedown, and couldn't remember whether or not I'd put the chair back, or whether I had rearranged the contraband just as I'd found it.

'I'm busy.' The casual smile I attempted felt more like a grimace.

'I see.' He licked the dollop of cake mixture from his finger. 'Playing hard to get, are we?' My throat dried up.

'Maybe.'

'I might as well tell you that you're on a hiding to nothing, babe. That little ticker of yours is going like a trip hammer.' His mouth hovered beside my ear, his hand wandering to the middle of my ribcage. 'You're just dying for me to ravage you. Go on, deny it.'

'If you don't mind –' I peeled his arms away – 'I'm trying to make a cake.'

He leaned against the worktop, right in my way, and flicked his eyes cheekily over my *Stand Back, Genius At Work* apron. I kept my hands busy in the bowl.

'If you say so.' Shoving a half-smoked cigar in his mouth, he didn't bother to light it, giving it a cowboy chomp instead. He went to the fridge and pulled out the wine bottle, refilling my glass and taking down a fresh one for himself. 'But I know I'm right. I can read you like an open book.'

I dared to meet his impenetrable gaze and hoped to God he was joking.

Chapter Six

NEE-NAW! NEE-NAW!

IN MY EXPERIENCE, one of the most effective ways to take your mind off your own problems is to get involved in somebody else's. By indulging in a bit of unashamed ambulance-chasing, you'll soon be reminded that you're not the only one trying to keep a lid on a can of worms. Besides, Julia had come speeding to my rescue more times than I care to count, so it was fair dinkum that I should now do the same for her.

I popped in to Julia's small but perfectly formed PR company on the loose but passable pretext of wanting Sara's opinion on some swatches. If there was one person who knew Julia even better than she knew herself, it was the redoubtable Sara, yet ever since Julia had promoted her from PA to business partner because of her immaculate conception, Sara had become harder to pin down than a hedge-fund manager facing cross-examination at The Hague. Her mobile constantly went straight through to voicemail, and judging by Dudley's weary message-taking manner on their home phone last night, he'd hardly seen hide nor hair of her himself lately.

Sara invited me towards the comfortable visitor's chair on the opposite side of the desk, picked up the telephone and hit a button.

'Hold my calls,' she barked in her firm, Lancashire, whiplash tongue. 'And bring us in a couple of coffees, would you?' Hanging up, she flashed me a wicked smile. 'I bloody love ordering people around.'

'I'm not keeping you, am I?' I dropped into the chair, grateful to take the weight off my feet after foolishly deciding to walk all the way from the tube rather than grabbing a cab or jumping on the bus. There are some pockets of London that were rudely ignored when it came to handing out the underground stations, and Lots Road, round the back of Chelsea and Fulham near the river, is one of them. My supposedly pleasant stroll from Sloane Square tube had started off well enough, the balm of high summer lulling my strappy sandals into a false sense of security, urging them to turn off the main drag and wind around the quiet residential back streets instead of pounding up the Kings Road with the die-hard shoppers and map-flapping tourists. Fifteen minutes into my ill-considered decision, I might as well have had blood pouring out of my shoes for all the pain they were causing me. Typically, there wasn't a taxi to be had for love nor money.

'Keeping me? Course not,' Sara said.

'I've decided to give the house a bit of a facelift.' I waggled the paper samples that I had ordered from Peter Jones a week ago. 'And seeing as you're the only one among us that's still on the right side of thirty, I thought you might be able to give me an idea of what's considered stylish these days.'

'Give 'em 'ere,' she said, reaching out and taking them from me. 'Nope.' She cast the first aside. 'Nope.' And the second. 'Nope. Nope. Urgh!' She turned the next one upside down and scowled at it. 'You're joking, right?' I shrugged. 'Nope.' Sling. 'Definitely not.' She dropped the last one to the carpet. 'There's your answer. They're all shite. And why would you want to mess with Rick's house anyway?' The door opened and a wide-eyed minion crept in to deliver the coffee tray. 'Thanks,' Sara said without bothering to look up. She waited until the serf had backed away and closed the door, then poured coffee for both of us, needing no prompting to be reminded of how I take mine. I'm sure she has a photographic memory. 'So that's done then. What else?' she said, pushing one of the cups towards me and pulling the paper wrapper off a mini-muffin.

'Um. Nothing really.' My intention had been to surreptitiously interrogate Sara about Julia's dreadful condition while innocently discussing swatches, yet I suspected that I had been rumbled the moment I walked in. These young women are so much cleverer than we used to be. I suppose it's because they were brought up with Game Boys and personal computers while we were raised to struggle along with Fuzzy Felt and blunt pencils. It's no wonder I feel like a dinosaur when measured up against the Saras of this world. With my strategy blown clean out of the water, there was nothing for it but to concede defeat, go home and regroup. 'I'll finish my coffee, then I'll get out of your hair.'

'No rush.' Sara swung back in Julia's chair, the luxury of the office suiting her well. Matt black walls. Expensive contemporary artworks. A classic, retro-style white desk with spiky, space-age chrome legs. The open page of her desk diary was chock-a-block with scribbled lists under urgent headings.

'I can see you're swamped.'

'That's the main thing,' she whispered. 'Look really, really busy – even when you're not.'

'But you must be rushed off your feet without Julia here?' Bullseye. Back on track with Phase One complete: put Sara at ease then artfully steer the conversation around to Julia.

'Not any more.' Sliding open a hidden desk drawer, Sara pulled out a packet of cigarettes then got up to open the window. 'Sure, the first few months were a bit of a nightmare. You just have to learn to delegate. No point having a dog and barking yourself, is there?' She pulled out a cigarette and played with it.

'I expect she'll start thinking about returning to work soon.'

'You don't need to hurry her along on my account.' Sara tucked the cigarette behind her ear, took a swig of her coffee and licked her lips thoughtfully. 'Nothing's on fire. We're raking in the cash. Tell her to put her feet up and relax. I've got used to running the place without her.'

So far, so good. Time to gently segue to Phase Two: find out what she knows.

'Has she said anything to you?'

'About what?' The ball I tossed her bounced limply to the floor.

'You know, about coming back to work?'

'Oh, that. No. Not really. If you ask me, work's the last thing she's interested in right now.'

'Really?' I tried to appear surprised. 'I wonder why that is?'

'Who knows?' Sara averted her eyes for a split second. And there it was. She knew something. And what's more, she knew that I knew she knew something. We sat silently for an awkward moment. There'd be no point in my trying to crack her open without resorting to torture, and even then I wouldn't put money on the outcome. She still kick-boxes to keep fit, and I once saw her punch a hole in a door without wincing, just to prove that she could. I'm glad I wasn't born in Lancashire. I doubt I'd have survived.

'How's that big marine of yours?' Sara neatly batted the ball back into my court. 'That was the best bloody no-wedding reception I've ever been to in my life. Took me days to get past the hangover.'

'He's fine.' I smiled. 'And Dudley?'

'The same old mind-numbing Dud.' She peered over the top of her cup with a fatigued expression. 'I've come to the sad conclusion that my husband is the human equivalent of beige.'

'You must come for dinner soon,' I suggested soothingly. Us married couples have to stick together from a social point of view. The last thing we need is to go out in public and be reminded that there's still a smorgasbord of available men out there, although why on earth she had chosen to get married at her age, I really don't know. Mind you, I can talk. By the time I was twenty-four, I'd made the worst decision of my life, but that's another story.

'Only if you promise to deep-fry his head.'

'Oh, come on! It can't be that bad!'

'Wanna bet?' She got up from her seat and pulled herself into an unapologetic stretch, flexing her youthful curves beneath an elegant Diane von Frankenstein wrap-dress. 'The minute I get home it's like I've stepped inside a parallel universe where normal human interaction is banned. Honestly, Helen, he's got absolutely no personality. It's like being married to a bath sponge.' Shaking the tension from her shoulders, she clicked her head this way and that, pulled the cigarette from behind her ear and stuck it in her mouth. 'It's my own bloody fault. I should never have married him in the first place. God knows, you lot warned me what he was like.'

'So why did you, then?'

'Dunno,' she shrugged. 'I think I just fancied getting married. You know, good excuse for a new frock and a bloody great piss-up. Besides, at the time he seemed to tick all the right boxes.' I wondered if there had been one that said 'dull as ditch-water'. Check.

'He's good husband material,' I reminded her with a wag of my finger. 'Nice looking, a successful lawyer with a good career, mad about you no matter how horrible you are to him.' It suddenly occurred to me that maybe Dudley was a masochist. They do exist, you know. They're the kind of men who nip off to a specialist prozzie at lunchtime to have their gonads stamped on. Well, well. I always knew there had to be something going on under that tediously polite exterior of his.

'So *you* shag him, then.' Sara threw the cigarette on the desk and frowned at it.

'Fair enough,' I said with a small, defeatist shake of my head. I imagine having it off with Dudley would be a bit like having sex with a Debenhams mannequin, only a lot less exciting. I could only sympathize with her. Let's face it, bad sex is a sad fact of life that most women will encounter at some point in their lives. At best, it'll manifest in a one-night stand as a result of having the old beer goggles on; at worst it'll turn out to be a lifelong endurance test with a husband whose idea of foreplay is to unbuckle his trousers while shouting, 'Brace yourself'. Sara's been grousing about Dudley's personality-bypass ever since the day she got back from their honeymoon. I had to concede that maybe the girl had a point.

'Me working a fourteen-hour day is a godsend as far as I'm concerned.' Sara said, continuing to eye up the cigarette on the desk. 'I like being here. It gives me a sense of purpose. So you can tell Julia from me that if she wants to get me out of this office, she's gonna need a dozen men armed with crowbars. Got it?'

'Got it,' I said.

We sipped our coffees, turning private thoughts over in our heads before I decided there would be no harm in taking a spoon out of her Lancashire hotpot and calling a spade a spade.

'Do you think Julia's suffering from post-natal depression?' I held my breath.

'I knew you were going to ask me that.' Sara picked up the cigarette, snapped it in half and threw it in the waste-paper basket. 'Wallpaper samples indeed.' She gave me a mildly amused smile. 'That's Sally's department, isn't it?'

The mere mention of Sally's name sent a bolt of bereavement through me. Oh, how I missed being able to mosey up one short flight of stairs for a perfectly mixed margarita with my fabulously dysfunctional sex-bomb neighbour whenever I was feeling gloomy. Leaving Sally behind had felt like having a limb cut off. I know he and Paul are just a stone's throw away, but it's just not the same.

'God, I miss him,' I sighed. 'Now the only person I can turn to for a bit of spontaneous company is Helga, and believe me, it's hardly the same thing.'

'I'll say.' Sara took a sharp intake of breath. I allowed myself a brief interlude, picturing Sally's rippling body grinding me into the dust, ramming the brakes on just as my imagination was handcuffing me to the bedstead. I forced myself to concentrate on the far more serious subject at hand.

'I'm worried about her,' I said, lowering my voice. 'Have you seen her lately?'

'Not much.' Sara put her cup down. 'But I know what you mean.'

'So you've noticed it too?'

'Yep.'

'Do you think we should force her to see a doctor?'

'Nope.'

'Why not?'

'I've already tried that.' Sara flipped back a few pages in her diary. 'Drove her to the surgery myself and took Frankie off her hands for the afternoon. Bloody hell, that kid's got a pair of lungs on him, hasn't he?'

'I think that would be enough to send me scatty,' I said, nodding.

'Anyway, she came out saying the doctor thought she was just fine.'

'Eh? Of course she isn't fine! Any idiot can see that!'

'She was lying,' Sara said.

'How do you know?'

'Her left eyebrow twitches.' Sara took another cigarette from the packet, only this time she lit it, drawing the smoke deep into her lungs and holding it there for a moment before letting it out in a giddy cloud beside the open window. 'Everyone's got a tell. You know, they touch their ear or fiddle with their fingers. With Julia –' she pointed her cigarette at me – 'it's all in the left eyebrow.'

THAT NIGHT, under the cool white blanket of a deceptive moon, I sat out in the courtyard, listening to the steady drone of traffic rising up above the chimney pots, watching Rick whistle his way incompetently around the kitchen, stacking the dishwasher badly with the aftermath of our dinner, scratching his head and wondering why the door wouldn't close. He lifted a couple of plates out and gave it another go, the contents crashing around as he rammed the door shut with his knee.

'Just leave it!' I called through the open window. Come morning, I'd only end up fishing out half a dozen broken glasses again.

'Nope!' he shouted back bravely. 'I'm gonna do my fair share around here. You made dinner. I'm gonna clear up afterwards.'

I wondered if that had been the deal with his five thousand previous wives, or if this was a new habit he had decided to adopt purely for my benefit.

A couple of minutes later, Rick emerged with two glasses of wine. 'That was fucking ace,' he said, setting the drinks down on the table and letting out an appreciative burp. 'Although I might as well have been eating on my own, for all the company you've been this evening. You've been like a cat on a hot tin roof these last few days. Now, are you gonna tell me what's up, or am I gonna have to torture it out of you?'

I felt my mouth curve into an uneasy smile. 'I'd like to see you try.'

'Ah.' He picked a cigar out of his pocket and lit it, the smoke clouding around his head, not a hint of breeze to chase it away. It was one of those balmy

73

London nights, hotter than July, the air thick with deliciously vile city pollutants and a few determined grains of mutant pollen searching for somewhere to spawn. 'I've got that sussed actually, babe.' He took a long drag, let out a perfect smoke ring and filled his lungs with the rest. 'I'm going to withhold sexual favours until you go out of your mind with frustration and tell me what's going on in that head of yours. Cunning, eh?'

'I see.' I picked up my wine glass and warmed the deep red claret in my hands. 'And how long do you think it will be before I buckle?' Rick looked at his watch. 'Very funny,' I said. 'I'll have you know that I can go for years.'

'Really? Blimey. I need a ten-minute break every couple of hours, myself.'

He pulled his chair closer to mine, his face taking on an earnest expression. 'What's up, gorgeous?'

I suddenly remembered what Sara had said about Julia's left eyebrow and tried to visualize every muscle in my face, freezing them into abeyance.

'Nothing,' I said, with an air of peaceful repose.

Rick leaned back in his seat. 'You know I trust you implicitly, right?'

Oh God. That's all I need. A category five guilt trip on top of a grilled Dover sole and a massive slice of lemon tart. Unsurprisingly, I'm one of those predict-able women who turn to the pantry shelves in times of emotional crisis. If I don't snap out of it soon, I'll be snapping out of my trousers instead.

'I wouldn't normally go sticking my nose in where it's not wanted, but there's something bugging you big time and I want to know what it is.' He stuck the cigar between his teeth and chewed it towards me, waiting for an answer.

'I'm sorry,' I mumbled. 'I suppose I have been a bit off-colour lately.'

'Wanna tell me about it?'

'Not particularly.' I hid behind a sip of wine. Whichever way I looked at it, there was simply no excuse for my having ransacked his wardrobe. No matter what I had found in there, it was inadmissible, having been obtained by deception without the relevant warrant. I had run through it in my head a thousand times over and come to the same conclusion: if a man had done that to me, I'd shove a size ten boot up his jacksey and tell him to be on his bike. There wouldn't be a single thing that he could say to me that would make me change my mind. The very thought of somebody sifting through my things, snooping around like some kind of deranged bunny boiler? Nope. No excuse on earth would get them out of that one. Suralan Sugar? You're fired.

'I thought we'd promised each other no secrets,' Rick said softly.

No shit, I thought to myself. Anyway, I seem to recall

that it was him who said 'no secrets' while I hid my face in the duvet, crossed my fingers and waved a rope of garlic behind his back.

'Don't take any notice of me.' I had already decided to say nothing, and forced an enigmatic smile, dipping my eyes to the flagstones. Despite my protestation of innocence, I could tell that he was determined to keep me there until he had got a satisfactory answer. I took a deep breath. There was nothing for it but for me to deploy the ultimate weapon in feminine self-defence. 'I'm just being silly,' I said coyly, batting my eyelids. 'You know what us women are like.'

'Oh really?' he said. 'Then how do you explain this?' He reached into his pocket and pulled out a half-empty bottle of herbal tranquilizers. My heart skipped a beat. Exhibiting the evidence in the middle of the table, Rick tucked the cigar back in his mouth. 'That was full on Monday. I found them hidden behind the coffee. The only reason I noticed was because I'd never seen them before and wondered what they were.' He picked the bottle up and read aloud from the label. 'Relieves worry, stresses and strains during difficult times,' he quoted. 'And judging by what's left, I'd say you've been eating these things like Smarties.'

'Helga?' I attempted.

'Don't give me that.' Rick took a big slug from his wine glass. 'Helga using a herbal remedy? I don't think so. She probably takes half a kilo of pure Afghan for a headache. They're yours, aren't they?'

'I'm sorry,' I mumbled, silently cursing myself for having been so careless. 'I didn't want to say anything.'

'About what?'

Quick, woman. Think of something that doesn't involve the words marriage, you, and second thoughts.

'It's Julia,' I blurted. 'I think she's got really bad post-natal depression and she's refusing to do anything about it. I'm at my wit's end.' Once I'd started, my mouth seemed to switch to autopilot, shovelling sentence after sentence, burying the festering corpse of my guilty little secret beneath a haze of hysterical rubble. 'She looks a complete mess. The house is a bombsite. If I didn't know better, I'd even say that she's regretting having the baby.' I felt tears welling up in my eyes, as though I needed to turn on the waterworks just to hammer home my sincerity and throw him off the scent. 'I've been over to see her virtually every day, but she just won't listen to me. I've never seen her like this before. It's like – ' drum roll, wait for it, wait for it – 'like she might go and do something really stupid.' Ta-raaaaa!

'Jesus!' Rick leaped up from his seat. 'Why the fuck didn't you tell me?' He began to pace the courtyard, pulling at his hair. 'And you've been worrying about this all on your tod?' He stared at me incredulously, threw his cigar in the nearest plant pot and marched towards me. 'You poor angel!'

I felt myself instantly suffocated by his huge embrace.

'I can't believe you've been carrying all this around on your shoulders. I'm so sorry I didn't notice. Shit.' He squeezed me harder. 'I'm such a dickhead.'

Chapter Seven

DADDY DAY CARE

'How long do you think you'll be gone?' David asked tentatively as we left him on the doorstep in sole charge of his wailing son.

'Not long,' I lied. 'Julia needs to get out of this place before she goes cabin crazy.'

'So a couple of hours maybe?'

'Sure.'

Had I told him the truth, he'd only have found a million excuses and left us holding the baby, as usual. Julia loitered on the doorstep, fretting at the squalling infant in her husband's inept arms, riddled with motherly guilt.

'Just hurry up!' Leoni yelled from the car. 'As long

as he knows which hole to shove a rusk in, what's the bloody problem?'

I bundled into the back with Sara, who had wisely chosen to spread a bin liner over the seat first. The inside of Leoni's biohazard car is a bit like the really grotesque moments in *How Clean Is Your House?*, only much, much worse. Julia seemed not to notice any of this as she heaved herself into the front with Leoni, sitting heavily on a handful of rubberized chips.

'You're not still driving around in this old dustbin, are you? I thought you were going to buy yourself a spanking new Mini with your winnings.'

'I thought about it for about ten seconds,' Leoni said, ramming the car into reverse and ploughing up the corner of Julia's lupin bed. 'Took one out for a test drive but Millie honked up in the back. I knew I shouldn't have let her eat that jar of Nutella before we left. At least it reminded me that there's no point in having a half-decent car while the freeloaders are still using it as a municipal tip.'

'I can't be gone too long,' Julia said, fretting and chewing at her ragged fingernails. 'David's developed a phobia about baby poo. Even the thought of it makes him dry-retch.'

'Well, that's just cheese of the hard variety, I'm afraid.' Leoni ground the clapped out Fiat into first gear and kangarooed off the drive without bothering to check whether or not there was anything coming. How she's still alive is one of the great mysteries of the world. 'If I were you I'd have slipped a couple of spoons of Senokot in Frankie's formula this morning and let the kid shit for England.'

'He'd never cope.' Julia's neck craned towards her disappearing house. 'So just a quick pub lunch, then I'd better get home.'

'No lunch,' Sara said, poking a gentle finger at Julia's flabby muffin tops. 'And no more baby talk, either. You've been kidnapped, and there's nothing you can do about it.' A rowdy cheer went up. 'Sorry, boss, but you left us with no choice.'

'Arsehole!' Leoni screamed out of the window, shaking her fist at the cyclist who had dared to put his hand out to signal a right turn. 'Do you pay road tax? Eh? *Eh?* Bloody moron.' He wobbled violently as she hurtled past him, almost knocking him off his bike. 'Probably a fucking vegetarian,' she muttered to herself.

Forty death-defying minutes later, we drew up on the Old Brompton Road, smoke belching from the exhaust as Leoni shunted her way into the space on the free meter she'd shot across the nearside lane to claim, narrowly missing an old lady with a tartan trundle-cart.

'Right, you.' Sara was out of the car like a whippet, pulling Julia's door open. 'Out.'

Julia mutely obeyed, stood on the pavement and looked around blankly, as though she'd never seen this part of the world before. 'Where are we going?'

'Back to the land of the living,' Sara said. 'Now look lively.'

Leoni kicked her door shut and didn't bother to lock it. 'Has anybody got half a million quid in loose change for the meter?' I fished all the shrapnel out of my purse and fed it into the machine. 'We can't take her in there looking like that,' Leoni hissed. 'Chuck a horse blanket over her head or something.'

'No problem.' Sara moved us along impatiently. 'Stefano said for us to go round the back. He's going to do her in his private room. You know, when I called him to make the appointment, he said he thought she must have died.'

'She has.' Leoni made like a zombie. 'I know I bloody well did.'

'Put a sock in it, troublemaker.' I elbowed her hard. 'The whole point about today is to try and help Julia feel a little bit better about herself, so drop it with the grim reaper stuff, OK?'

The parking meter ate everything in my purse then demanded a whole lot more, forcing us to search our pockets for every last fluff-bound coin.

Sara flipped open her phone and scrolled down as we walked. A small glimmer of recognition passed over Julia's face as she realized where we were taking her.

'No!' she gasped. 'I can't!'

'Yes you can,' I said, tightening my grip on her arm.

'Stef?' Sara barked into her phone. 'It's Sara. She's here.'

After picking our way past the rat-infested bins behind the smart neighbouring bistro, we heard the latch go on the stainless-steel security door at the back of the salon that Julia had once frequented as regularly as clockwork, come hell or high water. The thought of shampooing and blow-drying her own hair used to be anathema to her. Nowadays, it was all she could do to muster the energy to drag herself into the shower.

'Dear God!' Stefano's manicured hands rushed to his startled face, his eyes widening in horror. '*Julia?*'

'I'm afraid so.' Sara pushed her through the door.

'What the hell happened?' There was no disguising the shock in Stefano's voice, his tanned, Botoxed face contorting into a picture of disgust as he reached out to touch for himself the appalling car-crash state of Julia's once perfect hair.

'She had a baby,' I explained.

'Yeah,' Leoni nodded. 'And now everybody's insisting that I'm not allowed to say I Told You So.'

'Oh, you poor daaaaaaarling!' Stefano threw a comforting arm around Julia's shoulder. 'Why didn't you ring me? You know I do an emergency call-out service. I've lost count of the number of blow-dries I've administered while my clients are having their giblets sewn back together!'

'Do I look that bad?' Julia bit her lip and hung her head.

'Bad? No. You just look like you've given up!' Stefano wagged a stern finger at her. 'What have I always told you?'

'Natural beauty just isn't natural,' Julia chanted sulkily.

'Thank God you brought her in through the back door,' Stefano breathed at Sara. 'She'd have cleared the salon in five seconds flat looking like that.'

We followed the great Stefano's wiggling, snake-hipped bottom up the stairs, past the line of gushingly autographed Hollywood photos, Julia leaning the bulk of her weight on the banister rail of the narrow staircase as we trudged up behind her. Leoni prodded me in the back, flashing her eyes and pointing to the size of Julia's rump. *I know*, I mouthed at her.

Stefano's private room, nestled on the second floor above the hum of the traffic, was strictly reserved for those A-listers who wouldn't be seen dead in something as common as a public salon. Kitted out like Marie Antoinette's boudoir, it was the perfect over-the-top mélange of loud fabrics, salvaged antiques and chinoiserie, offering sufficient additional seating for any respectably star-sized entourage to hang around and leech in comfort. Leoni flung herself on the red velvet chaise longue and kicked off her shoes.

'Hello?' She pointed at the glass-fronted chiller cabinet and the neat rows of sparkling crystal champagne flutes set out above it. 'Are those just for decoration?'

'You just go ahead, sweeties.' Stefano flicked the back of his hand at us, being far too distracted by Julia's dishevelled appearance, and guided her to the hallowed Seat of Stefano, in which he had teased the locks of some of the world's most famous (and infamous) women.

Everybody knows that Stefano's real name isn't Stefano. It's Steve, but he had decided that Steve just wouldn't cut it in the cut-throat world of celebrity hairdressing. Everybody also knows that Steve isn't gay either, even though he wears frilly shirts and minces around like he's chewing a toffee in his bottom. It's all about image, he says, and when he started off in the fame game in the late Seventies, there was nobody who did it better. Women felt far safer in the hands of a flamboyant fruit who purported no sexual interest in them at all, and were far more likely to pass on gossip about their indiscretions to someone who had surely heard it all before. Hence the kiss-and-tell book he's been working on for nearly thirty years, no punches spared, which he refers to as his self-invested personal pension scheme. Rumour of its existence has led more than one panic-stricken star to reach for the nearest libel lawyer, but Stefano plans to revert to his real name once the shit hits the fan and move to a country with no extradition treaty.

After carrying out his initial examination of the patient, Stefano took a step back, pressed his chin into his hands, then reached for the phone.

'Carlo? Send Cheryl up here immediately. I have a major eyebrow situation that needs her magic touch.' His eyes lowered discreetly to Julia's legs. 'And tell her we're going to need wax. *Lots* of wax.'

'DAVID?' Leoni lay back on her chaise as Julia's screams of agony rose from the treatment couch behind the gilded screen. 'Julia won't be home until tomorrow. Uh-huh. Yep. That's right.' She put her hand over the receiver and faked a big bored yawn at us. 'Well, you're just going to have to deal with him yourself, aren't you?' She listened intently for a while. 'Rubbish. Of course you can. It's a baby. Not the global economy.' She reached for her glass, drained it and waggled it at Sara for a refill. 'Don't give me that "he needs his mother" bullshit,' she snapped into the phone. 'Now that your wife's mutilated breasts are finally off the menu, you've got no excuse. Right? Now go and make up half a dozen bottles and stop whingeing.' Sara gave her a big thumbs-up and charged her glass. 'We're all staying over at Helen's –' she fired me a question-ing shrug which I answered with a brief nod of sure, why not – 'and if you dare to so much as ring us even once, one of you had better be dead. Do I make myself clear?' She barely gave him a moment to answer. 'Good. Now shape up and get on with it. Byzie-bye!' She hung up.

'Ever thought about applying for a job in the diplomatic corps?' I asked.

'Bloody men.' Leoni set about her third glass with the same gusto as the first. 'Give them a baby and an empty house and anyone would think you'd asked them to hack their own penis off with a picnic knife.'

'He'll be crapping himself,' Sara said, arranging herself attractively on the pouting red-lipped sofa set beneath the sun-streaming window. Another shriek of pain sailed out from behind the screen. 'Suffer it, baby!' Sara shouted.

'Bollocks!' Julia yelled back. 'You're all going to die!'

'Just finish that bottle and stop complaining,' Leoni bellowed. 'We're not taking you shopping with Axminster legs, and the last time I saw a moustache like that it was attached to a walrus.'

'Aaaaaarrrrrrggggh!' Julia's blood-curdling scream rattled the windows. Sara looked at us and winced.

'Armpits,' she said, clutching at hers painfully. We all sucked breath over teeth in sympathy. Five minutes later, Julia staggered out from the torture cell, wrapped in a pink silk dressing gown, her face a mass of angry red welts.

'Bloody Norah,' I said.

'Thanks a bunch,' Julia sniffed. Stefano cooed at her

kindly and offered her an ice pack for her upper lip, guiding her back to his star-studded chair. The girl called Cheryl slipped out from behind the screen, waving a waxy spatula at us.

'Anyone else while I'm at it?'

'No thanks,' I blurted quickly.

Sara ran a hand down her satin-smooth legs. 'I'm good,' she said.

'Mmm,' Leoni frowned, then stood up and unbuckled her trousers and had a quick shufty in her pants. 'Why not?' she announced. 'It's all a bit *Out of Africa* down there. How about a Brazilian?' Clearly, the champagne had done its work.

'Don't do it,' Sara warned her. 'I've been there, and I'm telling you, it ain't worth the pain.'

'Marcus will think I've taken a lover.' Leoni's brain started grinding away with the usual chain-reaction of far-fetched calculations. 'I can start slipping out all the time, saying I'm going to Sainsbury's and coming home with nothing but a smile and a dab of foreign aftershave. Then I can make sure he gets a glimpse of my new billiard ball. He'll go wild with envy. It'll be brilliant.' She got up and headed for Cheryl's couch, taking the bottle with her. 'I might be needing this.'

'Oi!' Sara reminded her sternly. 'You've got a car parked up the road which says you should have stopped drinking about half an hour ago.'

'Let them tow it away.' She flung her belt aside and started dropping her trousers. 'It's a shit-heap anyway.'

THE BEST PART of three hours later, the four of us spilled out into the street, just a tiny bit the worse for wear. Leoni's car was now sporting a yellow metal boot, the big sticker across the windscreen angrily shouting, 'Stop! Do not attempt to move it!' Leoni rummaged in her bag for a lipstick and scribbled a few choice obscenities on it.

'Isn't that better?'

I fell into step next to Julia, her glossy locks bouncing in the sunshine, all traces of grey obliterated. I reached out to touch it, its silky finish positively gliding through my envious fingers. I wish I had hair like that instead of having to make do with a headful of mousiness that refuses to grow much past my shoulders.

'Your hair looks amazing,' I told her.

'Yeah. And my face looks like it's been stuck on a sizzling skillet.'

The redness had gone down a little, but not much. In view of her appearance, we revised our plans and decided to abandon the notion of trailing around the shops making spontaneous purchases while slightly drunk. I have a wardrobe full of that kind of stuff anyway, thanks to Leoni's predilection for stopping every hour on the hour for a stiffie whenever we go for a shuffle around the shops together. I stuck my hand out and flagged down a passing cab.

'Come on, everyone. Let's go back to my house and knock up a cupboard surprise.'

'I've got a better idea.' Leoni clambered in, her bag clanking suspiciously with the two bottles she'd shamelessly sprung from Stefano's fridge. 'Let's nip round the corner first and knock up Captain Sexypants. I'm gagging for a shag and I have a feeling that today might just be my lucky day.'

STANDING ON THE DOORSTEP set across from the leafy garden square, I felt an involuntary wave of nostalgia as Leoni leaned her finger on the button. The speaker on the entryphone crackled into life.

'Yoo-hoo!' sang Leoni.

'Let me guess,' came the distinctive South American drawl from the world's most provocative man. 'It's my lover-girl come to see her aunt Sally.'

'You betcha, baby,' Leoni purred back. 'Let me in, let me in, or I'll blow your—'

'Leoni!' I smacked her arm.

'Is that Helen I hear?' Sally's salacious laugh lifted from the speaker as the catch on the front door buzzed a loud and clear welcome. We tramped up the wide staircase, passing my own abandoned flat on the first floor, turned the corner on the landing and headed up the second flight towards the sleek salsa rhythm drifting down the stairs.

'Hey, girls.' Sally was waiting for us, languidly leaning the full height of his taut body against the door frame and beaming his half-moon smile, which cut a flash of pearly white across his gorgeous, sun-kissed face. He hadn't bothered to button his shirt in the afternoon heat. It just hung open like a wicked invitation, loosely skimming his outrageous physique.

'Now *that* – ' Leoni kept on walking until her face made full contact with his bare chest – 'is what I call a real man.' She tossed her head back wantonly and pressed her breasts up against him. 'Oh, go on, Sal,' she pleaded. 'Just once. Then I can die a happy woman. I won't tell anyone. Promise.'

'Of course you will,' said Sally, sliding his taunting hands down her body. 'If you were capable of keeping a secret, baby, I'd have done you a long time ago.'

'Please!' She nuzzled against him. 'I've had my downstairs done specially.'

Peeling Leoni from his chest, Sally opened his arms and enveloped me in a divine mixture of crushed citrus, sweet herbs and a heady dose of dangerously potent pheromones. 'Hey, neighbour. You have no idea how much we've been missing you around here.' I had the instant urge to start bawling. In that moment, all I wanted to do was to come home and pretend that nothing had changed. To rush down one flight of stairs, open up my mothballed flat and convince myself that I had never left. As if sensing it, Sally held on to me for a moment longer than he needed to. 'Margarita time?' he murmured into my hair.

'Deffo.' Sara slapped his pert behind and barged straight in.

The rabble moved to the sitting room where they sat cooing over the pile of rough sketches spread around on the low coffee table. Now, I don't know much about art, but I know what I like, and Sally's illustrations are nothing short of spellbinding. You've more than likely seen them now and again in the glossy magazines. He somehow manages to capture the very essence of the human condition in a few, brief lines. A complex expression, told all at once in a single stroke of his pen, set against a kaleidoscopic background. His sense of colour seems to transcend any notion of the expected, but always looks just right. None of his work remains in the apartment, as every piece is sold before his pen touches the paper. I asked him once how he could bear to part with any of them, to which he just smiled and said that he had been put on this earth to bring pleasure to other people.

I gave Sally a hand in the kitchen, reaching automatically for the basket of limes while he emptied half a bottle of tequila over a jug of crushed ice. 'I've been bored without you,' he drawled. 'Now I have no one to play with.'

'Me too.' My eyes refused to behave and kept flicking down to the damp skin beneath his open shirt. It's no bloody wonder that I've been missing this place so much. The eye-candy deprivation has been worse than giving up chocolate for Lent.

'You never come to see me.' He nudged me seductively.

'I can't.' I began cutting the limes. 'I'm still trying to get used to the sight of Rick naked.' I pointed my knife at his open shirt. 'And that's not bloody helping, all right?'

'Sorry, baby,' he said, and slipped it off with a naughty smile, dropping it to the kitchen floor. I felt my temperature surge. Bloody phwoooooooooar. The scream of approval when he took the margarita tray through to the sitting room almost brought the ceiling down. Sara turned up the music and kicked off her shoes.

'Come on, big boy,' she said, shimmying her shoulders at Sally. 'Show me what you got.'

Sally had hold of her in an instant, thrusting his hips into hers, locking them together before throwing her into a dizzying spin. While they danced a sinful salsa around the carpet, Julia lay back on one sofa and stretched her legs across my lap. Leoni perched herself on the arm of the other, snapping her fingers to the infectious beat, calling encouragement and salivating over Sally's killer moves. He pulled Sara close and stuck to her like Velcro, bending her athletic body into the kind of shapes that would shatter my spine in an instant. Julia's hand found mine and squeezed it hard.

'Oh, to be young again, mmm?' she whispered. I was going to answer her with one of my stock-in-trade platitudes, but it dissolved on my tongue. I nodded quietly and watched Sara's smile as Sally dipped her low and kissed her neck.

'Thanks,' Julia said quietly.

'What for?'

'For kidnapping me today. I think I needed it.'

'It's not over yet.' I pulled her shoes off and dropped them on the floor, rubbing her feet. 'You're on a pink ticket until we take you home tomorrow, so you just sit there and chill, OK? Anything you want, just ask.'

'You have no idea how much this means to me.' Julia's nostrils began to flare. Oh no. Not here. Not *now*. 'I've been so wrapped up in looking after Frankie that I've forgotten how to look after myself. It's full on, Helen. Twenty-four hours a day. I barely have time to fart, never mind anything else.' She glanced down at her manicure. 'You know, it's been so long since I've painted my nails that they actually look weird to me right now. How bad is that?' She sighed. 'I just don't know if I can do this, Helen. It's like I've been catapulted into the middle of a black hole where I've ceased to exist as a person in my own right.'

'Sshhh,' I said, tugging on her sleeve. 'Now don't start all that again. Come on!' Julia nodded and tried to put on a brave face. I slipped out from under her legs and moved along the sofa, reaching out to give her a hug. 'We're all here for you.' I gathered her up and found her clinging to me. 'Nothing has changed.'

Her lips found my ear.

'I have to tell you something,' she whispered.

As she began to speak, the whole world seemed to move into slow motion, like that moment when you knock a box of eggs off the worktop then watch them almost float to the kitchen floor before everything speeds up again and they explode into the most almighty mess. I couldn't believe what I was hearing. I pulled back from Julia sharply. '*What* did you say?'

She leaned in close to me again, gripping my hand.

'I don't know who the father is.'

Chapter Eight

I'M SORRY,
I'LL REPEAT THAT

'HEY, TREACLE!' Rick emerged from his study the moment he heard our voices, grabbing Julia's hand and kissing her enthusiastically on both cheeks. 'Wow, Jools! You look a million dollars, girl!'

'Rick.' She returned his affection with a smile. 'It's been much too long.'

'Hi, babe!' The kiss I got was a lot more intimate than Julia's and tasted of freshly chewed Cohiba. It's OK. I'm getting used to it.

'Hi,' I said stiffly, unable to keep the agitation out of my voice.

Julia and I had hot-shoed out of Sally's place within thirty seconds of Julia delivering her bombshell. Quite what I had said by way of an excuse I can't even remember, only that we left behind three bemused expressions and a suggestion that Leoni crash at Sara's for the night. It wouldn't have been wise to leave her where she was. She's been trying to copulate with Sally ever since the day she first clapped eyes on him, only now that he's married to Paul, the chances of him having another one of his rare female interludes have all but disappeared. Leoni's biding her time, and swears blind that she'll get him to turn one day if it kills her.

'What have my two favourite girls been up to?' Rick pulled off his tie, signalling the end of any pretence of work for the day, and opened up his collar, undoing a couple of buttons. A brief flashback of Sally's rippling torso popped inappropriately into my head. Oh well. If one can't have steak, might as well settle for a burger. At least this one comes with a decent-sized gherkin on the side.

'Nothing much,' I said, barely trusting myself to speak. Julia stole nervous glances at me, no doubt awash with remorse for her disclosure and having some major second thoughts about having opened her margarita-lubricated mouth. My jaw ached with tension. I couldn't even look at her.

'Girlie stuff,' Julia added. 'Can I just nip to your bathroom?'

'You know where it is,' Rick said. 'Help yourself.'

I was already on my way to the kitchen. 'Julia's going to be staying here tonight.'

'Great!' Rick said. 'I'll take you both to dinner at Tony's, if you like. That'll get the old tongues wagging, eh?' He checked Julia was out of earshot. 'How's she doing?' he asked, his voice hushed with concern. Why he couldn't be like every other man and just bugger off, I don't know.

'Fine,' I said, matter-of-factly. 'And if you don't mind, I think we'd better give dinner a miss.'

'Oh.' He sounded disappointed and hung around while I slammed a few drawers and put the kettle on for a cup of tea that I didn't want. 'Er, you all right, Hell?'

'Bloody marvellous,' I snapped.

'Is something wrong, gorgeous?' Oh, just piss off, will you? I'm really not in the mood for all this touchy-feely stuff right now.

'Wrong?' I turned on him. 'What could possibly be wrong? Christ! Can't I have just one tiny little mood to myself without you giving me the third degree?' He backed off, real fast, holding his hands up in submission.

'Jeez,' he said. 'I was only tryin' to help.'

'Well, don't.' I threw up my arms. 'In fact, if you want to help, you can bloody well go out and find something to do on your own for a few hours. I need to speak to my sister in private, if you don't mind.'

'That's nice, isn't it? You're chucking me out of my own house?'

'No,' I banged the kettle down on the worktop. 'I'm chucking you out of *our* own house, OK?'

'Fine.' He picked up his keys from the kitchen table. 'I know when I'm not wanted.'

'Hallelujah,' I said, yet, like a sucker for punishment, Rick insisted on coming in for a goodbye kiss.

'Laters.' *Mwah*. 'Sure you I can't talk you into a quickie? I love it when you're angry.'

I pointed at the door. 'Out!'

JULIA HELD BACK until the coast was clear before daring to put in an appearance. I sat waiting for her, fingers drumming against the kitchen table, tight with unexplained fury. I had no idea where the anger had come from. Maybe it wasn't anger at all. Maybe it was something else. That's the thing about extreme emotions – most of them feel weirdly similar. I suppose it's all about the sentiments we decide to attach to them. Fear, hate, love, hostility – they all seem to set off the same raft of symptoms. The uncontrollable heartbeat. The surge of adrenalin. All normal, rational reasoning flying straight out of the window. This was no time to get hysterical. This was serious. Really serious.

Tentatively, Julia stepped into the kitchen. I stared at her as though seeing her for the first time, my eyes renewed.

'Sit down,' I said, then went to Rick's study to fetch the decanter of his best Armagnac. I had a feeling we were going to need it. As I pulled up the chair opposite hers, Julia's face wrenched itself into exactly the demeanour I remembered from our childhood whenever she got herself into steaming hot water. Like the time she sneakily borrowed Mum's one and only half-decent piece of jewellery, a Pinchbeck rabbit brooch with garnet eyes and a pearl tail, then promptly lost it somewhere between our front gate and the local flea-pit cinema one Friday night on her way to see *Carrie*. I attempted to corral my galloping thoughts into some kind of order.

My mind flew back to last September, and to the romance Julia had vehemently denied as summer segued into autumn. Her ex-fiancé, once the love of her life, and a European count, of all things (although Leoni prefers to shorten that particular handle to something altogether less royal), had turned up out of the blue, showering her with his newly divorced attentions. I had asked her outright whether or not she was playing away from home. At least, I thought I had. I sifted through my memory banks to find the exact point at which she had lied to me, but nothing came through. Perhaps I hadn't asked her directly at all. Perhaps I'd beaten around the bush like I usually do, allowing her to neatly sidestep the question. Well, let that be a lesson to me. Next time, I'll shine a Nazi lamp in her face and hammer a few toothpicks under her nails.

Julia uncorked the decanter and poured us each a frighteningly deep snifter.

'Say something,' she said.

'Like what?'

'Anything.'

'Let me guess,' I said icily. 'Count Stanislav von Westenholtz.' I picked up my glass and took a hit. 'Well, Julia. I've got to hand it to you. I'm shocked. Truly shocked.' She turned her head away. 'It's no bloody wonder you've lost your marbles. I'm surprised you're able to sleep at night.'

'I'm not,' she said.

'It's no less than you rightly deserve.' I shook my head judgementally. I know all marriages have their ups and downs, but getting pregnant by another man? That really takes the biscuit. I suppose it wouldn't seem quite so appalling if David weren't such a lovely bloke. What would this do to him? I quickly forced that minor detail from my reeling head. Julia stared grimly at the decanter. 'What are you going to do?' I asked, although, frankly, I'm not sure that I wanted to hear any more.

'I don't know.'

'Well, that's useful.'

'I just needed to tell somebody.'

'Thanks a bloody bunch, Julia. Now I feel as bad as you do.'

'I doubt that very much.'

The pair of us sat there and sighed a lot. Oh, what a mess. What a bloody, bloody mess. There was nowhere to go with this one. Nowhere to go but down, straight into the gaping jaws of hell.

'How long have you known?' I asked, although why this should matter seemed kind of academic right now.

'Since day one, I suppose,' she admitted ruefully. 'I think I was in shock. I mean, me? Pregnant?' Enough said. 'I had a hard enough time getting my head around that, never mind anything else. I guess I just shoved the paternity question out of my mind, thinking that it would all just go away and nobody would be any the wiser.'

'Brilliant.' I shook my head.

'I didn't know I was going to feel like this.'

'Does David suspect anything?'

'No!' Her whole body jerked upright. 'And you're not to say anything to anyone, either!'

'Of course not,' I said gravely. 'What the bloody hell do you think I am?' When the chips are down, the least us women can do is stick together. It's what we're famous for. 'How sure are you?'

'About David?'

'No, you idiot. About the baby. How sure are you that it's not his?'

'I'm not.' Julia bit her lip. 'I mean, I just don't know. My system's been on the blink for so long that I wouldn't have a cat in hell's chance of pinpointing the moment of conception.'

'Do you still love him?'

'Yes!' She glared at me incredulously. 'Of course I do!'

'Then why the bloody hell did you go and sleep with Stan?'

'Because I was bored.'

'*Bored?*' This just gets better and better. '*Is that it?*'

'No, of course that wasn't it!' She threw her hands in the air. 'I was bored shitless with my whole life. I was over forty and having my grey hairs dyed out every six weeks by a woman half my age.' She began shouting. 'You try fighting to keep an impossible fig-ure you should have given up on years ago! I was sick to death of worrying about how long it would be before my face slid into my pants.' Her fist hit the table. 'For fuck's sake, Helen! What do you want me to say? That I was stupid and selfish and callous without thinking about the consequences? Well, I was! And you know what? At the time, I loved every second of it.' The fury flashing in her eyes told of a thousand other reasons that she would never even try to explain. 'I was all those things I never thought I would be, OK? Satisfied?'

'So you decided that jumping into bed with Stan would fix all that, did you? Bloody hell, Julia. I thought you were supposed to be the intelligent one.'

'What am I going to do?' Julia pressed her face into her hands, her wedding ring catching a shaft of light from the halogen spots overhead, glinting its condemnation.

'Nothing,' I said, more harshly than I had intended. 'You've made your bed, so now you can bloody well lie in it.'

'Nothing? How can I do nothing?'

'You and David are going to bring up this child together and you're never going to mention another word about this ever again. Not to me, not even to yourself. Do you hear me?'

'No can do, I'm afraid.' She got up from the table, picked up her drink and poured the rest of it down the sink. 'The guilt is eating me alive.'

STILL WIDE AWAKE after an hour of counting black sheep and having eaten half an elephant tranquillizer, I felt Rick slide into bed beside me, keeping to his side, trying not to smell of garlic and cigars. I guessed he'd taken himself off to Tony's for dinner on his own with nothing but his voracious appetite for company. They take good care of him there. Always have done. It was a moonless night, and I'd heard him stumbling around in the dark, trying to brush his teeth and get his clothes off without putting the light on and disturbing me. I moved along the cool sheet and lay against him, feeling his arm come about me, snuggling into his chest hair. It stank of cigars too.

'Sorry,' I murmured, feeling deliciously hazy from the brandy and pharmaceuticals. 'I had a bit of a rough day today. I didn't mean to snap at you.'

'No worries, babe.' He kissed the top of my head. 'You sure there's nothing I can do?'

'You can help me deliver Julia back to her house tomorrow, if you like. After the day we've had, I expect she'd appreciate a lift.'

'Sure thing.' He tightened his arm around me. 'Anything else?'

Well, as he himself said, I was bound to buckle sooner or later.

THE BENTLEY swung lazily into Julia's drive, the huge tyres eating the gravel and churning deep tracks in their wake. Julia and I were settled comfortably together in the back, discreetly holding hands while Rick played chauffeur up front. Having mopped up what was left of our Armagnac hangovers with a couple of hand-raised pies in a crooked pub we found along the way, I hoped against hope that Julia would take heed and find a way to reconcile herself with her terrible secret. It was as though the ramifications of what she had told me were only just beginning to sink in. The way I saw it, she had no choice other than to sweep it under the carpet and move on. Fast. It was that cut and dried. There was nothing to discuss. I felt her hand become clammy in mine. Taking a tissue from my bag, I pressed it into her palm.

Rick switched the engine off, leaned an arm over the back of his seat and tugged his forelock at us.

'That'll be three shillings and sixpence, miss.'

'Want to come in for a cup of tea?' Julia gripped my wrist forcefully.

'Thought you'd never ask.' Rick was out of the car in seconds, pulling the door open for us. The warmth of the day invaded the air-conditioned interior in an instant, bringing with it the scent of newly mowed lawns and a sweet waft from the few remaining lupins that had somehow survived Leoni's Evel Knievel wheel-spin yesterday morning. Yesterday morning. Is that all that it was? It seemed like years ago. Like another time and place before everything changed. Everything was different now. Tainted. Spoiled. And I was guilty by association. Rick proffered his hand and helped Julia from the back seat while I let myself out of the other side. I looked up at the house, then at Julia.

'All quiet on the western front,' I said. 'That's got to be a good sign.'

Right on cue, a full-blooded Frankie wail rose from an open window upstairs. He must have sensed that his mother was home and decided to give her due warning that he was not best pleased about her having gone AWOL. Rick leaned through the driver's window and gave the horn a little honk before sealing off the bat-mobile with a wave of his key. Our footsteps scrunched along the gravel to the front door, but before Julia could get her key into the latch, David was already there, wrenching it wide open for us, a sheepish grin on his face.

'God, I've missed you!' He flung his arms around Julia. 'You look great! Had a good time?' David led her in, giving Rick and me a casual, 'Hi, you two!'

'Wotcha, mate.' Rick shook his hand. 'Still in one piece, then?'

'Course!' David smiled. 'Come on in! I was just about to open a bottle of something decent.'

I must say, for a man who'd been left holding the baby and forced to take an unscheduled day off work, David seemed remarkably relaxed. The newspaper lay open on the otherwise spotless kitchen table. The floor shone here and there with wet patches where the mop had been. There wasn't so much as a hint of mess anywhere. And if my nose was to be believed and that was stale cabbage I could smell, he'd even gone to the trouble of making himself something vaguely nutritious for lunch then cleared away every last scrap of it before his exhausted wife came home. Well, well. Good man. Wonders will never cease. Julia looked about the place and seemed completely flummoxed.

'Everything all right, darling?' she asked.

'Sure!' David busily buried a corkscrew deep into the neck of an expensive-looking claret.

'Where's Frankie?'

'Upstairs,' he smiled, concentrating on the bottle.

'Didn't I just hear him crying?'

'Did you?' David ripped the cork out and passed it under his nose. 'I can't say that I heard anything. Rick? Sling us a couple of those glasses, would you?'

Julia caught my eye and I had to agree with her – there was something not quite right here.

'Coming right up, mate.' Rick made himself at home, picking up some clean glasses from the draining board and running a tea towel over them, pretending that he knew his way around a kitchen.

'Has everything been all right while I was gone?' Julia looked up at the ceiling, straining her ears for any further sign of Foghorn Frankie.

'Stop fussing.' David glugged a good inch or so into each of the huge balloon glasses. 'Sit down and have a glass of wine.'

'I might take one of those outside and spark up if

that's all right with you,' Rick said, holding up a half-smoked stogie.

'Be my guest. Don't suppose you've got an extra one, by any chance?'

'Does the pope shit in the woods?' Rick pulled the leather Cohiba case out of his pocket and tossed it to the table.

'Where's the baby-listener?' Julia suddenly demanded, scanning the worktops.

'No need,' David said breezily. 'Everything's perfectly under control.'

Then something caught Julia's eye.

A lilac cardigan, hung neatly on a hanger, with a headscarf placed between it and the wood to avoid catches, the whole ensemble hooked on the back of the kitchen door. I followed her gaze, the pair of us instantly coming to the same, hideous conclusion. There is only one person I know in the whole world who is anal enough to do that. Julia and I looked at each other.

'Mum,' we chorused.

'Is that Julia I can hear?' Our mother's shrill voice tore a hole through the walls a good ten seconds before she came striding into the kitchen.

'Richard!' she positively dashed towards Rick. 'What a lovely surprise! How wonderful to see you. Gosh! Don't you look well!'

Julia and I locked eyes, our expressions deadpan.

'Hello, Joyce!' Rick swept up her hand and planted a big smacker on the back of it. 'How's that for a bit of fresh air on a summer's day?' He stepped back and admired her floral, non-crease dress.

'Did you bring the Bentley with you?' she began, peering out of the window. 'Oh yes. There it is. Very nice.'

'Hi, Mum.' I administered the obligatory kiss.

'Hello, dear.' She allowed me to peck her powdered cheek, then moved on to Julia. 'Julia? Well I must say that your hair's looking rather better than it was the last time I saw you.'

'Mum.' Julia kissed her reluctantly and fixed a glare of daggers on David. 'What an unexpected surprise.'

'Would you like one of these, Joyce?' David made for safe ground and offered his mother-in-law a glass of wine.

'At this time in the afternoon? Good gracious, no. I might have a very small gin and tonic later. Anyone for a cup of tea?' She reached for the kettle and started marching around the kitchen as though it were her own, fetching the milk (which she had previously decanted into a jug, of course) from the fridge, and taking the warmed pot from the Aga. The atmosphere in the room thickened like lumpy gravy. 'So where did you two girls go running off to yesterday?'

'Nowhere,' Julia said.

'Just taking a bit of time out, Mum,' I added. 'Julia's been sitting around staring at these four walls for long enough.'

'Hmph.' Mum threw the tea towel over her shoulder. 'Perhaps I should have done the same thing and abandoned your father to fend for himself when you were a baby. But things were different in my day. You couldn't just drop everything and go gallivanting off whenever the fancy took you. That poor boy's been yelling his head off for his mother. It's a jolly good thing that David called me.' The kettle came to a rapid, angry boil. 'Still,' she said with a small sniff, 'I'm here now.'

'Great.' Julia's face fell into a sulk.

'Where's Dad?' I glanced out into the garden hopefully. Maybe we could salvage something of the afternoon and get the old man to dismantle Mum's hair-trigger detonating device.

'Oh, he's long gone, dear.' She waved her hand at us. 'Hopeless around babies. He hung around for a couple of hours yesterday, but once he knew that you two weren't coming back, he went home.'

'Yesterday?' Julia scowled at David accusingly. 'And at just what time did David call you?'

'Oh, about eleven, I suppose.'

In other words, about an hour after we'd made our escape.

'And you didn't think to check with me first?' This time, Julia ignored Mum's presence and addressed her husband.

'I thought you'd be pleased,' he said defensively. 'I know how tired you've been lately. And now that you're not feeding Frankie yourself any more.' Dear, oh dear. I've never seen anyone skating so fast towards the thinnest patch of ice on the pond.

'Not feeding him *myself*?' Julia rounded on him. 'And since when did anyone else feed him?'

'Now, now, dear,' said Mum, busying herself with the tea bags. 'You know very well that this is women's work. I told you that I would be here the minute you got him on the bottle. I think someone's been telling little porkie pies, hmm?'

'Give me strength.' Julia's knuckles shone white as she gripped the back of a kitchen chair.

Rick feigned deep interest in the cactus on the window ledge.

'Would anyone else care for a cup of tea? I'm making a whole pot anyway. I can't understand these people who squeeze a bag around in a mug. It's so uncivilized.'

'I'll have one,' David said obsequiously. 'Seeing as you make the best cuppa in the world.' I flashed my eyes at Rick.

'Er, yeah. Go on then, Joyce. I don't suppose you brought one of your home-made cakes with you, eh?' Why, you slimy, toadying bastard. Just for that, I hope she bloody well has and that you shatter your teeth on it.

'I'm afraid not, Richard,' Mum said, wagging a playful finger at him. 'But I did bake one this morning!' She turned triumphantly to the worktop and lifted a tea towel away from the concrete slab she'd made earlier. I was tempted to stay and watch her try to get a knife through it, yet the twitch at the corner of Julia's mouth demanded I take evasive action before the cake knife ended up embedded in David's skull.

'Come on.' I grabbed a couple of glasses from the table and nodded Julia towards the back door that leads out to the baize-smooth bowling-green lawn. She has a man come and do it for her once a week. A man she can rely on. 'Let's go and see if you've got any fairies down the bottom of your garden.'

'Bloody bastard,' she spat as we trudged past the well-kept flowerbeds. 'I'll kill him. So help me God.'

'I'm sure he meant well.'

'No he bloody didn't. Lazy git. Haven't I got enough on my plate without the battleaxe breathing down my neck and criticizing my every move?'

'Just calm down. Right now, it seems to me that you need all the help you can get. All you have to do is keep out of her way and let her do all the work.'

'So that she can make me look totally inadequate, you mean?'

'Does she do that to you as well?' This was a turn-up

for the books. Ever since I could remember, Mum couldn't have made it plainer that Julia was her favourite. It was always Julia this and Julia that. Anyone would have thought that I was just an unfortunate accident that came along a few years later to throw a spanner in the works.

'Of course she does. Nothing's ever good enough.'

We shared a sigh of camaraderie.

'I wish the old man had stayed,' I said, suddenly missing him awfully.

'Are you kidding me?' Julia took a big swig of wine. 'He was probably beaming like a Cheshire cat all the way home. I expect he'll be up the Royal Oak having a few jars with the allotment brigade without being put on a half-hour time limit by Boadicea.' She sank to the grass and lifted her face to the low afternoon sun. 'God knows how I'm going to get rid of her.'

'Well, don't look at me.' I dropped to the ground and joined her. 'I'm fresh out of silver bullets.'

'It's no good you know, Helen.' Julia shook her head sadly at the never-ending stretch of cloudless sky. 'I can't keep up this charade much longer. It's like the whole thing is sitting on the tip of my tongue, morning, noon and night.'

'You mustn't say anything.' I hushed my voice to a whisper.

'How can I bring up a child without knowing who the father is?'

'Does it matter?' Even I knew that I was grasping at straws here.

'Of course it bloody matters.' She finished her wine in two enormous gulps and let the empty glass roll into the flowerbed.

'Right,' I said decisively. 'Then there's nothing else for it.'

'What?'

'You're going to have to get a DNA test. Then you'll know for sure.' Julia lay back on the grass and stretched her arms over her head.

'If only it were that simple,' she muttered.

'Trust me,' I said. 'It is.'

Chapter Nine

TESTING, TESTING

A FEW YEARS AGO, when I was newly thrust back into the Real World and left to fend for myself, the inimitable Sara attempted to drag me kicking and screaming into the twenty-first century by teaching me how to use email. I say attempted, because we never really got out of the starting blocks. I did try to warn her, but she'd taken no notice of my snivelling, insisting that it was child's play. Unsurprisingly, she was soon forced to admit defeat and gave up trying to hammer a square peg into a round hole. What can I say? My heart just wasn't in it. From the way she had gone on at me about it, I'd been left with the distinct impression that not being au fait with online technology was a capital offence. It was a very worrying time for me. Anyway, suffice to say that, despite the trauma Sara put me through, I'm still here, living testament to the theory that you really can survive in this fast-moving world as a fully qualified techno-twit.

I skirted around the silver laptop sitting on the desk in Rick's study like a cat circling a suspicious cushion. Julia and I had agreed that she could have no hand in the sourcing and supply of the necessary laboratory equipment. If she were to get caught – well, let's just not go there. No. I would have to take on that part of the task myself and, according to Julia, I'd be able to find all the information I needed just by typing a few choice words into something called a search engine. Sounded simple enough. The typing certainly wouldn't be a problem. I've done plenty of that in my time, having learned at school on a rusty old Imperial that had probably seen trench action in the First World War. Then I was unleashed into the workplace to feverishly discover the heady speeds of an electric IBM golfball that went *ping* at the end of each line. I've even used a word processor once or twice. Yes. I thought you'd be impressed.

I opened the laptop. The screen burst into life and made a satisfying little digital bing-bong sound. So far, so good.

'Hell-yen?' Helga barged in. I slapped the laptop shut. 'You vart coffee?'

'Is it that time already?' I looked at the clock. Gracious. Had I really been pissing around for over half an hour already, getting nowhere? 'Yes please, Helga.'

She eyed me knowingly.

'You make spy?' She squinted at the laptop.

Well. There was no point in denying it, seeing as I'd been caught with my fingers well and truly in the till, and no point in trying to give a complicated explanation either, seeing as Helga could barely string a sentence together despite having lived here for the best part of five years.

'Yes. I make spy.'

'Ah!' she nodded. 'You good. Me make spy with hutsbant. Me know he look, erm, eez . . .' her brain began to fizzle. 'Eez, POOMPH!' She mimicked big breasts and several miscellaneous porn websites.

'Oh,' I said, nodding understandingly. 'Does he indeed. Typical bloke.'

'*Da.*' She tutted and shook her head. 'Tippick block. Tits, *da?*' We sighed together, united in our opinion. It's the same, the world over. 'Hmph,' she decided. 'I look his computer too.'

'Really?' The notion of Helga navigating her way around a piece of modern technology blew a fuse in my head. 'You know how to use one of these things?'

'*Da!*' she said. 'I find man with big *moskovoya*. Is make picture for looking on computer. Is very nice.' The duster twitched in her hands. 'I make picture for him also.'

'Eh?' I hoped I had misunderstood. 'You mean, you put pictures of yourself on the Internet?'

'*Da*! Lots of picture!' She muttered to herself, flicking through her internal and somewhat limited vocabulary. 'Lots of people. It like, erm, you make meet if you want.'

'You meet?'

'*Da*. We meet for make sex.'

'Helga!' Hold the front page. 'I don't believe it!'

'You believe!' she snapped, storming towards me. I automatically lifted my arms to protect my head. The laptop was open in a second as Helga expertly sparked up the browser, tapping away at the keys. 'Look!' she pointed.

God forgive me, but I couldn't help myself. And don't say that you wouldn't have taken a peek either. The hairs on my arms stood on end. I've seen those television advertisements for Internet dating sites, but this . . . well, this was something else entirely. Under a flashing red-banner heading announcing 'Bored Russian Housewives' sat a set of toe-curling pictures, some of which were visually unintelligible (i.e. what the hell is *that*?).

'Is women,' Helga explained without a shred of inhibition. She clicked the pad below the keyboard. Another page loaded. My eyes nearly fell out of my head. 'And this is man, da?' I squinted at the screen. A man? Are you absolutely sure it's not a horse? I blinked and turned my head up the other way. Nope. It was a man all right. I looked at her, my mouth agape. She gave me a salacious smile. 'Is good, *nyet*?'

'Dear God,' I mumbled. Helga sniggered to herself as she tapped a few more keys and the horse-man disappeared, the computer screen now an innocuous, wavy blue space. She closed the lid.

'Ja mik coffee now, *da*?' I just sat there, dumbstruck. 'Mit wodka?'

'Not in mine, thanks, Helga.' Like a lifelong punishment, I knew I'd never be able to get that picture out of my head, not for so long as I lived and breathed. 'You go ahead and help yourself.'

Ten-thirty is turbo-coffee time in the bleak Russian gulag Helga hails from. Guaranteed to hit your larynx like an oncoming Siberian express: two of those and you won't be going anywhere for the rest of the day. Believe me, I've tried. Helga scampered out of the door. I lifted the lid of the laptop again. Now come on, woman. It can't be that bloody complicated if numb-skull Helga can manage it. Every kid in the country knows how to use one of these things.

There was nothing on the screen that gave me even the slightest clue, just a row of little pictures along the bottom, each one of which meant something, presumably. Some were self-explanatory. A camera. A calendar.

A waste-paper basket. The rest could have been any old thing. I was obviously going to have to do this by a process of elimination. Right. Here we go. Click. Nothing. Mmm. Scratch, scratch. Staring at the screen. Click, click, click. Ah-ha! Something opened with pictures of spanners and filing cabinets and God knows what else. Now, I'm no Stephen Hawkins, but it didn't look very Internetty to me, so I tried to get rid of it. All I had to do was to work out how to undo what I had just done.

The study door opened again. The aroma of fresh coffee. I was so engrossed in what I was doing that I hardly noticed as the cup went down on the desk. A warm hand covered my eyes.

'Guess who?' Rick growled.

I clean jumped out of my skin.

'Rick!' Thumpity-thump, thumpity-thump. 'Will you please stop creeping up on me like that!'

'What ya doin'?' He leaned over me and peered at the screen.

'Aren't you supposed to be in a meeting somewhere?' I span round in his black leather world-domination chair.

'Nah!' He cracked his knuckles, sat himself on the edge of the low cabinet and took a slurp of coffee. 'Complete bloody waste of time. Spud did a background check on the bloke's company and he hasn't got a pot to piss in. I told Ange to ring him and tell him to sling his hook. Mind you – ' he glanced at his Piaget – 'he's probably already there, so she can tell him in person.'

'That'll make her day,' I said. 'I expect she's sharpening her machete as we speak.' Mindful that this little diversion tactic was only going to last for so long, the moment was fast approaching when I'd have to explain to him why I was sitting at his desk trying to hack into his computer. Right. Say something really interesting and throw up a smoke screen. 'And how is the lovely Angela?'

'What do you care?' he smiled. 'You hate her guts.'

'I'm trying to take an interest in your work. You know, like a good wife?'

'I shouldn't worry about it. She's not your biggest fan either.'

'Charming! It's not as though I've ever done anything to offend her, except to breathe in and out.'

'Waddya expect, babe? I think she was hoping I'd declare my undying love to her one day and make an honest woman of her.' I stood up from the desk, affected a weary yawn with a big stretch, and softly closed the laptop as I brought my arms back down to my sides. Smooth. Very smooth. 'So, what were you looking for?' He nodded towards the desk.

'Looking for?' I adopted a suitably puzzled expression.

'On the computer.'

'Computer?' I glanced at it as though I'd never seen it in my life. 'Oh, that.' I wrinkled my nose. 'Nothing. I was just looking at it.'

'Oh yeah?' He raised an eyebrow at me. 'Not that I mind. You can look at anything you want to.' Don't worry, mate. I already have.

'I've been thinking,' I said innocently. 'It's pretty hopeless my trying to take an interest when I can't even work a computer. I think it's high time I dragged myself into the twenty-first century and at least got my head around how to send an email, don't you?' I waited for a casual enough pause to pass before adding, 'And the Internet, of course. In this day and age, only an idiot doesn't know how to surf the net!' Jargon too. God, I'm good. I sat down again.

'Blimey,' he said. 'You do surprise me. I thought you were a confirmed Luddite.'

'It's never too late to teach an old dog new tricks.'

'I'm glad it's you who said that and not me,' he smiled. 'OK, twinkle, round you go.' He twisted the chair around so that I was facing the desk again. 'Just open the top and I'll show you what to do. And if you're a very good girl – ' I felt his breath close to my cheek – 'I'll take you out and buy you one of your own.'

'HI.' USHERING JULIA IN, I checked the street to make sure she hadn't been followed.

'Is he out?' she whispered.

'Yep.' I put the chain on the door (a new industrial-sized version that was, I hoped, Helga-proof). 'Everything's upstairs.'

We crept up to the top of the house to the dungeon, the smallest of the six bedrooms and roughly the size of a priest hole. Nobody ever goes in there, unless they've been very, very naughty. I opened the bottom drawer of the tiny dresser, lifted the linen aside and pulled out the big manilla envelope that had arrived yesterday morning. That had been a close shave, hanging around by the door three days in a row, feeling as guilty as sin, waiting for the postman to arrive. I'd virtually ripped it out of the letterbox before he'd let go of the other side. I expect he thinks we're harbouring a man-eating Hound of the Baskervilles in here now. Julia and I sat down on the bed. I tipped the contents out.

'Bloody hell.' Julia picked up one of the three smaller envelopes that fell out. Each one was labelled with a different colour sticker, with space for the person's name, date of birth, ethnic group and signature. 'Alleged father,' she read from the sticker. 'Shit. This is really bad.'

'I know,' I said. The sight of all the forms suddenly lent a terrible gravitas to the situation. 'There's a pair of swabs in each of those envelopes,' I pointed out. 'They're just long cotton buds, really. You've got to get a sample from you, another one from Frankie, and, of course, one from David.'

Julia picked up the detailed instructions and started to read.

'No tea, coffee or tobacco for four hours. Blah blah blah. Wash hands. Yep. Yep.' She scanned further down the page and paused. 'Cheek swabs?' She looked up at me. 'How the bloody hell am I supposed to get a cheek swab out of David without raising his suspicion?'

'Don't worry.' I sifted through the papers. 'I did a bit of research about that. Hang on a minute. I know it's here somewhere. I printed it off the Internet myself.' Big wow. Deafening applause. 'There's a whole load of other stuff they can use. Here it is. Listen to this. Blood—'

'Blood?! Well, that's no sodding good, is it? What am I supposed to do? Stick a syringe in his artery while he's asleep?'

'Shhh.' I held up my hand. 'Let me finish. Blood stains, like you get on a used Elastoplast.'

'Sorry.' She nodded. 'Right.'

'Clothing, like baseball caps, which have been close to the head where a few cells might have rubbed off. And underwear.' We both looked at each other and pulled a face. 'Dental floss, ear wax –' blurgh – 'electric razor clippings. Does David use an electric razor?'

'No.'

'Floss?'

'Sometimes, but he throws it straight in the loo and flushes it.'

'Never mind. Chewing gum, so long as it's sugar-free. Hair, with the follicle attached, of course.' I could feel myself getting into my role. This was better than *Columbo*. 'A licked envelope, you know, with a bit of saliva.' Julia was concentrating intently, staring at the carpet. 'Nail clippings, and, well . . .' I put the sheet down. 'We don't need to go through the rest of the list.'

'Why not?'

'Because we're talking samples from a dead body. Unless you've got some other way of getting hold of a slice of David's liver.'

'Oh.'

'So that gives us a bit more scope, doesn't it?' I did my best to sound positive and cheerful. 'I thought you could offer to give him a pedicure or something.'

'That would be a first.' She picked up the other envelopes and had a look inside. 'Mind you, needs must, I suppose.'

'Well? What do you think?'

'Seems straightforward enough.' She sounded hesitant.

'Is there a problem?'

'I can't take these home with me.' Julia pushed the envelopes away. 'God knows, with Mum in the house it would be asking for trouble. She's already "tidied" every drawer in the house and had a good old snoop around.'

'That's terrible.' I mirrored her scowl of disapproval. 'She's got no respect for other people's privacy.'

'I'll have to bring Frankie over here,' she concluded. 'You don't mind, do you?'

'What, with Mum?'

'I know.' We sat and frowned. 'Maybe I can get rid of her, although she's showing no signs of leaving anytime soon. Bloody David. Pretending to hang on her every word and hinting about braised beef and mashed potatoes and "nothing like a full English breakfast, is there, Joyce".' She let out a puff of female frustration. 'He knows I don't cook. I never cook. I *hate* cooking. It's a complete and utter waste of my time. If he wants something that badly, he can pick up a Delia Smith book and bloody well make it himself. If you can read, you can cook. All this bollocks about *oh-I'm-not-very-good-in-the-kitchen*.' Her mewling impression was pretty much spot on. 'He just can't be bothered. And why should he have to so long as Mum's there waiting on him hand and foot and giving me the evils?'

'Look,' I said. 'You just do whatever you need to do. If she turns up here with you, I'll get her out of the way somehow and keep her distracted. Now all you have to do is pin David down and rip a couple of his fingernails out. Oh yes.' I suddenly remembered. 'There is one other small thing.'

'What?'

'It's just that . . .' Hmm, how to put this. 'Well, apparently it's completely illegal to gather a DNA sample from somebody without their express permission. That's why they're supposed to sign all the forms too.'

'Great,' Julia said. 'And what happens if I get caught?'

'Oh, nothing much.' I shrugged. 'I think I might have seen something about a massive fine. And a prison sentence, maybe.'

'Perfect.' Julia got up. 'Next time you make one of your almond cakes, you'd better practise hiding a nail file in it.'

Chapter Ten

THE NAME'S BOND. JAMES BOND

'GOT IT?' I don't know why I was asking Helga if she could manage. It was me who was struggling. We'd been at it for hours, my aching limbs ready to snap clean off.

'*Da*,' she said through gritted teeth as she lifted her end clean off the floor.

'OK.' The sparrow's kneecap muscles in my arms were already starting to quiver. 'Over there.' I bucked my head towards the space we'd cleared by the south-facing window and we shuffled across the carpet together before gratefully depositing the sofa on the other side of the sitting room. 'That's it.' I dusted off my hands and consulted the list that had arrived with Lily's monstrous bill. It was no bloody wonder she could afford to jet off to China to grab a couple of bottles of magic tincture every time she felt a wrinkle coming on. Writing out the enormous cheque, I'd felt positively fleeced in return for a few cushion covers and a list of nonsensical instructions. No pointy or pokey things with sharp corners. No single items, matching pairs only. No clutter, not that there was ever any here in the first place.

Helga took a sharp intake of breath. '*Chto za huy?*' She threw herself to the patch of carpet where the sofa had been. There, cowering under Helga's furious glare, lay a mark, about the size of a ten pence piece, that looked suspiciously like dried guacamole welded to the velvet pile. '*Govno!*' She began to pick at it with her fingernails, muttering unintelligible expletives under her breath before scurrying off to the kitchen and coming back with a blowtorch.

I sat on one of the reshuffled seats and tried to reacquaint myself with the space. It certainly felt fresher – more open if you like – and the introduction of Lily's recommended accent colours with a few bright scatter cushions and a matching pair of voluptuously curved red vases on the mantelpiece seemed to have made all the difference. Spooky. Perhaps there was something to be said for this feng shui nonsense after all.

Helga hummed to herself contentedly. She keeps the house like a shiny new pin, which doesn't leave much room for her to exercise her Russian stain-busting techniques. For her to find a rogue blemish lurking somewhere is like the Queen discovering a stranger standing in her bedroom. Heads will roll, and she won't be satisfied until all evidence of the offender has been obliterated.

'Do you want to take any of this stuff home with you?' I asked. She sat back on her knees and squirted what remained of the mark with a pile of caustic mousse. 'Helga?' No response. I think she may have been counting in her head. 'Hell-ga!'

'Huh?' She blinked. I pointed to the bags of rejected household objects and soft furnishings sitting out in the hallway waiting to be consigned to the nearest charity shop. There was no point in hanging on to any of it. Lily had been quite firm with her instructions to sling it all out before Rick could salvage anything and make a fuss about it.

'You take?' I asked. 'They're only going to Oxfam, so you can have anything you want out of there.'

'Ah.' She knocked her forehead with her fist. '*Nyet*,' shaking her head in defeat. 'Agan.'

'You,' I pointed at her, 'take this – ' I waved my arms

at the bags – 'to your home? You take home. *Da?*' Big nod and a smile of encouragement. Her eyes widened.

'You make *present?*' she squealed.

'*Da*, Helga. Present from me and Rick.'

'Reek make present?'

'Yep.' Suddenly she was on me like an alien face-hugger, the sweet aroma of yesterday's vodka intake clinging to her pink overall.

'You good Hell-yen.' She stood back, grasping my shoulders, then slapped her chest. 'To-marrow, I bring present for you.' Helga's idea of a suitable gift is the remains of her breakfast wrapped up in tin foil.

'No need.' I patted her hand before removing her fingers from my collar. 'I hope you can get some use out of it.' If I didn't know better, I might have thought that was a tear I saw welling up in Helga's right eye rather than a splash of industrial carpet cleaner. 'Come on,' I said. 'Time for a coffee break.'

The futuristic steel kitchen had been brought back down to mother earth with a set of pale linen Roman blinds softening the light in place of the aluminium slats that had been there before, and a pretty row of delicate potted orchids running along the length of the window sills. On Lily's recommendation, all the knives had been removed from the magnetic strip on the wall and put away in a drawer instead. Whether or not this was part of her feng shui formula or just a common-sense move in any marital home is something I'll probably never know. Either way, the overall effect had been a runaway success. It no longer felt like a sterile operating theatre, and Helga and I slumped gratefully to the kitchen table and admired our handiwork.

'Much better, don't you think?' I said as I poured a slug of Stoli into her mug.

'*Da.*' She nodded approvingly around the room, took the bottle, and insisted that I keep her company, slinging a double Kremlin measure in mine. Well, why not? You can't say that we hadn't earned our vices today, and after lunking all that furniture around, my legs were like jelly anyway. I braced myself and took a swig.

'Helga? Can I ask you a personal question?' Bearing in mind that she probably wouldn't understand a word anyway, I soldiered straight on. 'You and your husband.'

'Hutsbant?'

'Yes. You and Mr Helga.'

'Ah. Boritz.'

'Is that his name? Boris?' After all this time, a hazy picture began to form of the man Helga shared her life with. His name was Boris, and for some inexplicable reason, he had chosen to marry Helga. That in itself said something about the man.

'*Da.* Boritz. He, umm –' grinding of brain cells – 'how to say. He fat.' She filled her cheeks with air, blowing up like a pufferfish. 'Big fat pig. He like to eat the pig fat.' She did a quick impression of Mr Helga eating lumps of lard.

'Are you happy together?'

'Ha-peee?' Helga struggled with the question, gulped down some more coffee and reached for the vodka bottle. 'Ha-peee.' She experimented with the word for a while and thought about it. '*Nyet*,' she concluded. 'We married. What for happy?'

'But don't you want to be happy?'

'Me?' Another huge slurp. 'Me happy. He no happy. He fat.' She held her hands out by her sides. 'Faaaaa-t.' Then blew a raspberry.

By the time I got down to the bottom of my mug, I could barely see the hand in front of my face thanks to Helga's insistent top-ups. Sometimes you just have to go with the flow. The vodka flow, that is. To reject a Russian's offer of hospitality is tantamount to slapping them in the face and calling them a ponce, and they're not the kind of people to back down from a fight easily. It's their national sport. An hour later, Helga seemed largely unaffected by her flammable refreshments, while I found myself stumbling around in the hall.

'Let me call you a taxi,' I suggested, trying not to slur my worms. 'You can't possibly manage all this on your own.'

'*Nyet*.' She punched my arm. 'I strong!'

'I know, Helga, but there's an awful lot of stuff here.'

'Pah,' she spat, then loaded herself up like a pack-horse and staggered out of the door towards the bus stop, leaving me blissfully alone.

Upstairs, the bedroom beckoned, bedecked as it was with new, crisp white bed linen instead of Rick's standard-issue charcoal grey, an enormous vase of cut flowers on the dresser and half a dozen deliciously expensive perfumed candles dotted around at strategic intervals. Although I had drawn the line at removing the television set, Helga and I had dutifully dragged the bed to the adjacent wall to face east/west rather than north/south. If you line your body up to the earth's magnetic poles while sleeping, it sucks all the energy out of your brains, apparently. Seemed like a load of old cobblers to me, but why risk it? After a quick run around under a hot shower to strip away the morning's hard labour, I lit a couple of the candles and slipped between the sheets on the pretext of seeing if I could detect any discernible difference. That's my excuse, anyway. It was definitely nothing to do with the vodka coma settling over me like a Dickensian pea-souper . . .

That damned Daniel Craig just wouldn't take no for an answer, his body crushing me up against the silk-lined walls of the Parisian hotel suite with the enormous four-poster bed just inches away. 'No,' I murmured, trying to force my head away from his urgent lips. 'Yes,' he insisted, tearing the shirt from his rock-hard body, forcing open my silk robe, his gun ready to go off at any second. He was too strong for me. There was nothing I could do but succumb. I felt myself thrust down upon the cool sheets, his hands all over me, my skin on fire. 'Oh God,' I groaned. 'Oh, yes. Mmmm.' His hot breath on my face, his mouth on mine, then moving down, down . . . holy mother of Jesus . . . the faint aroma of an expensive cigar . . . Eh? My eyelids began to flicker, my consciousness flooding back into the room . . .

'Mmm,' growled Rick. 'God, you're fantastic.'

Eyes wide open. Rick lying behind me, his hands on my knockers, my shameless body quite obviously having a whale of a time while my subconscious had quite clearly been somewhere else entirely. I made a quick inventory of the situation. Me fast asleep, partially inebriated, having my favourite Daniel Craig dream. Husband comes home, finds the missus in bed naked, in the middle of the afternoon, freshly showered, candles lit, roses in vases. It's an open-and-shut case, m'lud. A gilt-edged invitation if ever there was one. Oh well. Best not rain on his parade. The *moskovoya* didn't feel like it was in any mood to change its mind anyway, so I closed my eyes and tried to scramble back into the four-poster with James Bond while Rick in the real world had his wicked way. And . . . action.

*

IF ONLY I'D checked out of the bedroom window before answering the front door. Mum looked me up and down disapprovingly. 'Helen?' Great. Perfect bloody timing, as usual. 'Why on earth aren't you dressed, dear?' She shoved me back inside, lest I should be seen in my dressing gown by some mere mortal passing in the street. Julia brought up the rear with a sigh, struggling a sleeping Frankie through the door in his buggy.

'I just took a shower,' I explained, resisting the temptation to add, 'and then had rampant fantasy sex with 007.'

'In the middle of the afternoon?' Oh, for heaven's sake. Here we go again with the correct-time-for-every-thing routine. The mouth turned down into its usual curve of displeasure. 'Why can't you shower in the mornings like normal people?' She began looking around, taking in every detail of the entrance hall. 'Goodness me,' she said, her eyes wandering freely. 'This is all rather grand, isn't it?'

'Hell?' Rick boomed down the stairs. 'Was that the door?'

'Yes!' I shouted back.

'Well tell whoever it is to piss off and get your arse back up here. I haven't finished with you yet!'

Mum's jaw dropped.

'I'm afraid the furniture moving will have to wait,' I

yelled up the stairs, then, turning to Mum, I said, 'We've been having a little change around. I was a bit sweaty.' Julia turned her face away, muffling her snigger behind an ineffectual cough. 'It's Mum!' I shouted up to Rick. 'And Julia!'

Frankie started squirming in his seat, opened his eyes, then his mouth, and let out a howl of protest.

'Thanks a bloody bunch,' said Julia wearily. 'I'd just managed to get him off to sleep and you two have to start screaming at each other like a pair of banshees.'

'Julia! Language!' Mum screeched. 'Oh, there, there.' She bent down and set about trying to unbuckle the NASA mechanism on the buggy belt, displaying her enormous rump, packed into a pair of powder-blue Marks and Spensive slacks. Rick did a double-take at the size of it as he came down the stairs to greet us. How he'd managed to get his clothes on that quickly was something of a miracle, but there was nothing to be done about the post-coital flush in his cheeks.

'I'll just pop upstairs and get myself dressed,' I said, deliberately bumping my way past him, feeling his fingers nip my bottom.

'Hi, Jools!' Rick stayed where he was and raised a hand towards Julia rather than bringing her in for a kiss. After what we'd been up to, probably best not to get too close. 'Joyce.' He offered her a small bow.

'Richard!' she gushed, charging at him, babe in arms. He put out his hands to stop her, patting the baby's screaming head.

'Hello, little fella!' Tickle, tickle.

'Waaaaaaaaaaah!'

'Did you bring the milk?' Mum barked at Julia. 'Just look at him! The poor thing's half starved to death!'

'WHERE IS IT?' Julia stuck her head around my bedroom door.

'Upstairs. Exactly where we left it.' I hopped around the room trying to get my trousers on, then grabbed a fresh shirt out of the wardrobe. 'You get up there and do the one for you. Then at least that's one of them out of the way. I'll make sure that Mum stays put and doesn't go wandering.'

I ran down the stairs to find Rick showing Mum into the sitting room. As he reached the threshold, he slowed and stopped in his tracks.

'Blimey!' He turned to me. 'What's been going on in here?'

'Do you like it?'

'Where's the African mask that was on that wall?'

'I moved it.' I said, quietly polishing another small fib on my sleeve. 'And a few other things. I hope you don't mind.' He frowned for a moment.

'And where's the vase that was on that—' He stopped and looked around quickly. 'Table. Where's the side table gone?'

'Upstairs,' I said. Mum settled herself and Frankie on one of the sofas, never taking her eyes off us, lapping up every awkward word.

'Oh dear. Has she been imposing herself on your lovely house, Richard?' Mum steered the bottle into Frankie's yelling mouth. He clamped his gums around it and began sucking like a Dyson.

'*Our* house,' I snapped at her. Sensing the tension, Rick slung a casual arm around my shoulder.

'She can burn the whole place down and start again if she wants to, Joyce. I've got no taste of my own any- way. All this was done by some poof in a frilly shirt who makes a living taking advantage of ignorant barrow- boys like me.'

Mum tried not to look disgusted. Any word that even suggests a leaning towards homosexuality is the height of vulgarity in her dictionary, especially after the wedding fiasco. It's just not normal, she says. That's why she changed churches following the scandal with Father Mulholland after a young deacon had been caught polishing his conscience in the confes- sional.

'Well, I must say,' Mum said, 'I wouldn't have thought you would have wanted her to change a single thing after going to such expense with a *proper* decorator. It's a very elegant house just as it is. She'll only go and spoil the effect.'

'Oh, put a sock in it will you, Mum?' I flung myself into one of the other sofas. 'Why can't you just chill out and stop finding fault with everything I do? It's really boring.'

'I'm not!' She widened her eyes at me, unused to being taken to task.

'Yes you bloody are.'

'Helen!' She glared at me. 'How dare you use language like that at your mother!'

'I'm sorry.' I stood up again, unable to settle. 'But I'm forty years old and I really don't need your uninvited opinions any more. Does anybody else want a drink?' My morning vodka-fest with Helga had just about worn off, and this was no time to sober up.

'I'll get it,' Rick offered. 'What do you fancy?'

'Don't care,' I said. 'So long as it's a large one.'

'Isn't it a bit early for that?' Tsk-tsk, cluck-cluck.

'There!' Hands on my hips. 'You just can't help yourself, can you?' Mum looked towards Rick in the hope of garnering some support, but he'd wisely turned his back on the pair of us, rummaging around unnecessarily at the drinks cabinet.

'I'll just get some ice,' he said, and left.

'You shouldn't speak to me like that in front of Richard,' Mum hissed through her teeth. 'Whatever is he to think?'

'What does it matter to you? He's my bloody husband, and I don't go around telling him how to dress, or what to say, and when it's all right to fart.'

She glared at me.

'It's never all right to . . .' Her mouth puckered. 'Pass wind.'

'Oh, get over it, Mother. You're living in some nineteen-fifties *Woman's Realm* fantasy world. Can't you see how stressful it is? Things are different now. You have to stop trying to impose your blueprint on me and Julia. It's just not helpful.'

'Oh yes,' she stiffened. 'And I suppose you think it's perfectly all right to spend the afternoon swanning around in your dressing gown? Well, let me tell you something, young lady.' Oh, please do. 'Not everybody has the luxury of too much time on their hands. I didn't even have a washing machine until the pair of you were both well into primary school. My whole day was spent scrubbing and cleaning, washing your father's shirts, scraping away at muddy potatoes.' Drone, drone, drone. I'd heard the same lecture a thousand times over, and each time it drove me just a little bit closer to parenticide. I bit my tongue and held it before it could lash out and slice through her throbbing jugular. 'It was all about discipline. Making the best of a bad lot. But, oh no, you young women think you've got it all worked out.' Rick came back with the ice.

'Gin,' I whispered as he walked past me. 'Fast up before I strangle her.'

'I'll have you know that I gave everything up for your father and you children,' she moaned. 'I could have done anything I wanted to. I could have joined the Royal Ballet and been a prima ballerina.' With an arse like that? I seriously doubt it. 'But no. My own dreams were ruthlessly cast aside without any consideration for my feelings.' She made a sweeping hand movement, took a deep breath, and unleashed one of her spectacular sighs. I wondered if now would be a good time to disclose that I happened to know exactly why she had married Dad. She was up the duff. He'd told me himself so that I might have something warm to cling to whenever she got on her high horse with me. The words burned on my lips, but I'd been sworn to secrecy. I hadn't even shared it with Julia. Dad had been quite particular about that.

I heard Julia's footsteps at the bottom of the stairs.

'Sorry, Mum.' I said softly. 'I just think you should loosen up a little and learn to relax a bit more. You never know, you might even like it.'

'Here,' Rick said, handing Mum an icy gin and tonic. 'Go on, girl. Force yourself.'

'Oh! Thank you, Richard.' She reluctantly took the glass from Rick's hand, smiled at it tightly, took a sip and almost gagged on its strength. 'Good heavens –' splutter, splutter – 'that's terribly strong.'

Rick slipped me a sideways glance.

'Nah,' he said, pulling a cigar from his pocket and shoving it in his mouth. 'It's a traditional blend, so it tastes much stronger than it actually is. It won't do you any harm, Joyce. Trust me. Hey, Jools!' Julia entered the fray and tried to act as though she hadn't just done a DNA swab. 'Wanna drink?'

'Sure,' she said with obvious relief. 'Why not? Load me up with whatever she's having.'

A long, terrible squelch sounded from the nappy department, shocking the room into silence.

'Oh dear,' Mum said politely. 'I think you had better excuse me for a moment.' I was out of my seat like a rat up a drainpipe.

'I'll do it!' I said. 'You just sit there and enjoy your G and T.' I grabbed the nappy bag from the floor beside her. 'I'll have him freshened up in a jiffy.' Scooping Frankie from her arms, I slung the bag over my shoulder and made for the dungeon.

IT FELT LIKE I'd been gone for hours. After dealing with what I can only describe as the most gruesome nappy ever known to mankind and hosing Frankie down with a fire extinguisher, I discovered that Julia had left a bottle of sterilized water in the bottom drawer with a note saying that I had to somehow swoosh Frankie's mouth out because he'd just been given a feed. That's easier said than done in a three-month-old baby. Oh well. At least Helga would have a few bonus stains to tackle when she came in tomorrow.

Getting Frankie to open his mouth was no problem. He was flapping it around like an arctic tent anyway, bawling his lungs out simply because he could. After several abortive attempts, I finally managed to get the swab inside his cheek for a couple of seconds. That would just have to do, I thought. Returning it to the envelope, I quickly shoved it back with the others, covered it with the spare sheets, pushed the drawer closed and scrambled up from the floor. The door opened. My heart went into arrest.

'Hey, babe! So this is where you got to! What you doin' all the way up here?'

'Hi!' I shrilled, gathering Frankie up from the bed. Two seconds earlier and I would have been caught red-handed. 'I thought it would be the best bet just in case we had any unexpected accidents. We wouldn't want that on our bedroom carpet, would we?' And there it was. The perfectly delivered inter-spousal lie. Seamless. Effortless. Undetectable.

'Good thinking.' He held the door open for us. 'Here. Let me take him.'

Rick took hold of Frankie and slung him confidently over his shoulder, balancing him with one strong hand, the tilt of Frankie's small body just so, leaving Rick's other hand free to carry the nappy bag too. There was no air of trepidation, no fumbling, just a practised touch that had handled many babies over the years. I watched him go down the stairs ahead of me, and, for a split second, stole a fleeting glimpse of what it might have been for the two of us to have shared a child of our own.

'And then –' Mum's volume had gone up several decibels since I'd left the room, and she was leaning forward in her seat, practically bellowing at Julia – 'she fell over, right outside the door to the village hall, and crushed her nasturtiums!' Julia let out a mighty guffaw. 'It's true!' Mum screeched, acknowledging Rick's return to the room with an unsteady wave of her empty glass. 'About time she was knocked down a peg or two, I say. She never stops going on about how she manages to take first prize every year at the horticultural society, and nobody likes a braggart. Your father couldn't have been happier about it, not that he said anything, of course.' She sat back and sighed to herself in satisfaction, letting out a tiny, accidental burp. 'His carrots were a triumph, you know.' Rick took the glass from her hand and replaced it with a fresh one. 'Oh, I really shouldn't, Richard!' Mum slurred at him, grasping hold of the glass without further ado. 'I'm just being sociable, you understand! And you're quite right! This gin isn't strong at all, is it?'

'So, how long do you think you'll be staying for?' Julia slipped the question neatly under her radar.

'Oh, I don't know, dear.' Mum unflinchingly downed a clear two inches in her first sip. 'I wouldn't want to outstay my welcome, but David doesn't seem to be in any hurry to give up his cooked breakfasts, now, does he?'

'We'll be fine, Mum,' Julia urged her. 'It'll be a lot easier for me to get back to normal once we're on our own, and if I need any help with Frankie, I'll call you.'

'Are you sure, dear?' Mum's left eye began to droop slightly.

'Positive.'

'I know!' Rick puffed at his cigar excitedly. 'Why don't we have a whacking great roast around here on Sunday? Then you can go home afterwards!'

'Brilliant!' I shouted, a little too enthusiastically.

'Frank can drive down or we'll—'

Mum cut him off. 'Oh, I don't know about that, dear. Driving in London?' She started tutting.

'Then I'll send a car for him,' Rick said. 'Anything you want, Joyce. I just think it would be nice if we could have a proper family get-together. Nobody's let me play host yet.' He looked at me proudly. 'I think it's about time my wife and I put our home on the map.'

Chapter Eleven

PISPRONUNCIATION

I LOVE GOING OUT for a swanky dinner now and then. The prospect of having a plate of Michelin-starred scran slapped down in front of me that some other kitchen slave has grafted over never loses its appeal. Granted, at my age lunch is the wiser option, allowing that much longer for the calorific onslaught to mulch down before I drag my overfed carcass into bed, dying of chronic heartburn while having cheese nightmares. But when push comes to shove, in the absence of lunchiepoos, dinner will do just as nicely.

Rick seemed uncharacteristically tense this evening as he sat back in the comfort of his usual chair and allowed Tony to go through the traditional procedure of faffing about unnecessarily with our napkins while he ran through the specials. Perhaps he'd had a bad day at the office. He wasn't himself at all, and I soon gave up on trying to make small talk and let my eyes wander around the room instead. Even on this unremarkable Tuesday evening, the place was virtually full as usual, save for the odd banquette held back in case a head honcho from the movie business should drop in looking for a reassuringly expensive *amuse-bouche*. I was now officially one of their 'regulars', which, I imagine, might go a long way on a CV should I find myself unexpectedly thrust out into the job market again.

'Thanks, Tone.' Rick accepted the napkin into his lap. 'Bring us a nice big Chivas on the rocks and a glass of champers for the missus, would ya?'

'Of course, Mr Wilton.' Tony slithered away, trousering the crisp note Rick pressed into his hand.

'This is nice,' I whispered, leaning across the table. 'Feels like we haven't been here for ages, doesn't it?'

'I thought I should take you out for an airing.' Rick smiled at last. 'No point in having a gorgeous new wife if I can't show her off once in a while, is there?'

The waiters greeted us like old friends. After missing our own wedding party on that fateful day in May, I doubted that any of them would forget us in a hurry. Boy, that had been some hoolie, by all accounts. Following the high drama in the registry office, we had slipped away into the night long before witnessing the messy end, but judging by the six-page theft and damages bill that had been politely presented to Rick upon our return from Vegas, things had gotten pretty ugly that night.

'Before we get too settled . . .' Rick picked up his drink and rolled the ice around his glass. 'Is there anything you want to tell me?'

I looked at him dubiously.

'Like what?'

'Oh, I dunno.' He took a long sip, savouring the whisky for a while before swallowing, briefly tightening his lips over his teeth before delivering his standard *ahh* of appreciation. 'I just wondered if there was anything you might not have mentioned to me that maybe I ought to know about.'

'I don't think so,' I said, slightly bemused.

'Are you absolutely sure about that?'

This time, I detected a distinct whiff of something highly suspect in his manner. His dark demeanour told me this was not the regular sort of pre-dinner conversation we usually went in for. The skin on the back of my neck prickled. Oh God. It was a loaded question. I wondered if I had been talking in my sleep. OK. Don't panic. Just deny everything.

'I love you,' I said limply. Rick likes it when I tell him I love him, regardless of whether or not it sounds like I mean it.

'Well, that's a start, I guess.' He stared into his glass.

'What's that supposed to mean?'

'Love's not enough, Hell.' He put his drink down. 'Not if we're gonna make a cast-iron couple. Know what I mean?' I got that horrible sinking feeling inside. 'I thought we'd agreed no secrets,' he said. 'That's where the rot starts, babe, and once it's set in . . .' His hand wandered vaguely towards his breast pocket, hesitating momentarily over the publicly banned cigar tucked within. Slave to his addiction, I'd become accustomed to the sudden brief absences demanded by his beeping nicometer.

'Do you want to step outside for a smoke?' I asked. Suddenly I was desperate for him to bugger off for a couple of minutes so I could hurriedly throw together some kind of vague strategy for whatever accusation he was about to hit me with. Maybe he'd found out about wardrobegate. All I knew was that it was quiz time, and I had no lifelines left. 'I don't mind,' I urged him. 'I'll be fine here.'

'Nah,' he said. 'It'll pass in a minute. The old dear always said that those things would kill me one day. Mind you, she could talk. Bloody fag-ash Lil on four packets a day. She was still smoking like a chimney the day she fell off the back of that cruise ship.' He picked up the menu and gave it a casual once-over, not that he ever orders anything outside of his three favourites. Lobster, if he's not particularly hungry, a table-heaving steak if he is, or a shepherd's pie if he's feeling sorry for himself. 'What do you fancy?' His eyes remained on the menu.

'You,' I said, hoping to curry favour.

'Good. Then you won't mind if I run something past you that's been on my mind for a couple of days.'

'Sure.' Uh-oh. My heart picked up a couple of paces, a granny knot slowly forming in my stomach.

'And I don't want you to think that I was checking up on you, all right? It was just one of those things.'

'One of what things?' (Huge Tom and Jerry gulp.)

'You probably don't know this, Hell, but when you use the Internet, the computer you're on automatically racks up a record of all the websites you've looked at.' My chest opened up like a cavern. 'It's called the history, and it just sits there in case you want to go back to something you found earlier.' He finished his Scotch and put the glass down heavily. 'So, like I said before, are you sure there's nothing you want to tell me?'

'I—' I looked away, my face as red as a bowl of Helga's borscht. 'I don't remember.' I felt my resolve crumbling under his laser-beam glare. 'I mean, I didn't know—'

He reached out and grabbed my hand.

'I'm not having a go at you,' he said firmly. 'Whatever you choose to do is up to you. I'm big enough and ugly enough to know that I can't tell you how to live your life, but we're gonna sit here like two civilized adults and have this thing out, OK?'

Tony materialized by our table, announcing his presence with a wave of his pad. 'And what can I get you two lovebirds?' he simpered.

A cyanide pellet. And make it snappy.

'I'll have the shepherd's pie, Tone,' Rick said flatly, handing his menu back. I dithered with mine a little longer, umming and aahing over the halibut, knowing that whatever I ordered would move around in my mouth like sawdust, assuming I could keep my fork steady enough to get it there in the first place. I copped out and ordered the lobster instead, hoping it would occupy my fidgeting fingers.

'Excellent choice.' Tony marvelled at my brilliance, shaking his head in admiration as he floated away.

Rick sat in silence, waiting for me to make the next move. There was nowhere for me to go.

'I promised I wouldn't say anything,' I whimpered, trying not to wring my hands. I'd been rumbled, big time, and there was absolutely nothing I could do except take a deep breath, face the music and sing like a canary. Rick fixed his slate-blue eyes on me.

'Promised who, exactly?'

'Julia.'

'You what?' His brow furrowed. 'Julia?'

'Please don't judge her,' I gushed, rushing head-long into the whole sorry mess. 'I know what it looks like, but you have to believe me – she knows it was a terrible mistake, and she's been beside herself with worry.'

'Julia?' Rick repeated incredulously. 'You're not serious?'

'I know,' I said. 'I had a hard time believing it myself when she first told me. Can you imagine what a shock it was? It's no wonder she's been in such a state. I said that she should just forget the whole thing and move on, but she won't have it.'

'I don't understand.' Rick pressed his hand to his forehead. 'Why the fuck should she want to—'

'Shhh! Nobody knows about it. Nobody except me. And now you.'

'I wouldn't bloody bank on that.' Rick inspected his empty glass. 'The Internet isn't exactly the discreetest place in the world, is it?'

'You can't say anything!'

'Don't worry. I won't.' From the stupefied expression on Rick's face, he was still having some trouble processing the information. 'But what the bloody hell was all that stuff doing on my laptop? Hasn't she got one of her own?'

'Of course she has! That was me,' I admitted shamefully. 'She could hardly go looking for the information herself, could she?'

'Information?' Rick raised an eyebrow. 'Is that what you call it?'

'Well, how else should I put it? Research?'

'Blimey,' Rick said. 'Talk about using euphemisms.

I'll have to remember that next time I paint myself into a corner.'

'I had no choice. Can you imagine what would have happened if David had caught her?'

'Oh yes.' A tense smile clouded his face. 'I can imagine exactly what he'd have done. Bloody hell, babe. You really had me going there for a minute. I thought you'd been living some kind of double life on the sly. Fucking hell – Julia.' He lowered his voice. 'Would you bloody Adam and Eve it?'

'I'm so sorry, Rick. I really meant to tell you, but my hands were tied.'

Our wine arrived. After the rigmarole of its introduction and ceremonial uncorking, Rick waved the waiter away and took charge of the bottle himself.

'No, babe,' he said, pouring thoughtfully. 'It's me who's the sorry one. I dunno what I was thinking of. You really don't wanna know the stuff that's been going through my head these last couple of days. It's been the worst time of my life. I really thought I was gonna have to get used to living without you. It just goes to show you.' He laughed uncomfortably. 'You never know what's going on behind closed doors, do ya? I thought those two had a really good thing going together.'

'They did.' I took a grateful sip of wine, trying hard not to knock half the glass back in one go to calm my shattered nerves. 'I must say, you're taking the news a lot better than I did.' Mind you, after that business with the Italian waitress back in the Eighties, I expect Rick's no stranger to the trailer-trash entertainment of paternity testing. 'I'm afraid I wasn't nearly as cool about it as I might like to have been. I guess I'll have to work on that.'

'I dunno.' Rick played with his cutlery. 'I suppose, if you want to be callous about it, it's only sex, but if that had turned out to be you, I don't think I could have coped with that.' He picked up his glass and sighed.

'Only sex?' I gawped at him. 'With an unidentified baby and a mother on the verge of an epic breakdown? I think the minor detail that she went and had sex with another man is the very least of her worries right now.'

'Eh?' The glass hovered midway to Rick's mouth. 'What the bloody hell are you talking about?'

'I—' The look on Rick's face said it all. My diaphragm snapped tight, sending a spasm of panic through every cell in my body. My mouth went dry, my lips instantly sticking together. Please tell me that I didn't just say that last thing out loud. The best I could do was to muddy the waters with a drop-lob. 'What do you mean, "what am I talking about"?' I said accusingly. 'What are *you* talking about?'

'The dodgy housewife services and photos of massive todgers I found racked up on my laptop.' I felt the blood drain from my face. 'And now –' he put the glass down and fixed his eyes upon me – 'why don't you tell me what *you* were talking about, young lady?'

SUNDAY HURTLED ROUND at lightning speed with no thought for those of us who wished it would never come. I busied myself in the kitchen, pretending to listen to some jolly-hockey-sticks grand dame I'd never heard of on *Desert Island Discs* while Rick sat at the table bashing a mountain of vegetables. The pair of us tried our best to act as though nothing was wrong, the tense atmosphere chewing right through the granite work-tops. Once the cat had clawed its way out of the bag, Rick had been so shocked that he'd just sat there, concussed, like a slab of concrete, cutlery in hand. He had barely uttered another word over dinner, and the pair of us had hardly touched our food, sending Tony into a blind panic when he caught sight of our aban-doned plates. That night, as we had readied ourselves for a passionless bed, Rick explained to me that he wasn't cross that I'd left him in the dark about the whole thing. He wasn't even disappointed. He was just hurt, because it meant that I didn't trust him, and he'd have to think about that for a good long while before he was prepared to talk about it. Then he had turned over without giving me a kiss and gone to sleep, while I had lain there wide-eyed, trying to tap into the positive chi while feeling like a heel. Not only had I scored a stupendous own-goal of grandstand proportions, I'd also let Julia down in the most spectacular way. It was a gargantuan double-whammy, and of one thing I was certain – she was going to kill me. Goodbye, cruel world.

I hauled the joint out of the oven, a thumping great leg of organically plundered pork under a thick blanket of perfectly scored crackling, and basted it for the millionth time. I knew it was Rick's favourite roast, but he'd been so preoccupied that he'd not taken much notice of anything since getting up this morning. He hadn't even tried to sneak the odd crunchy morsel off the end of the meat while I wasn't looking, like he usually does.

'Better get those spuds in the oven,' I said, loading up the tray and sliding it on to the free slot above the meat. The doorbell went. My heart lurched and I went to the door.

'Hi, Mum,' I said, pecking her on the cheek. Julia was right behind her. 'Where's David?'

'Dragging half the contents of Mothercare out of the car.' Julia jabbed a thumb over her shoulder. 'Hi, big boy,' she said, smiling at Rick. It was all he could do to look at her.

'I'll go and give him a hand,' he said uncomfortably, walking out into the street.

'What's the matter with him?' Julia said, frowning. Mum leapt in with an immediate diagnosis.

'Hungry, I expect. You know what these men are like, sitting around starving themselves to death rather than lifting a finger in the kitchen. Your father's like that.' She marched into the sitting room. 'He'll go for hours, getting all tetchy because he's hungry. Yet can he be bothered to make himself anything to eat? Oh no. Nor me, for that matter. Then the moment I get up and mention that I'm making a sandwich, it's all, "Oh yes, dear, that would be lovely". You know, I've sat there for hours, knowing very well that neither of us have had a single thing since breakfast, just waiting to see how long it will be before he gets up, but he never does. Still, that's men for you.'

'He knows,' I hissed sideways at Julia, grabbing her arm as she hung her jacket on the stand. She shot me a horrified glance. Without warning, David appeared in the doorway with Frank Junior strapped into the car seat. 'David!' I smiled brightly, kissing him on the cheek, deflecting attention from his dumbstruck wife. 'Need a hand there?'

'It's OK,' he said. 'I've got it.'

Rick lumped in the rest of the baby equipment, then lugged Mum's colossal suitcase into the hallway. 'Fancy a brewski, mate?' he said, slapping David on the back.

'You bet.' David followed him to the kitchen.

'Is he here yet?' Mum asked.

'Who?'

'Your father, dear.'

'No.'

Julia hid her face from Mum and mouthed at me, *'What do you mean, he knows?'*

'I'll tell you later,' I muttered through clenched teeth.

'Well, that can't be right.' Mum examined her watch. 'He said he'd be here by twelve and it's almost half past. I wonder where on earth he could have got to?' Big sigh. 'Probably stuck in the middle of Piccadilly Circus going round and round, refusing to ask for directions.'

I poured us all a glass from the bottle of Prosecco I'd opened half an hour before, having been in dire need of a barge-load of Dutch courage. Julia sidled up to me, but before we could make a furtive exchange, the men came back, beers in hand.

'Isn't this great?' David settled himself on the sofa next to Mum and plonked the baby seat on the floor beside them. Frankie grumbled, half opened his eyes, let out a rippling fart, then promptly fell back to sleep.

'Awesome,' Rick said cynically. I concentrated on handing out the drinks.

'Isn't there anything to nibble on?' Mum glanced critically at the bare table.

'I thought best not,' I said. 'We've got five tons of roast pork to get through in a little while. I didn't want to spoil everyone's appetite.'

'Never mind,' she sighed. 'I suppose I shall have to sit here and wait for lunch to be served just like everyone else.'

'I've got some olives in the fridge if you'd like something to pick at,' I offered.

'No thank you, dear,' she replied, lifting her nose distastefully. 'They make me feel squeamish. I've never got on with foreign food. It's not good for the digestion, you know.'

After five minutes of wrist-slittingly banal conversation, a car horn sounded urgently from the street. Julia leaped up and raced to the window.

'It's the old man!' she said, peering out into the road. 'Looks like he's got himself a bit hot under the collar.'

Rick was already on his way outside, pulling Dad out of the car and pointing him towards the open door of the house before jumping behind the wheel of the old Volvo himself and shooting off in search of a parking space. Sundays are always a bit touch and go around here, and the clampers like to ruin as many weekends as possible by immobilizing anyone stupid enough to think that they might actually take the day off and rush to church to save their fallen souls.

'Dad!' I went to greet him. 'You made it!'

'Hey!' He gave me a hug. 'So this is where you've been hiding out, is it?' He dropped his voice to a whisper in my ear. 'Very nice, kid. Looks like you've done all right for yourself. Your Mum will be puffed up like a pheasant on pension day in the post office.'

Julia cut in and threw her arms around him.

'Hi, Dad!'

'Julia!' Dad groaned under the force of her vice-like grip and gave her a kiss. 'Where's that little grandson of mine?'

'Right here.' David strode up and shook Dad's hand. 'How you doing, Frank? Good to see you.'

'You're late!' Mum said, brandishing her wrist at him. 'We've all been wondering where on earth you could have got to. Why didn't you ring? You could have been involved in some terrible accident on the motorway, for all we knew!'

'Hello, dear.' Dad bent down and placed a weary kiss on his wife's forehead. 'No such luck, I'm afraid. I did think about parking on a level crossing and taking a nap –' he threw Julia a sneaky wink – 'but then Julia would never have been able to get rid of you, would she?'

'Frank! Really!' Mum patted her hair in irritation. 'You shouldn't joke about things like that. People get killed on the roads every day, you know.'

'Yep,' Dad sighed. 'Lucky buggers.'

The front door banged. 'You were just in time, Frank.' Rick reached out his hand and gave Dad's a hearty shake. 'Found you the last free space just around the corner. Let me bring you a beer.'

'Not if he's driving!' Mum gasped. 'Get him a soft drink. Do you have any orange squash?' I saw Dad cast one of his long-suffering grimaces at Rick.

And so it began. An excruciating two-and-a-half-hour

interlude of brittle conversation and stolen glances across the dining table with no opportunity to slide away and whisper in corners. Julia, wound tight like a coil, barely managed one measly roast potato. Mum watched on approvingly, congratulating her on her marvellous self-discipline, observing how she'd noticed the weight positively dropping off her this last week or so. By three o'clock, both Mum and Frankie were snoring in front of the *EastEnders* omnibus, while the men sat out on the patio enjoying Rick's offer of a nice fat cigar. I unloaded the second batch of crockery from the steaming dishwasher, while Julia leaned up against the sink, silently watching the men being men through the kitchen window.

'Well, I suppose that's it then, isn't it?' she said. 'So much for keeping this a secret. Thanks a bloody bunch, Helen.'

'Don't worry. He's promised me he won't say anything.'

'Oh really? And since when did a man's promise mean Jack shit?'

WITH EVERYONE GONE, a deathly hush descended upon the house. Rick loped into the kitchen, pulled up an ashtray and fired up his third cigar of the afternoon.

'Well, that wasn't the most awkward lunch of my whole life then, was it?' he said sarcastically, flicking the match out and snapping it in half before dropping it in the ashtray. 'Tell you what, Hell. You women sure know how to make a bloke feel like a complete—' He stopped short of using the word he had automatically reached for. 'You have no idea how bad I felt, sitting there talking to David and making like everything's OK. Poor bastard. He's got no bloody idea, has he? And as for your sister . . .' He shook his head. 'I know I've been no saint, but Jesus, Hell.'

'Tell me about it.' I threw the dishcloth into the sink. 'I wish she'd never told me in the first place.'

'Does she know that I know?'

'Of course she does!'

'Christ.' He sucked on his cigar hard, disappearing temporarily behind a huge cloud of smoke. 'What did you tell her that for? It's no bloody wonder she was looking at me like I had seven heads.'

'She's my sister. It's bad enough that I broke her confidence. The very least I could do was save her the embarrassment of having to lie to you as well. You've got no idea what she's going through.'

'Nah,' he said. 'I suppose not. When you gonna get the results back?'

'End of the week. Thursday maybe.'

'Bloody hell.' He sat down at the table. 'And what's she gonna do if it's not his?'

'Don't ask me.' I sat down next to him, and we sank into silence for a while. For a moment I was tempted to take the cigar from his fingers and have a good old go on it myself.

'You know what, babe?' Rick picked up my hand and played with my wedding ring. 'I know this has all been really difficult for you, and I don't mean to harp on, but there's one thing that's still bothering me.' Oh no, not again. I wasn't sure how much more grilling my skin could take.

'What *now*?' I whined.

'Well.' He stuck the cigar in his teeth and looked me straight in the eye. 'Julia's predicament still doesn't explain what all those photographs were doing on my laptop.'

'Oh, for God's sake.' I buried my head in my arms and spoke into the cold, hard surface of the kitchen table. 'Please don't make me go there. It was nothing to do with me.'

'Then you already know what I'm going to ask you.'

'Yes,' I sighed. 'Although why you can't just trust me and leave it—'

'I'm sorry, babe, but you know what us men are like. One-track mind and all that. This old heart of mine really needs an explanation.'

'All right. Fine.' I stood up sharply and marched towards the study.

Booting up his silver laptop like an old pro, I launched the web-browsing window with a couple of confident clicks. 'Right,' I said, vacating his seat and insisting he sit down. 'Go on then, smartypants. Find that website.' I stood over him as though supervising a child on a vile homework assignment, huffing indignantly while he drilled down through the pages. As the offending site loaded, Rick cleared his throat uncomfortably and tried not to look at the screen. 'Go to the women's section,' I commanded, 'and type in Cif-lover.'

'Syph?' He grimaced at me. 'That's disgust—'

'Just do it!'

'OK, OK!'

'C-I-F, hyphen, L-O-V-'

'I know how to spell,' he grumbled, tapping at the keys.

'Clearly.'

'What am I supposed to be looking for?' He sat and waited for the screen to load.

'You'll see.' I sauntered out of the study. 'And don't say that I didn't warn you.'

Chapter Twelve

WHAT WOMEN WANT

I DON'T KNOW WHY men complain about women being such complicated creatures. If they could only be bothered to take their heads out of their arses for long enough, they might just find that keeping their women-folk happy is a lot easier than they think. Sure, we all like to have a good old moan now and then – if they had to do half the things we do, they'd never bloody stop – but what isn't helpful is when they start up with the automatic defensive mechanism that refuses to listen and brands us all a bunch of screaming, nagging harridans. They're terrified that they might actually have to make an effort and do something, so far better to throw their weight around, then go off in a huge, manly huff. It seems to me that it's only women who really know how to look after a woman. With Julia's life heading down the plughole faster than a pint of Mr Muscle sink unblocker, I knew that there was only one sure-fire way to bring a little sunshine back into her life. She needed a present. Something really fabulous. And that's exactly what I had in mind.

'This is rather unusual,' said the woman behind the desk as I concluded our second meeting in as many days. Initially, she had seemed rather reluctant to entertain my custom. I expect the unconditional cheque I offered her helped. She had slipped it in her desk drawer and miraculously pulled out all the stops, offering me a choice of her very best merchandise. I'd given all three options a thorough going-over that morning, and we had finally agreed terms on the pick of the bunch.

'I'm sure it will work out just fine,' I reassured her, standing up to take my leave. 'And if it doesn't, you can keep the finder's fee anyway.'

'Are you positive you don't want to see any others?'

'No thank you,' I said. 'I have a feeling that she'll be very happy with this one.'

'Until tomorrow, then.' She stood up and shook my hand.

Out on the street, the hordes of West End office workers heading towards the lunchtime sandwich bars reminded my grumbling stomach that it hadn't been given so much as a cornflake since last night's thrown-together supper. I'm not quite in the swing of it yet from a marital catering point of view. In my determination not to fall into the trap of becoming The Little Woman At Home, I'm having to keep a very tight rein on my predisposition towards predictable routine. If I start cooking every day, then Rick will soon start expecting it, and before I know it he'll be coming home wanting his dinner on the table at the allotted time and I'll have no one to blame but myself. I'm not bloody well going there again. The trick is to retain the all-important element of surprise. Keep the catering unpredictable, like the train services. Maybe I'll cook. Maybe I won't. It all depends on whether or not there are leaves on the line, or the wrong kind of snow. I joined the queue in Pret and grabbed a sandwich to stuff down while I made my way across town for the meeting I had arranged for eleven-thirty. Busy, busy, busy.

'IT'S A NICE ENOUGH PLACE,' breezed the estate agent with an air of casual disinterest. Quite who he thought he was I really don't know. Little Lord Fauntleroy sprang to mind. He had far too many buttons on his over-tailored green tweed suit, and a ridiculous polkadot handkerchief sprouting foppishly from his top pocket. After turning up half an hour late, he must have spent all of two minutes giving my flat the once-over before rolling out the standard patter about the haemorrhaged state of the current rental market.

'With the ways things are at the moment, I can't guarantee that we'll be able to find you a tenant unless you're prepared to undercut everyone else.' He ran his finger along the mantelpiece, inspecting it for dust. Bloody cheek. I'd drafted Helga in yesterday, unleashing her on the drop-zone fully armed, and she'd gone through the place like a dose of salts. Luckily for him, she wasn't here, otherwise I suspect she'd have taken him by the ankles and heaved him over the balcony.

'I'm not overly concerned about the money,' I said curtly, opening the French windows in the hope of dissipating the pungent fug of his cloying aftershave. 'I just want to make sure that it goes to somebody respectable who's going to look after the place.'

'Don't they all,' he chortled to himself. 'I'd advise to you remove anything expensive.' He aimed a glance of warning at the antique chandelier hanging from the ceiling rose. 'One stray cork and that thing's history. We see it all the time. Better safe than sorry, eh?'

Before I could respond, the serrated buzz of the intercom interrupted my urge to tell this oily little upstart exactly what he could do with his advice.

'Excuse me a moment.' I smiled tightly, then went to the entryphone and released the door downstairs. There was no need for me to peer over the balcony. I already knew who it was from her secret code. Two short buzzes, one long one, then a third persistent blast as Leoni jammed her finger on the button until I answered it.

'Every landlord has to accept an element of wear and tear,' he continued from somewhere behind me. 'As long as they don't completely trash the place and pay the rent on time, that's about as much as you can hope for these days.' He copped a quick feel of the curtains and made a few notes. 'I'll get somebody over to take a couple of photographs, then we'll run up the details and see if we get any bites.'

'Wotcha!' Leoni said as she burst in, shamelessly sporting the Dior sunglasses she had liberated from my bedroom drawer some weeks earlier and adopted as her own. 'Sorry I'm late. The boys were trying to skive off school this morning, lying in bed making with the old cancerous coughing routine. I told them if they didn't shift their arses in ten seconds flat, I'd bloody give them something to feel ill about. Hello?' She dumped her bag and marched up to the slick-haired sleazebag playing property mogul in the sitting room. 'Do I know you?'

'Edward Mainwaring,' he announced with unbridled pomposity. 'Albrights estate agents.'

'Oh, really?' Leoni looked him up and down. 'Selling or renting?'

'Letting,' he corrected her.

'Good. Just checking. She's left this place to me in her will, you know. If I catch anyone trying to flog it without my permission, I'll break their legs. Understand what I'm saying?' He twitched his clipboard in uncertain response and tried not to look scared. Having made her point with a well-placed snarl, Leoni lost interest and returned to her bag, conjuring from its depths a big screw-cap bottle of cheap Sainsbury's wine and disappearing off to the kitchen.

'If there's nothing else for now,' I hinted, edging towards the door.

'Oi, Gunga Din!' Leoni shouted. 'You got anything to eat round here?'

'No,' I yelled back. 'Sorry.'

Little Lord Fauntleroy hung around like a bad smell, refusing to be ejected. 'There's a basic contract and a few details about commission rates we ought to run through before I go.' He began extracting some papers from the trendy leather document folder tucked under his arm.

'Perhaps we could do that another time.' Oh, just get out you ghastly little creature.

'If I could just leave you a copy of our—'

'Thanks.' Leoni reappeared with a full glass in her hand, snatched the papers from his fingers, pushed him out onto the landing and shut the door in his face. 'You're not seriously going to give that little shit a key, are you?'

'Perhaps not,' I muttered. 'But right now it looks like he's the best of a bad bunch. I'll have to trust somebody sooner or later. Why not him? They've got a good reputation.'

'You'd have to be completely out of your mind,' Leoni said, tapping a finger on her temple. 'He's the kind of git who pretends to be trying to find you a tenant when what he's really doing is using the place as a shag palace and passing duplicate keys around his friends for fifty quid a pop.' She sucked in a huge mouthful of wine, swilled it around her teeth before swallowing it, then passed the glass to me with a grimace. 'Here. Take this. I'm sure it'll taste OK after the first couple of glasses. Mind you, at three bottles for a tenner, who's complaining?' I followed her to the kitchen. 'Why do you want to get an agent anyway? Last thing we need is a slimy little bastard like that leaving a slug trail all over your carpets. Find a tenant yourself. If they do anything wrong, you can always get Rick to come over and smash their faces in.'

'Hmm.' I took a sip of wine while I thought about it, the acidity sending a splitting pain into the little hollow beneath my ears. 'Urgh!' I stared at the glass.

'Do this!' She threw her head back and gargled the next mouthful. 'Kills off the taste buds.' Her stomach let out a long, lingering groan. 'So what are we going to do about food?'

'Pass,' I said. 'I didn't think to get anything in, seeing

173

as I was only dropping in to play Tour Guide Barbie. I'd have popped out to Waitrose and rustled up something delish had I known you'd want feeding.'

'Don't talk to me about cooking,' she spat. 'I'm so sick to death of preparing food that I've gone on strike. Haven't been to the supermarket for over a fortnight. Everyone's been living on prison rations chiselled out of the back of the freezer and whatever they can order from the milkman. I'm just dying for Marcus to have a go at me about it so that I can give it to him both barrels about why anything to do with food should be my department, just because I'm a woman. He's refusing to rise to the bait, as usual.'

'Do you want me to see if there's a tin of soup in the cupboard or something?'

'Soup? I wasn't born at the top of the food chain to eat bloody soup. All I've had today is a banana and a cup of Baileys. Wanna go out to Mario's for a late lunch?'

'Like this?' I motioned down at my scruffs.

'Mmm. Perhaps not.' Leoni flicked her eyes up and down my shabby figure. 'And your hair looks like something's been nesting in it too.'

'Cheers.' I clinked my glass against hers and moved out onto the balcony.

Pulling one of the wrought-iron chairs out from the tiny tête-à-tête table, I sat myself down and gazed out across the street to the communal garden square. I wished I had taken more advantage of it now, joined the garden association or something, or turned up now and again when that old Chinese lady came along to do t'ai chi with the yummy mummies. It wasn't a particularly big garden when measured against the grand scale of some of the better known squares, but, dare I say, it was prettier than most and had been spared the indignity of a tennis court or too many benches. Propped on my elbows, I sunk my chin into my palms and watched the street below going gently about its business, realizing just how much I missed being able to sit at an invisible vantage point and spy on the world unseen. Certainly, the courtyard at the back of Rick's house was nice enough, but it was completely private, not overlooked by anyone, with the price of not being able to overlook anyone else either. And where's the fun in that?

I heard the radio go on in the kitchen. A bit of white noise and squelching as Leoni retuned it to Radio 2. A sudden burst of an old Carly Simon number about kissing with confidence that I hadn't heard for years. The volume going up. Leoni making herself quite at home, no doubt turning my immaculate kitchen into a bombsite in the process of trying to find something vaguely edible. I didn't mind. Let her enjoy it. It would be someone else's space soon enough.

'Yoo-hoo!' A familiar sing-song voice carried up from the pavement. I lifted my head over the parapet and looked down into the street. Paul waved an armful of shopping bags. 'I wondered why your doors were open! Is that a private party or can anyone join in?'

'Paul!' I was so pleased to see him that I almost toppled over the balustrade. 'Come on up! But be warned – we've only got one litre of wine, so you might have to go and raid your fridge first!'

'You got it!' He danced around the lamppost and pirouetted towards the steps. I leaned further over the side.

'Bring snacks too! Leoni's in there licking the wallpaper!'

'OH, IT'S JUST LIKE OLD TIMES,' Paul simpered, leaning back on his chair and propping his bare feet up on the edge of the balcony. Not only had he come armed with two very respectable bottles of Sauvignon Blanc, he had also done a quick Wonder Woman wardrobe spin and appeared at the door in a pair of denim hot pants teamed with a white vest top, determined to soak up the last of the rare summer sun. In days gone by, we had spent many an afternoon hanging out here like bored teenagers, dangling the occasional arm or leg over the side, busy doing nothing.

'I really miss this place.' I tilted my head back, feeling the warm rays on my face. 'I've had three letting agents round today, and there's not one of them who seemed to appreciate how special it is. As far as they're concerned, it's just another pile of bricks and mortar with a commission attached.' Remembering Leoni's suggestion, I thought I might as well start putting the word around. 'I don't suppose you'd know anyone who might want to rent it?'

'Apart from me?' Paul pushed the heart-shaped sunglasses a little further up his nose. 'I always said that we should do swapsies if ever you moved out. Sally and I would kill for a little bit of outside space. He's always going on about the light not being right. It's enough to make him go stir-crazy being cooped up inside a sweltering flat on a day like this. You know what these exotic types are like.'

'What did I tell you?' Leoni threw the last handful of nuts in her mouth. 'I'm always right. It's bloody frightening, isn't it?'

'Are you serious?' I asked Paul levelly.

'Sure!' He got up and moved his chair a couple of inches to the right, following the trajectory of the sun. 'And with a bank account like yours, I'm sure we could come to a nice little neighbourly arrangement to even out the differential on the rent.' He fluttered his eyelashes at me.

'Crikey.' My brain started whirring. The perfect tenants, packaged up in a neat little parcel, tied with a red ribbon and delivered straight into my lap. Surely it couldn't be that simple?

'Then at least you'd know who's sleeping in your bedroom, and you know we'd take good care of the place.' You're telling me. Paul could easily give Helga a serious run for her money. I've never seen anyone else floss around the base of their taps.

'In that case – ' I picked up my glass and tipped it towards him – 'it looks like we may just have ourselves a cosy little arrangement.'

'Got any more nuts?' Leoni waved the empty bowl at Paul.

'Yes, thank you,' he sighed. 'But I'm afraid they're not on the menu.'

'When's Sally getting back?' She checked the time on her mobile phone. 'My buns need squeezing and I'm not leaving until I've had my rations.'

'Who knows?' Paul inspected his nails. 'He's in one of his funny moods at the moment and keeps wandering off. It's this weather, you know. I really ought to have him fitted with a tracking device so I can keep tabs on him. God only knows where he's got to today.'

'Uh-oh,' I said inadvertently, wishing immediately that I'd bitten my tongue off instead. Being a highly sensitive sort, Paul can detect a sexual nuance at four hundred paces.

'What?' He pulled his legs off the table and sat to attention.

'Nothing,' I said, floundering. 'He's probably wandering around art galleries in search of some inspiration.'

'Art galleries?' Paul scoffed. 'And since when did my Sally need to steal ideas from somebody else?'

'That's not what I meant.'

'I'll bet.' Leoni picked up her wine, wobbled it towards her mouth and slurped the last half-inch through puckered lips. 'You don't think he's having one of his lesbian moments, do you?' Paul's mouth dropped open.

'I beg your pardon?'

'Leoni!' I glared at her. 'Don't be so insensitive. Sally's a married man now.'

'What?' She refilled her glass. 'I'm only saying—'

'Oh, behave.' I slapped her leg playfully, trying to make light of the moment and fudge over Sally's track record of sleeping with the occasional woman when his hormones get the better of him.

'Why don't we ring him?' Leoni picked up her phone and scrolled drunkenly through the numbers, coming to rest on the name Stud. She pressed the handset to her ear and waited a while. A big smile crept over her face. 'Hello, tiger,' she purred. 'Guess what colour knickers I'm wearing.' Her eyes met mine. 'Nope – ' snigger, snigger. 'Nope.' She pulled at her waistband and peered down at her pants. 'Bingo.' Thumbs-up. 'Where are you? Oh yeah? Well never mind that. Hurry up and get your pert little love muffins straight back home. We're all hanging around waiting to have sex with you and Paul's refused to let me munch his nuts.' She listened intently for a moment, broke into a filthy cackle, then blew a kiss into the phone before hanging up.

'What did he say?' Paul demanded defensively.

'Never you mind,' she said, flicking through a few more numbers until she reached the name Arsehole. She hit the green button again and tucked the phone under her chin. 'Marcus?' she barked. Holding the handset towards us, we all heard him tell her crossly that he was in a meeting. 'Like I care.' Swig of wine. 'You've got to get the kids from school this afternoon.' A distorted voice blared out from the phone again. She snatched it to her ear tightly and growled. 'Don't you give me that crap. They're your kids as well as mine, and I'm telling you that either you get your royal fatness over there by half past three or they'll be wandering the streets, because I'm not bloody moving. All right?' She held the phone away and scowled at it while Marcus did his pieces, waiting until the storm had died down before delivering her second barrel of rock salt. 'Well, I can't,' she said defiantly. 'I'm pissed as a fart, so there. Sue me.' Marcus unleashed another torrent, which I couldn't quite make out except for the odd F-word. 'Yeah? *Yeah*?' she shouted. 'You and who's army?' I grabbed the phone from her before the situation went international.

'Marcus?'

'What the bloody hell's going on there?' he yelled.

'Marcus, I'm so sorry. I didn't realize it was so late. I asked Leoni to drop by and give me a hand with something this morning—'

'What? Like drinking a tanker-load of wine? Well, you can tell her from me that I've had it up to here with her. You know there's nothing to eat in our house? She's been feeding the kids a bag of chips on the way home from school and refusing to make me so much as a bloody cheese sandwich when I get home from work. What kind of a wife is that?'

'Mmm,' I sympathized.

'I bet you wouldn't do that to Rick, would you?'

'No. But the night is still young, Marcus. Give it a couple of years and ask me again.' Silence. 'Look,' I said, trying to reason with him, 'I know it's short notice—'

'Short notice? You mean her dropping me right in it? How much has she had to drink?'

'I don't know,' I lied casually, eyeing the third bottle, half empty on the table.

'Can she drive?'

'Drive?' I glanced at Leoni unsurely. 'Maybe a flock of sheep, if she had a big enough whip.' Leoni started sniggering. I flapped my arm at her to hush.

'I don't believe this,' he sighed protractedly.

'Oh, Marcus. This is entirely my fault. It's such a lovely afternoon, I guess we just got carried away.'

'Well, that's just bloody marvellous,' he grunted. 'I don't know why she doesn't just pack her bags and piss off, Helen. It would certainly make my life a whole lot easier. Then at least I'd know where I stand.'

'I'm sorry,' I mumbled.

Leoni rolled her eyes at me, pushed her thumb onto her nose and wiggled her fingers childishly. 'Tell him to go fuck himself.'

'So I'm supposed to just drop everything and go racing off to the school now, am I?' Marcus declared indignantly.

On any other day, I might have offered to go for him, but in that moment, all I could think was that Leoni had been racing off to the school virtually every afternoon for years. Although her timing could have been better, she was quite right. They were his kids too. Let him bloody well do it for a change.

'Looks like it,' I said. 'And count your lucky stars that it doesn't happen very often.'

He let out a huge sigh of inconvenience.

'All right, all right. Let me just finish up what I'm doing here, then I'll get over there. But you can tell her from me that I'm seriously unimpressed and I'll be having words with her.' Oooh. I bet she's really scared. Not.

'I'll do that,' I said. 'Bye.'

'Tosser.' Leoni got up and went into the kitchen in search of some more ice.

Paul polished his sunglasses on his vest. 'Sounds like situation normal in the Leoni household.'

'Yep.' I enjoyed a long, cool sip of wine. 'That's the joy of wedded bliss for you.'

'Any regrets about getting married?'

'Sure,' I said, reaching for my handbag. 'In fact, I think I've got a list in here somewhere.'

'WHERE THE BLOODY HELL have you been?' Rick said, pouncing on me before I could struggle my key from the latch.

'Oh, don't you fucking start.' Leoni barged straight past. 'I thought you were meant to be one of the good guys, but oh, no,' she tutted. 'You're already demanding to know her whereabouts twenty-four hours a day, just like every other insecure tosspot in the universe.'

'Leoni?' Rick watched her stagger off, her one-track mind no doubt in search of yet another bucketful of wine. 'What's she doing here?'

'Hiding from Marcus.' I pushed the door closed. 'I can't very well pack her off home in that state, can I? She'll have to crash here for the night and I'll send her by Parcelfarce in the morning.'

'It's here,' Rick caught my arm.

'What?'

'The envelope. It's here. On my desk in the study.'

'All right if I open this?' Leoni zigzagged into view, a bottle dangling from her hand.

'Course it is, treacle,' Rick said.

'No!' I corrected him. I took the bottle from her and steered her towards the nearest seat. 'I think you've had quite enough for one day, unless you're planning on waking up in the morning needing a brain transplant.'

'Life transplant,' she hiccupped. 'Though right now I'd settle for a straight lobotomy.'

'For heaven's sake, sit down and behave.' Leoni was incapable of arguing as I shoved her into a chair. 'And don't you move until I get back.'

YOU COULD HAVE CUT the atmosphere in Rick's study with a knife, him huffing his frustration, the pair of us locked in a Mexican stand-off.

'Just open it,' Rick said, chewing impatiently on his cigar.

'I can't do that! It's nobody's business except Julia's.'

'She should have bloody well sorted it out herself, then, shouldn't she?'

'I'll take it round to her first thing in the morning.'

'Listen, babe.' He struck a match from the pot on his desk and sucked his stogie back into life. 'I'm telling you, you're not gonna make it through the night in the state you're in.'

I felt as though my heart was going to explode, pounding away as it was, my throat strangled by the invisible rope of doom coiled around it. All I wanted was to get the news to Julia, but David would be home by now, and this was one conversation that I wasn't prepared to risk while he was in the same building. My pacing had reached fever pitch, up and down, up and down. Rick got up from his seat, took the envelope from the desk and thrust it into my hand.

'Open it,' he said. 'Then at least you'll know what you're dealing with.'

'No.'

Before I knew it, he had taken the envelope from me and torn it open. Flapping the folds out of the letter, he held it in front of my face like a repossession notice.

'Are you going to do the honours, or shall I?'

'I can't believe you just did that.' I snatched it from him and began to read. 'Case number blah blah blah, we have completed the paternity test with the result that there is a likelihood of ninety-eight per cent that the sample provided is—' I stopped reading. The next sentence stuck on my tonsils. The page froze in my hand. I sank into the chair and looked up at Rick.

'What does it say?'

'Here.' I passed the document over. 'Read it yourself.'

Chapter Thirteen

BABY, YOU CAN
DRIVE MY CAR

THE NEXT MORNING, I forced myself into a supposedly invigorating shower and tried to scrub away the
sleepless night filled with a terrible recurring nightmare
about being run over by a bus while wearing pop socks.
The image burned itself indelibly on my sleep-deprived
mind. A huddle of rubber-necking bystanders gathered
around as I lay there, poleaxed, in the middle of the
road, skirt above my knees, and even though I was
dead, I could hear the shocked gasps from a group of
clucking women who were openly thanking God that it

wasn't any of them. I stood under the soft jets of warm water, watching Rick trying to finish off his shave, patiently rubbing a hole in the steamed-up mirror yet again before finally giving up and feeling his way around the underside of his chin instead. By the time I slunk back to the bedroom hidden beneath a shroud of towels, he was suited and booted, ready to go and do battle at that mysterious office of his.

'I brought you up a coffee.' He bucked his head at the steaming mug beside the bed. I never thought I'd see the day when the only sort of coffee I wanted was one of Helga's thunderballs.

'Thanks,' I said. 'Any sign of the house guest?'

'Nope.' Rick stood in front of the dresser and knotted his tie, the sober blue stripes lending him a certain air of respectability. 'After the mess she was in last night, I'd be surprised if she regains consciousness at all today.'

'Great.' I dropped myself onto the bed and picked up the mug. 'That's all I bloody need.'

'You want me to stick around for a while?' He pulled his suit jacket on.

'No thanks.' I had quite enough to deal with today without having a man hanging around waiting for me to pay him some attention.

'I'm off then.' He presented himself to me for inspection, polished up like a shiny new apple, a tissue tucked into his collar to mop up the shaving nicks. 'I won't be late. Call me if you need me.'

'OK.'

'Well?'

'Well what?'

'Don't I get a kiss?'

'Oh.' I stood up automatically and planted one on his lips, shrinking away as he put his arms around me and tried to give it some meaning. Oh, for heaven's sake. Why can't men leave the kissing thing in times of crisis? It's like they think the world will stop turning if they don't force the issue just for the sake of their ego. It's highly irritating. While he pressed his lips against mine, I ran through the day's jam-packed agenda and remembered that there was one teensy-weensy little favour that I had forgotten to mention. At last, he broke away from my face, looking mighty pleased with himself. 'By the way,' I said lightly. 'Do you mind if I use the car today?' He blinked at me for a moment.

'The Bentley?'

'Er, yes.' Funny how men can go deaf and stupid when it suits them. 'Unless you have another car kicking around here somewhere that I can use instead?'

He laughed uneasily.'Why don't you just grab a cab?'

'I'd rather not.' I pulled the towel off my head and rubbed at the ends of my hair. 'I've got to drop Leoni back to her car, then I have to go and collect something I ordered for Julia, then I have to get myself all the way over to her house, and after she's read that letter, I may well have to drive her to the nearest airport to make a quick getaway. If it's all right with you, I'd really rather not be victim to the vagaries of public transport today. I have far too much to do. It'll be much easier if I can just drive myself.'

'It's a bloody big car,' he said anxiously. 'Sure you can handle it?' He shifted his weight uncomfortably from one foot to the other and looked at the carpet for a split second. Well, well.

'You don't want me to drive your car, do you?'

'Don't be daft, babe!' His smile was rigid, just that little bit too tight around the edges.

'You think I'm going to scrape it down every parked car in the neighbourhood and back it into the nearest lamppost, don't you?'

'Course not!' A tiny knot of apprehension appeared on his brow.

'You bloody chauvinist! I know that face. You don't trust me with it, do you? I'll have you know that I've had a full, clean driving licence for over twenty years, which is more than I can say for you, buster.' I brushed past him and took a seat at the vanity, turning on the hairdryer to drown out his protests.

'Aw, Hell! Don't be like that! It's a bloke thing! Of course you can use the car. What's mine is yours, babe!'

'Don't bother,' I shouted over the dryer. 'I'll go to that disabled shop round the back of Ebury Street once I'm dressed and buy myself one of those motorized spag chariots, shall I?'

Rick ducked out of the room and came back a couple of minutes later with the keys.

'Sorry, babe.' He put an arm around my bare shoulders and pressed the keys into my hand. 'You go right ahead.'

PUSHING OPEN THE DOOR of the guest room we had dragged and dropped Leoni into last night, I was hit by the grotesque stench of stale alcohol clinging to the wallpaper. It was hardly surprising. While Rick and I had been huddled in his study arguing over the envelope, Leoni had of course taken full advantage of being left unsupervised for half an hour and had got well and truly stuck into the brandy. By the time I got back to her, she was slumped on a sofa, trying to do the harmony to a song she was playing in her head. I think it may have been Take That's 'Shine', although her high notes were a couple of miles short of their target. My futile attempts to get her up the stairs were met with a stream of abuse and slurred demands to go out clubbing. She had then broken into a quick rendition of 'Le Freak', hanging on to the banister rail and thrusting her hips suggestively towards the weeping fig. Rick must have heard the commotion and came swiftly to my aid, picking Leoni up like a twig and throwing her over his shoulder before marching her up the stairs and flinging her down on the nearest available bed. She

thin sweater, I felt the distinct signs of rapid weight loss. I stood back to get a better look at her.

'Someone's not been eating properly,' I said, my voice more concerned than complimentary.

'I'm not bloody surprised. I haven't slept a wink, and the thought of food just makes me feel ill.'

'I've brought a little something to cheer you up,' I said. Julia glanced at my empty hands. I raised a finger and beckoned the gift that I had hidden behind the bay tree. A pleasant-looking girl emerged from behind the foliage and stepped forward. 'Julia, this is Odene.' The girl called Odene offered Julia an excitable smile. 'Odene, this is my sister Julia. The one I told you about.'

'Hello.' Julia accepted Odene's whimsical attempt at a handshake and looked at me, befuddled.

'Odene is a fully qualified Norland nanny.' Odene nodded enthusiastically and flashed her badge proudly. 'And she's all yours.' Julia's mouth dropped open.

'A nanny?' Tears sprang to her eyes. 'For me?'

'Well?' I said. 'Aren't you going to ask us in?'

It took Odene all of fifteen minutes to hand over the references I had already checked, drink a cup of sugary tea and make herself useful. The moment Frankie woke up from his nap, she insisted on taking command of her new charge and took him out for a stroll around the garden. Julia hovered at the door unsurely, watching her every confident move.

'How old is she?' Julia asked.

'Twenty-two,' I said. 'She's been working for a couple down in Dorking for the last year, but the dad kept making inappropriate suggestions and accidentally walking into her bedroom with nothing but a towel on.'

'Crikey. Poor kid. That must have been traumatic.'

'Surprisingly, no. She said it wasn't the first time it's happened to her. She's well used to it. It was the wife who turned out to be the bigger problem. She sacked her the minute she noticed she'd caught her husband's eye. Apparently he had a bit of a reputation for getting it on with anyone who sat still for long enough.'

'Where's she from?'

'She's living in a flat-share with four other girls in Clapham at the moment, but says that she'd far rather live in, if that's all right with you.'

'All right with me? Are you kidding?'

'She comes very highly recommended. Good family background. Absolutely loves babies. Hasn't got a boyfriend to moon over and swears she doesn't want one either after her last experience.'

'Where on earth did you find her?'

'From an agency, of course! Honestly, Julia, you really need to get that brain of yours back up and running again. She'll work five days a week, any five that you like, and says that she's happy to do extra hours so long as she gets paid overtime.'

'A nanny.' Julia shook her head incredulously. 'Why the bloody hell didn't I think of that?'

'Because you're too busy having a nervous breakdown.'

'Of course.' She nodded.

'I've covered her salary for three months. Call it an early birthday present. Mind you, if you decide to keep her, she expects to have the use of a car, so you'll have to sort that out yourself.'

'If?' Julia turned to me. 'Please tell me she brought her suitcases.'

'Not yet,' I smiled. 'I think she wanted to check you out for herself before making her mind up.'

'I don't know what to say,' Julia said.

'How about thank you?'

Odene trotted to the door, bouncing Frankie happily in her arms. 'He's gorgeous!' she gushed. 'And I just love your house! You wouldn't believe the place I'm living in at the moment. We're crammed in like sardines!'

'You can move in here with us, if you'd like to,' Julia suggested. 'There's a lovely spare room upstairs with its own en-suite bathroom. Would you like to come and have a look at it?'

'Oh, yes please!' Odene bounced on her heels and wagged her tail like a Labrador. 'I prefer to live with my families anyway, and I can do as much overtime as you like. I'm saving up to go to Australia for a year. My friend Michelle went last summer and never came back. Now she's working in a seafood shack and expecting a baby of her own! Isn't that just completely brilliant?!'

My face ached with the effort of keeping up with her enthusiasm – her radiant smile lit the place up like a Christmas tree.

'Wow,' I said, trying to sound young.

'I can move in whenever you like! All I have to do is go and pick up my stuff.'

'Don't you want to wait a while and see how it works out?' Julia said.

'Why?' Odene shrugged. 'Unless your husband's got arms like an octopus and you're one of those mothers who starts on the flaming sambucas before breakfast, I don't see what there is not to like!'

'Listen,' I said to Odene. 'Would you mind keeping an eye on Frankie for a little while? Feel free to have a wander round the house and take a look. I have a couple of things I need to speak to my sister about.'

'No problem!' Odene beamed. 'You just take your time. We're happy, aren't we, Frankie?' she said, twiddling his buttons.

'I'M SPEECHLESS.' Julia sat down at her dressing table, picked up the brush and set about her hair. 'Thanks, Helen. That's the best bloody present I could ever have wished for. I have a feeling that today might just turn out to be the happiest day of my life.'

'Not so fast,' I said gently. 'It's here.' I pulled out the envelope that had been burning a hole in the bottom of my handbag all morning and handed it to her. 'I already opened it,' I said. 'Sorry. I know I shouldn't have.'

She looked at it dispassionately.

'What does it say?'

'You'd better read it for yourself.'

'I don't want to.' She put it down next to her collection of expensive perfumes. 'I already know what's in there. It's written all over your face.' I could scarcely bring myself to meet her eyes. 'David's not the father, is he?'

'No.'

She leaned her elbows on the mirrored surface of the table and pressed her face into her hands. For once, words failed me. There was nothing I could say, so I sat down quietly on the bed, trying to blend in with the duvet cover. After what seemed like an eternity, Julia took a deep breath, sat up and gave me the kind of look you'd expect from an Elizabethan traitor waiting for their executioner to arrive.

'That's it, then,' she said.

'What are you going to do?'

'I don't know.'

'Is there anything I can do to help?'

'I wish.' She offered me a forlorn smile.

Picking up the envelope, Julia stood up and went to the window, which had been left open to invite the small breeze. It was a beautiful day outside, heavy with the rich scent of late-summer pollen, warm without being at all uncomfortable. Julia leaned against the window frame, took out the letter and read it. It stayed in her hand for a mighty long time, and I guessed that she was torturing herself, running the same inevitable sentence past her tired eyes over and over again. I looked away, embarrassed by her discomfort, having no place in that awful, disturbed moment. Julia took a small book of restaurant matches from the ornamental dish on the dressing table, struck one and held it to the corner of the paper. It caught immediately. She held the smoking page out of the window, the breeze fanning the flames instantly, and let the burning letter drop from her fingers, curling black and disintegrating before it reached the ground.

The knot in my throat grew to the size of a cantaloupe. I pinched the skin on the back of my hand hard. Come on, woman. Get a grip. This was no time to start howling. Julia stared out of the window unblinkingly, as though every last vestige of life had been sucked from her. I could feel her torment, the air around her supercharged, tightening around us like a rubber band.

'Come on,' I said firmly, jumping up from the bed and pulling open her wardrobe doors. 'Let's see if that body of yours has shrunk sufficiently to fit into some decent clothes.'

'Huh?' She blinked, miles away.

I gave her a big, decisive hug and pinched a small handful of her much-reduced flesh. 'If I'm going to take you out for lunch today, you can bloody well make an effort and stick a nice dress on.'

'Lunch?' She looked at me incredulously.

'We'll have to get a move on.' I ignored her distress and fiddled with my watch. 'I left Leoni comatose in one of the spare bedrooms this morning, so we'll have to drop back to my house first and scrape her off the mattress, then I vote we all go and have a major scoff-a-thon at Mario's. What do you reckon?' I summoned my very best beaming, happy smile. Well, why not? It wasn't as though there was anything either of us could do to change the situation, so might as well just say sod it and go out and do something constructive involving lots of food. It was either that or stand around here with long faces for the next two hours looking like somebody had just died. Besides, the evidence had just been neatly incinerated, and nobody need be any the wiser. It was over. She'd got what she wanted. The Truth. And what she decided to do with that was her own affair. From the look on Julia's face, I guessed she was in one of those moments when she wasn't sure whether to laugh or cry.

'But what about Frankie?' she said. A rhetorical

question if ever I heard one. What about Frankie? What about David? What about the father? What about the starving millions?

'What about him?' I shrugged casually. 'We've got Little Miss Sunshine downstairs. Why don't we kill a couple of birds with one stone? She can tag along with us, then go and grab some of her stuff while we have lunch. What do you say?'

'I don't know,' she said, squirming unsurely. 'It's bad enough trying to get him through an appointment at the baby clinic. I'm not sure if he's ready to—'

'Listen, Julia. I know exactly what you're thinking. But how many times have we sat in a restaurant and been subjected to a screaming kid while the mother sits there defiantly with an AK-47 hidden beneath her napkin, just willing somebody to make a fuss about it?' At last I saw the beginnings of a faint smile on Julia's lips. 'Yeah? Well now it's our turn. So let's cram that sorry backside of yours into something other than a shroud and unleash your kid on an unsuspecting public.'

SWEEPING AROUND the lazy bend at the end of Julia's tree-lined street, I fancied that I was really starting to get the hang of the Bentley. Provided you held in mind that it was roughly the size of a refuse truck, it was surprisingly effortless to drive. Just point it in the right direction, give the accelerator the merest suggestion of a press, and away you went, owning the tarmac in grand style. We had a bit of trouble getting the baby seat in, mind you. I think you're supposed to order one from Bentley, rather than Mamas & Papas, but Odene managed to get it wedged in, after a fashion, and clambered into the back with him. Forty-five minutes later, after dropping Odene off at her flat, we came to a convenient halt on a yellow line a few yards away from my front door. I left the keys in the ignition, just in case the clampers should be hiding around the corner rubbing their hands.

'If you see a yellow peril, drive around the block,' I told Julia. 'I won't be a minute.'

'Got it,' she said, and slid herself behind the wheel.

'Hell-yen!' Helga came pounding down the stairs the moment she heard my key in the latch, her face flushed with blind panic. 'Hell-yen! I sorry!'

'Whatever's the matter?' My eyes did a rapid-scan, looking for an expensive breakage.

'Is here!' She grabbed my arm and dragged me towards the kitchen. 'Is, how you say, erm . . .' A few garbled Russian words fell from her jabbering lips. 'Is PROOOMPH!' She gesticulated wildly. 'I not know! I sorry!'

Leoni sat slumped at the kitchen table, holding an ice pack against her head.

'Leoni?' I rushed to her side. She lifted her face

towards me, her left eye swollen half-shut. 'Oh my God!'

'You no tell me!' Helga wrung her hands. 'You no say! I go up!' She pointed to the bedroom above. 'I hear noise. I see person. I think is burgling!' I eased the ice pack from Leoni's head, revealing a huge egg-shaped bump.

'Oh, Helga! What on earth have you done?'

'Hit me over the head with a fucking vase,' Leoni spluttered.

'But your eye!' I took a closer look.

'Oh that,' Leoni sank to the table again. 'That was me. I fell over coming out of the shower and walloped my face on the corner of the bog.'

'Shouldn't we get you to casualty?'

'Nah.' Leoni waved the suggestion away. 'Helga gave me a couple of vodka coffees and a handful of diamorphine, so I'm not feeling much pain right now.'

'I sorry!' Helga wailed through a gust of vodka breath. Well, it was that time of day.

'It's OK, Helga.' I put my arm around her and gave her a reassuring pat on the back. 'I should have left you a note or something.' To be honest, the thought had crossed my mind, but I wasn't sure that she'd be able to read it. I've seen her struggling with the occasional newspaper headline, moving her lips like Snoopy, scowling at the words before throwing the paper aside and giving up. 'Next time I'll ring you,' I said. 'Really. It's not your fault.'

The Bentley's horn sounded urgently from the street.

'Bugger,' I said. 'Julia's outside in the car with little Frankie. We were going to pick you up and go out to lunch. Never mind. I'll go and tell her the change of plan.'

'What?' Leoni dragged herself to her feet, wearing the clothes she had liberated from my wardrobe while I was out. My invitation for her to make herself at home had obviously been taken at face value, and she'd gone for my one and only Escada shirt and a pair of brand new linen trousers that I'd only worn once. I waved the ensemble goodbye, knowing I'd never see any of it again. 'If you think I'm passing on a lunch invitation, you've got another think coming.'

'Leoni! You can't possibly go out in that state!'

'What state? I've still got my bloody arms and legs, haven't I? Just give me a minute. I haven't found my handbag yet.'

'*Ya pomogoo tebe*!' Helga rushed to the oven, opened the door, and pulled out Leoni's handbag. 'Is you bag? *Da*?'

'What's it doing in there?' Leoni took it from her.

'Ah,' Helga said proudly. 'I find. I keep. But now, you have back. Is present from me.'

'Thanks.' Leoni shoved it over her shoulder.

'I take money already,' Helga sniggered to herself.

'And no hard feelings, eh, Helga? Had I not been so hungover, I expect we could have had a good old-fashioned saloon punch-up. I quite like a bit of a ruck every now and then.'

'Ah.' Helga nodded unsurely. '*Ya ne panimayu tebia.*'

'Yep,' Leoni said. 'Whatever that means.' The car horn sounded again. 'Right then.' Leoni pulled herself up unsteadily. 'Fix bayonets. We're going over the top.'

'*BELLA SIGNORA!*' Mario positively sprinted his enormous bulk through the restaurant to greet us the moment we walked in. '*Ciao! Ciao! Bellissimo!*' His eyes fell upon the slumbering Frankie as Julia manhandled the baby seat through the door. '*Mamma mia!*' he said, clutching at his chest. 'Eez a bambino! Hey! Tommaso!' Tommaso abandoned his post behind the bar and rushed over.

'*Bella* Julia!' He kissed her cheeks. '*Che brava!* He beautiful like his mamma! *Congratulazioni!*'

Frankie woke up with a start to find two burly Italians grinning garlic into his face, prodding his chest with pudgy fingers.

'Waaaaaaaaaaaaaaah!'

'Hey!' They exchanged an approving nod at the size of the kid's lungs. 'He make the opera, no?!' Mario stood back and cleared this throat, threw out his arms and sang a couple of bars of his own football version of 'Nessun Dorma'. Frankie howled even louder, his face turning puce.

'What his name?' Tommaso beamed down at him adoringly.

'Frank Junior,' Julia said.

'*Bello!*' Mario nodded. 'Francesco! Come!' He pulled at my arm, directing us towards the big table in the middle of the restaurant, set for eight, but now ours to abuse as we saw fit. Taking the baby seat from Julia, he plonked Frankie right in the middle of the table so that he wouldn't miss anything. As he sat there and yelled like an air-raid claxon, the other diners shrank in their seats, hands going over ears, appetites evaporating. A bottle of champagne was thrust upon us.

'Perfect,' Leoni said, nodding, as Mario poured, having given Frankie the cork to suck. Might as well start the kid off early. 'The only way to get through a hangover like this is to get straight back on the horse.'

'Not for me.' I held my hand over my glass. 'I'm driving. I'll have some fizzy water instead and just pretend.'

'You no order food today,' Mario insisted. 'Juan make you special dish for celebrate. You just leave it to me, eh?'

'Thanks, Mario.' Julia handed back her menu and settled in her chair, flicking her gaze around the restaurant nonchalantly, refusing to make eye contact with any of the scowling customers.

'*Prego!*' Mario, glowing in the company of a bouncing baby, burst back into song and made for the kitchen, ignoring any attempts from his exasperated customers to secure just a little bit of service. I snuck a glance at Julia. She seemed to be elsewhere, staring at something way off in the distance, quietly contemplating her own thoughts. She caught my eye briefly, and for a moment I thought I saw a sliver of acceptance pass through her, deep down somewhere. I smiled at her, a smile of tacit understanding and lifelong love, and she returned it to me.

'Helen?' Julia raised her glass. 'I would like to propose a toast.'

'Oh, goody!' Leoni drained her glass and reached for the bottle. 'Just let me freshen up my glass. Can't do a toast with something you've already had a slurp from. It's a hundred years bad luck.'

'Had it not been for you,' Julia said, 'I'd be festering at home on my own searching for the earplugs and stinking of baby milk.'

'Fuck that,' Leoni nodded.

'So I'd like to say a big thank you, from the bottom of my heart, for taking me in hand and showing me that there is such a thing as life after childbirth.'

'Just you wait till he gets a bit bigger,' Leoni said. 'That's when the trouble really starts.'

'Zip it,' I told her. 'Julia's having a moment.'

'That's it, really,' Julia shrugged. 'So here's my toast.' She raised her champagne to my flute of sparkling water. 'Sisters.' She clinked her glass against mine.

'Sisters,' I said.

Leoni's face dropped.

'Oi! That's not bloody fair! It's not my fault I'm an only child!'

'Yes it is,' Julia said. 'I remember what you were like when you were a kid. It's no bloody wonder your parents called it a day. I expect your mum booked herself in for an early hysterectomy just to make sure.'

'That's blatant victimization,' Leoni said sulkily.

'Hey!' I tossed a breadstick at her. 'What have you got to complain about? You've been an honorary sister for years!'

'Have I?' Leoni brightened.

'Sure!' Julia said.

'In that case – ' Leoni lifted her champagne glass – '*salute!*' and she threw back half the glass in one deft swallow.

Under Mario's watchful eye, one bottle followed another, and we saw off a heaving banquet fit for Pavarotti and ten of his fat friends while Frankie brought the house down in between half a dozen hungry milk feeds. He eyed his mother suspiciously as we went through plates of antipasti drizzled with rich, fruity olive oil, baskets of home-made ciabatta still warm from the oven, and a big dish of slow-cooked osso buco that fell off the bone and melted on the lips. By the time the tiramisu arrived, I barely had room to breathe.

'Mario!' I implored him. 'Please! No more!'

'Speak for yourself, mate.' Leoni dug her spoon in. 'I'm not leaving until I've finished every scrap, and if it kills me in the process, so much the better.' As the wine went down, her volume went up.

'You'd better hurry up about it.' I tapped my watch at her. 'There's no way I'm going to have another one of those conversations with Marcus about his wife being in no fit state to get to the school again.'

'Tosser,' she said. 'I hate his guts. Just leave me here and tell him I've died. I expect he'll get the bunting out and throw a massive party.'

'Don't worry. I'll give you a lift,' I said, 'seeing as you're three times over the limit, yet again.'

'Good.' She finished her limoncello and licked the inside of the glass. Julia started cackling, being more than a couple of sheets to the wind herself. 'If alcohol's the only way I can get through life being married to a shit-for-brains single-celled organism, then so be it.'

'Excuse me.' The lady from the neighbouring table broke away from her conversation and turned in her chair, barely holding her temper in check. 'It's bad enough that we've been subjected to your screaming child all through lunch, but must we really listen to your filthy language as well?'

Leoni gave me one of her looks.

'Back off, fatso,' she snarled at the dumbfounded woman. 'Unless you wanna go outside and make something of it?' Leoni lifted her dark glasses, displaying the grotesquely swollen state of her left eye, which in the last couple of hours had taken on a painfully multicoloured hue. The horrified women at the other table took a collective intake of breath. 'Yeah?' Leoni lowered the shades back over her injury. 'You should see the other guy.'

THE CLOCK TICKED gracefully on the dashboard, issuing a suitably Jeeves and Wooster reminder that we'd cut it dangerously fine, madam. 'School run first, then I'll drop you home,' I said to Julia.

'You'll never get us all in the car,' she said. Ah. I hadn't thought of that.

'OK. I'll dump you and Leoni at hers first, then I'll double back and grab the kids.'

'Are you sure?' Leoni slid in and made herself comfortable in the back.

'Unless you've got a better idea, Einstein?'

'Nope.' Leoni started playing with the window and testing out the various personal comfort controls. 'Knock yourself out.'

The best part of an hour later, after depositing them on the pavement outside Leoni's house, I found myself lost in a throng of desiccated mothers and complaining children outside the gates of the local primary school. It was utter chaos. Kids running out into the road. Mothers screaming after them. Scuffles breaking out between rival groups of rutting ten-year-olds. A plastic SpongeBob lunchbox being hurled at some kid's head. I searched around desperately for Leoni's offspring, concerned that if I left the Bentley abandoned for more than two minutes around here I'd probably come back to find it propped up on bricks.

'Josh!' At last I spotted one of them in the affray. 'Over here!' Then I caught sight of William, hunched near to the ground behind his brother, trying to set fire to the bottom of his trousers with a match. 'William!' I ploughed forward, elbowing my way through, just like all the other mothers. 'Stop that!'

'Where's Mum?' They looked past me.

'She's waiting for you at home.' Perhaps best not mention the part about her being somewhat drunk and disorderly. 'I thought I'd come and pick you up as a special treat!' They glanced at each other warily. 'Guess what car I've brought with me?'

'Dunno,' William said, pulling himself up from the pavement.

'Just you wait and see! But first, I think you'd better hand over those matches, young man.'

'What matches?'

'The ones you're hiding in your pocket.' William

pulled his mouth into an enormous sulk and handed over the contraband. 'Good.' I said. 'I won't tell your mother about this. Just don't do it again.' Who was I kidding? They'd already learned how to make gun-powder and blown a chest of drawers apart in their bedroom. I tried to chivvy them along. 'Have you got everything?' William grunted some sort of unintelligible response. 'How about you, Josh?'

'S'pose,' he mumbled, kicking the toe of his shoe on the pavement, determined to scuff the leather down to the bone.

God, it was hard work trying to jolly the sullen little bastards along. Adults and children really shouldn't have to mix. They don't get on, don't like each other, and certainly don't speak the same language. 'Where's your sister?'

'Dunno,' Josh shrugged.

'You two wait here while I go and find her. Don't move a muscle. OK?'

Millie isn't particularly easy to pick out in a crowd. She's a petite little thing, like her mother. She's also a little bit shy and rather quiet, unlike her mother, and has no doubt been permanently damaged by the deranged battleground of a family home in which she lives. After a few tentative enquiries aimed at a couple of gum-chewing teenage mums, I finally found her tucked behind the flowering cherry in the corner of the playground, talking to her dolly.

'Hello, Millie!' It took her a moment to recognize who I was, her not having seen me for a month. Four weeks is a very long time in the life of a seven-year-old. 'Mummy sent me to pick you up from school today!'

'Where's Mummy?'

'She's at home, darling, making you something yummy for supper.' Yeah right. 'Come on!' I took her hand. 'You're going to have a nice ride in a very posh car, just like the Queen.'

Back on the street, William and Josh had located the Bentley and were busy showing it off to their friends. Snotty faces slid round the windows. Mucky hands grappled with the wing mirrors and smeared dirty marks all over the paintwork.

'Cor!' Josh shouted in my face. 'Can I have a go behind the steering wheel?'

'Best not.' I unlocked it with a wave of the key. 'It's Rick's, so we have to be very careful with it.'

'Oh, go on!' William pleaded. 'We won't break anything! Promise!'

'Next time,' I said, hoping they couldn't smell my fear. 'You two hop in the back. Millie, you jump in the front with me.' I opened the door for her and helped her climb in.

'That's not fair!" Josh shouted. 'I want to go in the front!'

'No!' William pushed him hard. 'I want to! I'm the oldest. I should go in the front!'

you like. I'm saving up to go to Australia for a year. My friend Michelle went last summer and never came back. Now she's working in a seafood shack and expecting a baby of her own! Isn't that just completely brilliant?!'

My face ached with the effort of keeping up with her enthusiasm – her radiant smile lit the place up like a Christmas tree.

'Wow,' I said, trying to sound young.

'I can move in whenever you like! All I have to do is go and pick up my stuff.'

'Don't you want to wait a while and see how it works out?' Julia said.

'Why?' Odene shrugged. 'Unless your husband's got arms like an octopus and you're one of those mothers who starts on the flaming sambucas before breakfast, I don't see what there is not to like!'

'Listen,' I said to Odene. 'Would you mind keeping an eye on Frankie for a little while? Feel free to have a wander round the house and take a look. I have a couple of things I need to speak to my sister about.'

'No problem!' Odene beamed. 'You just take your time. We're happy, aren't we, Frankie?' she said, twiddling his buttons.

'I'M SPEECHLESS.' Julia sat down at her dressing table, picked up the brush and set about her hair. 'Thanks, Helen. That's the best bloody present I could ever have

'A nanny.' Julia shook her head incredulously. 'Why the bloody hell didn't I think of that?'

'Because you're too busy having a nervous breakdown.'

'Of course.' She nodded.

'I've covered her salary for three months. Call it an early birthday present. Mind you, if you decide to keep her, she expects to have the use of a car, so you'll have to sort that out yourself.'

'If?' Julia turned to me. 'Please tell me she brought her suitcases.'

'Not yet,' I smiled. 'I think she wanted to check you out for herself before making her mind up.'

'I don't know what to say,' Julia said.

'How about thank you?'

Odene trotted to the door, bouncing Frankie happily in her arms. 'He's gorgeous!' she gushed. 'And I just love your house! You wouldn't believe the place I'm living in at the moment. We're crammed in like sardines!'

'You can move in here with us, if you'd like to,' Julia suggested. 'There's a lovely spare room upstairs with its own en-suite bathroom. Would you like to come and have a look at it?'

'Oh, yes please!' Odene bounced on her heels and wagged her tail like a Labrador. 'I prefer to live with my families anyway, and I can do as much overtime as

'Dog breath!' Josh shoved him back. 'Two minutes older doesn't make you the boss.'

'Ow!' William lashed out, kicking Josh's leg. 'Piss off!'

'William!' I covered Millie's ears. 'Don't use language like that!'

'Why not!' Josh had him in a headlock. 'Mum does!'

'Arseholes!' William yelled. I felt Millie's grip tighten on my hand.

'Now, stop that! Both of you! Or you'll be walking home. Do you hear me?'

The short drive back to Leoni's house was the longest five minutes of my life. I tried desperately to find the button on the dash that disabled the passenger controls in the back, but no luck. The twins were having a heyday messing around with everything they could find, wrestling with each other and trying to land punches and score points whenever I was forced to take my eyes off the rear-view mirror for a few seconds to concentrate on the road. Millie sat quietly in the front beside me, thumb in mouth, wide-eyed as she obeyed my yelled command not to touch anything. I felt terrible. The shout had been aimed at her brothers, who didn't take a blind bit of notice anyway, yet it was Millie who had flinched in her seat and nodded her golden ringlets at me immediately, quaking with fear. Poor little sausage. She's so sweet it makes your heart ache.

Julia was waiting outside Leoni's house, ready to load

Frankie back in and make a quick getaway before either of us could get stuck in the House of Hell. I waited until the boys had clambered out of the back before turning to Millie.

'I wasn't shouting at you, sweetie-pie,' I said softly, giving her nose a little beep. 'You're a peach.' She blinked at me like a lost chick. I got out of the car and came round to her side, then took her in to her mother.

'Thanks.' Leoni had her feet up on the sofa with the television on full blast. From the racket coming out of the kitchen, I assumed the boys were in there smashing a couple of walls down with a lump hammer.

'Sure you can manage?' I asked.

'Yep.' She flipped through the channels without looking up.

'What about feeding the kids?'

'Oh, they're all right,' she sighed. 'They know what a fridge looks like.'

I looked down at Millie. She looked up at me. 'Shall I make you and dolly a nice little sandwich before I go?'

JULIA WAS LOITERING by the car waiting for me. She seemed agitated.

'Sorry!' I picked up my pace and trotted towards her. 'Just had to rustle up a quick snack for the kids. Leoni's sparked out on the sofa.'

'Whatever you do . . .' Julia took a purposeful step towards me . . . 'don't panic.'

'Panic? Panic about what?' She opened the rear passenger door and stood aside.

It took a moment for the sight to register. I felt the skin on my cheeks go tight. There was mud everywhere, ground into the carpets, smeared across the back of the driver's seat. Huge streaks of black pen criss-crossed the central arm rest. And, if my eyes did not deceive me, the cream calfskin upholstery had been redecorated with a huge, gaping slash. 'Oh my God!' My fist rushed to my teeth. 'Oh *shit*!' I turned to face the house, my first instinct being to go flush out the culprits and give them a good hiding. And a fat lot of good that would do. Leoni had tried beating them for years, only to discover that it merely toughened them up and made them even more violent towards each other. 'Oh, *fuck*!' I stared at Julia. 'Rick's going to do his pieces!'

'Come on,' she said. 'Let's just get in the car and get the hell out of here before they can do any more damage.'

I flung myself behind the wheel, turned the engine over with shaking hands, revved the massive engine and screeched away from the kerb. 'Get on the phone!' I said, throwing my handbag at Julia. 'Ring the Bentley shop on Berkeley Square!'

'What's it called?'

'Christ! I don't know!' Julia took out her own phone and hit the speed dial.

'Sara? It's me. Yes. Fine. Everything's just fine. Listen, I need you to do something, fast as you can.'

Hunched over the steering wheel like a woman possessed, I hit the accelerator hard, leaning the car into the corners like a high-speed oil tanker. Frankie began to howl, struggling against the straps on his car seat, kicking his legs and making himself as uncomfortable as he could. Julia raised her voice, barking at Sara to be heard over the din. I raced towards the green light. Don't change. Please don't change. It went amber. Maybe I could make a dash for it. Just put your foot down, woman. Still six feet from the junction, it turned red and I bottled out, slamming on the anchors. And just when I thought things couldn't get any worse, there came the unmistakable sound of a baby regurgitating its lunch.

Chapter Fourteen

IT'S ONLY A
BLOODY CAR

'THREE *WEEKS*?'

'I'm afraid so, madam.'

'But surely it's only superficial?'

'It's a Bentley, madam. There's nothing superficial about a Bentley.'

'Oh God.' Any notion I had had about a quick fix and Rick being none the wiser went sailing right up the Swanee. 'What am I going to tell Rick?'

'Don't ask me.' Julia flipped a tic tac into her mouth. 'I've got more important things on my mind.'

'Want me to break it to him?' Sara fished a Juicy Tube out of her handbag and freshened up her lip-gloss. 'Bad news is my middle name.'

'No,' I sighed. 'I might as well take the rap and wait for him to go mental at me and say I Told You So. Why didn't I just get a sodding cab like he said?'

'It's only a bloody car.' Sara smacked her lips together and stuffed the tube back into her bag. The Bentley man bristled and bit his cheek. Julia's phone rang from her pocket.

'Hello?' Her eyes rose to mine. 'Odene! Where are you? Fantastic! Just tell the cab to pull up and hang on. I'll be right out.'

'Odene?' Sara asked. 'Who the bloody hell's Odene?'

'Julia's new nanny,' I said. 'She just went home to grab some of her stuff. She's moving in with Julia this afternoon.'

'New nanny?' Sara smiled at Julia. 'About bloody time! I was wondering when you were going to come to your senses and draft reinforcements in.'

'I hate to leave you in the shit like this.' Julia stuffed her phone into her bag and made ready to leave.

'Then don't,' Sara said. 'Send little mister stinky pants here back home with the nappy slave.'

'I can't do that!'

'Why the hell not?'

'She hasn't even met David yet!'

'So? She's got a tongue in her head, hasn't she? Go

on!' Sara pushed her towards the door. 'Just sling her your keys and tell her to get on with it.'

'I couldn't possibly—'

'Oh, for Christ's sake, woman.' Sara snatched Julia's handbag from her and picked Frankie up. 'Give it here. I'll do it myself. If she's gonna fit in with us lot, she might as well get used to being chucked in at the deep end, eh? I'll bung her some cash for the cab and give David a ring.' She flounced out into the street, sashaying her hips and swinging Frankie in his baby seat.

'This is just too weird,' Julia said shakily. 'The thought of being baby-free for a few hours is like being offered the Crown jewels. I just knew it. I'm a really bad mother.'

'No you're not,' I said, nudging her. 'He's in perfectly good hands, and I'll be buggered if you're going to leave me to face the music on my own when it's your sprog who chundered all over the back seat.'

'Bloody hell!' Sara was back in moments, dusting her hands off. 'Is she on the happy pills or something? When I told her it was sink or swim time, anyone would have thought that she'd just won the lottery! She told you not to worry about a thing. Come home whenever you like.'

'I'm stunned.' Julia leaned on me for support. 'Just give me a minute. I think I'm having a panic attack.'

'Madam?' The Bentley man loitered nearby. 'The car?'

'Oh yes,' I handed him the keys. 'Just get it done as fast as you can and call me when it's ready.'

'Of course.' He bowed slightly, clicking his heels together. 'And if Mr Wilton would like a courtesy car in the meantime, just let us know and we'll have one brought round at once.'

'Thank you.' I signed Rick's car away on the service sheet, wondering how on earth I was going to explain my way out of this one.

'RICK?' I knew he was here somewhere – the aroma of a freshly smoked cigar hung loosely on the air.

'Hey gorgeous!' he boomed from the study. 'Gimme a couple of minutes, would ya, babe? I'm on the blower to New York.'

'Sounds like somebody's in a good mood.' Sara pulled the shocking pink pashmina from her shoulders and threw it onto the chair in the hall.

'Not for much longer,' Julia said sagely.

'I don't know about anyone else,' I said as I trudged towards the kitchen, 'but I need a drink.'

'Allow me.' Sara pushed past. 'I reckon I've just about perfected my Martini recipe. Have you got a cocktail shaker?'

'*Naturellement*,' I said. 'It's in the cabinet in the sitting room with the expensive stuff.'

'Gotcha.'

I watched her leave the room and whispered to Julia, 'Gosh. I can't believe how much Sara's grown up these last couple of years. She's one gorgeous girl.'

'Makes you feel old, doesn't it?'

'Speak for yourself,' I said. 'I wouldn't want to go back to my twenties for all the tea in China.'

'That's because you were married to a complete jerk.'

'Easily done.' Sara came back with the bomb-making equipment and filled the shaker with ice from the dispenser on the fridge. 'Let's face it, the chances of getting it right first time round are pretty bloody remote.' She threw a decisive glance over her shoulder at us. 'You might as well know I'm divorcing Dudley.'

'You're what?' My heart turned over.

'Well, you said it yourself.' She slipped a soupçon of vermouth over the ice, swilled it round and drained it off in the sink, then poured in an enormous slug of vodka and slapped the lid on. 'I never should have married him in the first place. It's been a complete waste of nearly three years of my life.'

'Sara! Three years? Is that all?' When will people learn that marriage is not like a disposable coffee cup. 'You can't! You haven't even given it a chance yet!'

'Yes I bloody well have.' She held the shaker over her shoulder and gave it a thorough rattling. 'The way I see it, I can hang around indefinitely, waiting to see if he changes, which, let's face it, is what a really stupid person would do.' I snatched a laboured breath and pretended not to have been that person. 'Or I can cut my losses now and abandon ship before all the lifeboats are gone.'

'Have you spoken to him about how you feel?' I persisted.

'Nope. Tried that six months ago and all he did was mope around and look all injured for a week. I'm done wasting my breath. It's curtains.' Sara gave the cocktail shaker a whack against the worktop, loosened the lid, and poured the drinks straight up. 'Olive or twist?'

'Twist,' Julia said automatically.

'But he'll be devastated!'

'Tough nuggies.' Sara sheared off a few slices of lemon zest. 'I don't see why I should hang around and squander my precious youth on him just because I accidentally backed the wrong horse. He'll get over it. And if he doesn't –' she put the shaker down – 'then that's not really my problem, is it?' She picked up her glass and had a taste. 'Mmm.' She nodded. 'Pretty good, even if I do say so myself.'

I have no idea why a Martini is classed as a cocktail. From where I'm sitting, it's just a bloody great glass of vodka with a fancy name. The first sip sent an evil, icy finger down my spine. 'Mmm,' I said politely. 'Lovely.' Yeeuch.

'When are you planning on doing the deed?' Julia accepted the other glass from her.

'Next Friday,' Sara said matter-of-factly. 'We're supposed to be going down to Hampshire to visit his godawful parents. There's no way I'm doing another Little House on the Prairie weekend. I'll give him the good news, then pack him off to bleed all over his mother. She always thought I was as common as muck anyway. Cheeky cow. Where there's muck, there's brass.'

'Have you seen a lawyer?' Julia said.

'Julia! You should be showing her to the nearest branch of Relate, not encouraging her to abandon her marriage! Talk some sense into her!'

'Why? Sara's one of the most sensible people I know.' Julia took an unflinching gulp from her drink. 'She made a mistake, that's all. She's young, but she'll learn.' Sara smiled a silent thank you. 'Just because you didn't have the guts to dump your first husband.' My mouth dropped open. 'Oh yes.' Julia went back to her Martini. 'We all know you could have saved yourself an awful lot of trouble if only you'd grown a spine. Why should you want Sara to cling to the wreckage and be miserable just like you did?'

'How dare you!'

'What? It's only the truth! You should have told him to stick it and packed a bag the minute he showed his true colours.'

'Marriage is not about bailing out at the first hurdle!' Suddenly I was shouting. 'That's half the problem with people these days! They see all these ridiculous celebrities getting married and divorced at the drop of a hat, and before you know it, it doesn't mean anything to anyone any more.'

'Now listen,' Sara said, trying to step in, but Julia wasn't having any of it.

'Bullshit. You're just bitter that you threw half your life away on a man who couldn't give a toss about you.' The truth of her proclamation knocked the wind from my sails before I could leap to my own defence, so I jumped to Dudley's instead.

'Dudley loves her!' I insisted. 'He's been mad about her since the day they met, and she's acting like—'

'Like what? Like she should be grateful?'

Sara twitched uncomfortably. 'Hey, guys—'

'Well, she should!' I snapped.

'What a load of old crap.' Julia, hard as nails, refused to be moved and raised her glass towards Sara. 'Do yourself a favour and get out of there as fast as you can. Trust me. Things can only get worse.'

'It's not crap,' I spat at Julia. 'It's how two people build a life together.'

'Like the one you had, you mean?' A wry smile began on Julia's face, boiling my blood.

'Hey!' Sara had raised her voice. 'Come on! There's no need to start a fight about it!'

'You complete bitch.' I could feel myself trembling. 'You have no right to speak to me like that. I tried for years to make my marriage work, no matter how bad things got.'

'More fool you,' Julia said.

'Fool, am I? And who's the fool in your marriage, Julia, eh?' Julia straightened in her chair, shooting me a glare of warning, but I was unable to hold my tongue. 'At least I stuck to my end of the bargain, which is more than I can bloody well say for you, and now look at the mess you've gone and got yourself into. Well, I hope you're proud of yourself for setting us all such a great example.'

'Oh-oh.' Sara pursed her lips. 'Sounds like it's time for me to call a cab.'

'Stick around, kid,' Julia purred. 'Things are just about to get interesting.' Julia locked eyes with me, smiling tighty. 'Go on,' she said, folding her arms across her chest. 'Say it to my face.'

'Forget it.' I backed down, regretting the heat of the moment.

'Please.' Julia insisted. 'Be my guest. You've already chosen to share my news with your darling, precious husband. Why not just take out an advertisement in the *Daily Telegraph* and be done with it? I can assure you, if you're trying to hurt my feelings you'll have a bloody hard job. I don't have any left.' My face reddened and I looked away, unable to hold Julia's burning gaze. 'What Helen is trying to say,' Julia explained to Sara, 'is that Frank Junior isn't my husband's baby.'

'When did you get the results through?' Sara stepped forward to top up Julia's glass.

'This morning, although Helen took it upon herself to open the letter yesterday while she was having a cosy little dinner with Rick.'

'Oh, really?' Sara raised an accusing eyebrow at me.

'Hang on a minute,' I said. 'Are you telling me that you already knew about this?'

'Course I did.' Sara looked at me as though I'd just crawled out of an apple. 'Julia told me the minute she knew she had a bun in the oven.' I stared at Julia, dumbfounded.

'And you let me believe that you'd kept this to yourself?'

'Sara's my business partner. She doesn't count.' Julia said. 'Besides, at least she knows how to keep her mouth shut, unlike some people around here.' With each baby-free minute that passed, Julia seemed to shed her skin, transforming herself into a newer, sleeker version of the tough-nut ball-breaker she had been before any of this happened.

'I'm so sorry I broke your confidence,' I snapped, trying to hold my own in the face of their frighteningly closed ranks. My vain attempt at sarcasm withered on my lips as I realized just how feeble I had been. Julia looked at me in that way of hers, as if to say that it didn't matter. I felt heartily ashamed of myself. As my school report said, must try harder.

'So what next?' Sara asked.

'Another one of these.' Julia held up her empty glass. I nodded and pushed mine towards Sara. 'Then I vote we sit down right now and hold an Extraordinary General Meeting.' Sara shook up another tin of vodka. I felt a small pull on my sleeve and patted Julia's hand, the formality of a spoken apology unnecessary.

'For what it's worth,' I said, contributing my two-penn'orth, 'I've told Julia that she should put the whole episode behind her and bring up Frankie as her husband's child.'

'Then you don't know your sister very well,' Sara said dryly. I tried not to take offence, feeling usurped by their long-standing no-nonsense association. That Julia has always adored Sara is no great secret. I can see the admiration in her eyes. The recognition of that certain something in Sara's youthful vitality that reminds Julia of herself when she was that age. I hadn't even come close as a young woman. There wasn't a single achievement I could pin on my lapel and say I was proud of. With the exception of my almond cake, perhaps. And my pastry. Great pastry.

'Helen thinks I should just sweep the whole thing under the carpet and pretend it never happened.'

'Yeah, right!' Sara laughed.

'What's wrong with that?' I said, the warmth of the cocktail loosening my skin. 'I read in *Marie Claire* years ago that ten per cent of supposedly legitimate children are not fathered by the unsuspecting husband. Women have been lying about it for years, and so long as everybody agrees a pact of silence, I don't see what difference one more would make.'

'You're assuming that I'd be able to live with that on my conscience for the rest of my life.'

'Still,' said Sara, adding her perspective, 'you've got to admit, at least it's a plan.'

'I suppose,' Julia said. 'So let's call that "Plan A", shall we? Next?'

'You inform the father,' I said, determined to demonstrate that they weren't the only two people in the room capable of a bit of lateral thinking. 'And then you deal with whatever the consequences are.'

'That'd be interesting.' Julia smiled.

'Well, I don't see what alternative there is. Although the logistics would be a bit difficult, what with him living in central Europe.'

'Eh?' Sara looked at me quizzically.

'The dreaded Count Stanislav von Westenholtz,' I replied. 'He's Transylvanian, although I suppose they're all classed as Romanians these days. Oh well. That'll teach him not to mess around with a married woman. And with Frankie being a boy, that's bound to put the cat amongst the pigeons.' Sara frowned at me. 'He's a minor royal.' I flexed my superior knowledge of my sister's former lover, glad that I at last had something over the indomitable Sara. 'Had two children with his wife, prior to their divorce, but they're both girls. You know how these things pass down the generations through the male line.' I caught a glimpse of an unexpected silver lining. 'In fact – ' I looked at Julia – 'your son may very well turn out to be titled! How about that?'

'Let's not get carried away,' she said.

'And you know how much he adored you,' I barged on. 'He'll probably declare his undying love to you and demand that you get married immediately!'

'I'm already married.'

'Well, if you insist on taking this line, then I expect you won't be for much longer.'

Julia's phone began to ring. She grabbed it from her bag and looked at the screen.

'Talk of the devil.' She answered it. 'Hi, darling. Yes. I'm with Helen.' She listened for a while. 'I know. Sorry I wasn't there to introduce you and get her settled. Helen ran into a spot of bother this afternoon. Oh?' she looked up at us. 'That was nice of her, but I wouldn't get too used to it. I'm sure she won't usually cook for you. Really? Oh. Uh-huh. Uh-huh. Yes, she is very sweet and lovely. I told her to take the bedroom at the end of the corridor. OK. Yes. Will do.' She hung up. 'Well, well,' she said. 'Nothing's caught fire and David's suggested I stay over here with you and come back in the morning.'

'Pink ticket?' Sara shouted. 'Bloody brilliant! Let's go out on the tiles!'

'Excuse me.' I knocked on the table. 'Aren't we supposed to be having a serious crisis meeting here?'

'Oh, come on!' Sara said. 'It's hardly the fucking G8 summit, is it?'

'That's not the point. Julia has an important decision to make here. It's either take a vow of silence, or go and tell the father.'

Sara slid a marked glance across the table to Julia.

'Well?' she said. 'Are you gonna tell her, or shall I?'

'Whatever.' Julia took a serious swig of her drink. 'If you think she can handle it.'

'Handle what?' I got the distinct feeling that I'd missed something significant.

'Well,' said Julia. 'When I said that I didn't know who the father was, that's exactly what I meant.'

'Hence the test,' I said. Another loaded look passed between them.

'Helen.' Sara placed a hand of sympathy on my shoulder. 'Allow me to introduce you to Julia, holder of the most explosive little black book in London, shameless serial adulterer, recovering sex addict.'

'You what?' I stared at her in disbelief. Julia raised half an eyebrow by way of explanation.

'You'd better believe it, honey,' Sara confirmed. 'Your sister has shagged her way twice around the world with tread to spare. She's got about as much chance of identifying that baby's father as Lemar has of becoming the next prime minister. Believe me, our

Julia here makes Russell Brand look like a latter-day saint trussed up in a cast-iron chastity belt smeared with extra rations of wholesomeness.' Sara settled into her seat and picked up her drink. 'So. There you have it. Bags open. Cats all over the place. And now you know what kind of woman I've been dealing with all these years.'

'Is this true?' I gawped at Julia. She winked at me.

'Hey, ladies!' Rick burst in. 'Sorry about that! Got stuck on the phone to my financial man in the States.' I pictured the anonymous man in America and wondered if Julia had shagged him too. 'These bloody exchange rates are playin' havoc with his nerves.' Rick helped himself to the dregs of my Martini glass. 'So what's new?'

It took him all of two seconds to register the shock on my face. 'What?' he said, looking from one face to the next, then back again.

'Oh, nothing,' I said, shaking myself out of it.

'Er . . .' Rick rumpled his hair. 'I don't want to talk out of turn here, but are we all singing off the same hymn sheet?'

'It's OK,' I told him. 'Sara knows.'

'I see.' Rick tapped the side of his nose. 'Mum's the word, eh?'

'I suppose you could say that,' Julia said. 'Although if it hadn't come out of my fanny I'd be hard pushed to give you any guarantees.'

'Wotcha, gorgeous.' Sara stood up and shook Rick's hand, cracking his knuckles as they kissed hello. 'We're all a bit pissed, although your wife's several drinks behind me and Julia.'

'Excellent!' He nodded approvingly and reached into his pocket for a half-smoked cigar. 'Sounds like I've got some catching up to do.'

'Here.' Sara peered into the shaker. 'Reckon I can squeeze one more out of this thing.'

'Thanks, treacle.' Rick pulled up a seat. 'Make it dirty, would ya?' Sara obliged and tipped a bit of the olive brine into his glass. 'How's that fella of yours? I was just saying to the missus that we haven't seen you both for ages. I expect it won't be long before we're hearing the pitter-patter of tiny feet from you an' all?'

'I wouldn't bank on it,' Julia mumbled into her drink.

'Why don't you bring him over for dinner one of these days?' He got stuck into his Martini, giving Sara a nod of approval as he sank the first mouthful. 'You girls can hide in the kitchen and say horrible things about us while we crack open a few beers and talk cars.'

'Ah,' I said. 'Which reminds me . . .'

Chapter Fifteen

NO SEX, PLEASE. WE'RE BRITISH

THERE'S NOTHING like a nice hot sausage in the morning. Besides, it's a proven scientific fact that the only way to survive a Martini hangover is to eat your way out of it. Rick drew the short straw and was dispatched to the patisserie round the corner under strict instructions to come back with at least one carrier bag stuffed to the gunnels with anything that looked like it might help to absorb the damage. Although I'm not a big fan of sending men on errands, because chances are they'll use their initiative and get it completely wrong,

I felt we were relatively safe with this one. Rick's good at choosing pastries. When he was hog-mewling fat a year or so ago, he'd scoff at least two custard Danishes before his morning coffee. Now he gives the doughnut department a wide berth and makes sure he eats an apple every day. My, how times have changed, although I'm not sure that I agree with him that tobacco counts as a vegetable.

'Feeling any better?' Julia had been in a far worse state than me last night on account of her head start, so I'd issued her with a couple of cowabunga horse pills the moment she crawled into the kitchen this morning searching for fluids.

'Not really,' she groaned. 'Bloody hell. I used to be able to drink like a codfish and shake the effects off before I'd even got out of the shower. I bet Sara's already in the office.' She glanced at the time.

'It's nature's way of telling you to ease up on the booze,' I told her. 'Unless you want to end up looking like that old woman out of *The Shining* before you hit your fiftieth birthday.'

'Yeah? Well, nature can piss off.' She lay her head down on the cool surface of the table and mumbled into her tumbling hair. 'Right now the booze is the only thing I have to look forward to. Are you really going to make me eat those things?'

'Yep. Have you called David this morning?'

'No. Why should I?'

'Don't be obtuse.' I worried the sausages in the pan. 'It might be nice if you were to check that everything's OK with Odene and the baby.'

'I'm sure they would have called me if there was a problem. Besides, I can't ring home with my voice sounding like this, can I?' True. She'd rounded off the session last night with a couple of Rick's Cohibas and had woken up this morning sounding like a baritone with a heavy dose of the flu.

'So, have you managed to come to any kind of decision?'

'Oh, just leave off, would you?'

I put the fish slice down and wiped my hands on my apron. 'Now look,' I said softly. 'I know Sara painted you like the whore of Babylon last night, but it really can't be that difficult, can it? I mean, we all know how long it takes to cook a baby, so you should be able to pinpoint roughly when it happened and, well . . .' I didn't want to be overly graphic about it. 'Exactly how many men did you sleep with that month?'

'A few.' She shrugged.

'And do you know who they are?'

'Of course I bloody do!' She lifted her head and tried to look indignant. 'What kind of slapper do you think I am?' I opened my mouth to speak. 'Don't answer that. You can keep your saintly opinions to yourself.'

'Was Stan one of them?'

'Yes.'

'How many others?'

'Three.'

'*Three?*' I did my best not to sound aghast. By my calculations, that meant she had slept with four men that month, plus her husband. That's a different one for each week, depending on how you look at it. Mind you, she always was a fast worker.

'OK, four,' she snapped irritably. 'And one of them . . .' She paused. 'One of them I met on a train, so I don't actually know him personally, if you're going to get all technical about it.'

'On a train? Please tell me you didn't do it in the—'

'First class carriage.'

'Oh, Julia!'

'What?' she huffed. 'There was nobody in there except us, and the ticket inspector had already been through.'

'I'm surprised you didn't rope him in too and make it a threesome.'

'I don't do group sex.' She picked up her tea sulkily. 'Any more. Too risky. You have to have eyes in the back of your head.'

'I don't believe what I'm hearing.' I went back to the sausages and set about whisking up some eggs.

'I'm not some kind of freak, you know! There are thousands of mature, consenting adults out there who aren't ashamed to admit that they enjoy free, uncomplicated sexual encounters with other like-minded consenting adults. I don't go around advertising it, but you can tell, the moment you meet someone, whether or not they're up for it. And where's the harm in it? It's discreet and private. In other words, it's nobody's business except mine.'

'I'm not judging you,' I said judgementally. 'But some of us manage to enjoy sex perfectly well without straying from our husbands and partners.'

'Well, lucky old you.' She dropped a sugar cube in her mug. 'But you've only been married for three nano-seconds, so you're hardly in a position to compare your circumstances with mine, and I suggest we don't get into another conversation about your previous—'

'Don't go there,' I warned, pointing the fish slice at her.

'Exactly.' Neither of us wanted a repeat performance of yesterday's altercation. 'My sex life with David hit the death zone after a year or so. Everyone seems to think that it's normal to end up doing that once-or-twice-a-month duty shag, but I thought to myself, what a bloody waste. I used to love sex, and then I was supposed to make do with this lukewarm excuse for passion? I don't think so.' I wondered if that would happen to Rick and me. What a horrible thought. I pushed it to the back of my mind and made a mental note. 'Don't get me wrong. I didn't actively go out there looking for it. Then one day I had an opportunity.' She smiled to herself. 'He was gorgeous. Married, too. So I thought to myself, why the hell not? It wasn't as though he was going to get all heavy about it afterwards. He had just as much to lose as I did.'

'Who was he?'

'Just some guy I met at a business lunch.'

'So you went ahead and had sex with him, just like that?'

'Yep,' she said. 'And it was fantastic.'

'Julia!'

'Don't look at me like that! You bloody well asked. It's perfectly normal for two healthy, attractive people to have urges like that. The thing that isn't normal is forcing yourself to suppress your feelings. Anyway, if you ask me, extramarital sex has held more marriages together than anyone would care to admit. People don't like to talk about it, but we're all different, and anything that keeps the scales balanced at home has got to be a good thing, hasn't it?'

I busied myself with the toaster, the conversation now heading way outside my comfort zone.

'One thing I know,' I said. 'I could never pick up a stranger on a train and have sex with him just like that.' I snapped my fingers. 'It's grotesque.'

'What if he looked like Robert Downey Junior, only taller?'

'Don't be ridiculous.'

'OK.' She regrouped her thoughts. 'What if it were Sally?'

'Sally?'

'Yep. On a train. The sexiest man in the world. Just you and him, on a hot summer's day.' She took a sip of tea, moistening her lips. 'You can't tear your eyes off him. He can't take his eyes off you. It's hot in that carriage. Steamy. You can feel your dress clinging to your skin.'

'Stop it!'

'Huh.' She raised an eyebrow. 'You bloody well would.'

No, Julia. Not bloody well would. I bloody well did. Twice. In one afternoon a couple of years ago. Not that anyone will ever find out. After the damage it did to our friendship, I swore to Paul that it was my fault entirely and that I would take the sordid little tale of Sally's peccadillo to the grave with me. It's one of those pages in history that has been neatly plastered over although, boy, I do like to dust those pictures off and indulge myself in a furtive little trip down memory lane every now and then. That man is two hundred pounds of mind-blowing sexual Semtex. If I try really hard, I can still conjure up a little sliver of the way he'd shivered me timbers. I felt a couple of beads of perspiration forming on my brow and wiped them aside with the tea towel, passing them off as nothing more than the usual occupational hazard of sizzling a few sausages.

'It's the only thing that's kept me sane over the years,' Julia said. 'Why do you think I worked so hard to keep myself in tip-top condition?' So that's what it was all about. And here was me thinking that her knock-out looks had been a natural blessing. 'You never know when you're going to have the next close encounter of the naughty kind. It's the perfect incentive.'

'David would die if he found out.'

'But he's not going to, is he?' She reminded me of my solemn promise. 'If anything, he should be grateful that I've found a way to keep myself happy and satisfied all these years, otherwise I would have ditched him long ago.'

'What about . . .' I wrinkled my nose . . . 'you know, diseases? Didn't you ever worry that you were going to contract AIDS or come home with a nasty dose of something vile?'

'I haven't been sleeping with any old Tom, Dick or Harry, you know.'

'Yes you have! What about the man on the train?'

'High court judge.'

'No!'

'Oh yes. If my memory serves me correctly, he was wearing a pair of his wife's knickers. You'd be surprised.'

'If that's at all possible.' I took the sausages off the heat and transferred them to a warmed dish. 'Although I'm amazed you had time to find out what he did for a living.'

'It was the wig.'

'No!'

'Not on his head, you twit. It was in its box. Everybody's at it. Sure, there are risks attached, but I've never let anyone in unless they're wearing a jacket.'

'A jacket? Dare I ask?'

'Condom,' she explained. 'And I had myself checked out regularly just to make sure I hadn't picked anything up.'

'Like a fertilized egg.'

'Could have happened to anyone.'

'But it didn't happen to anyone! It happened to you!'

'Like I don't know.'

'And now you're going to have to find out which of those four men is the father.'

'Two.'

'I thought you said you'd slept with four?'

'I did,' she said. 'I think. But one of them had had a vasectomy, so it can't be him.'

'How do you know he was telling the truth?'

'Because I know his wife.'

'Marvellous,' I said. 'And what about the other one?'

'Definitely not. There's no way on earth I could have got pregnant that time.'

'Oh, don't tell me. You just sat there and held hands for the evening.'

'No. We had sex all right.'

'Then how can you be so sure?'

'Because it was a woman.'

'You *what*?!' The tomato in my hand burst its skin, squirting juice all down my front. Julia started laughing.

'Don't look so shocked,' she said soothingly. 'One has to ring the changes every so often. Besides, given the right circumstances, an experienced lezzer will move heaven and earth to turn a hardened straightie into a sister.'

'That's it!' I held my hands over my ears. 'La-la-la-la-la, I'm not listening!'

The front door went bang. Rick barged in and slung the pink carrier bag down on the table.

'Houston? We have pastries,' he announced. 'Did I miss anything interesting?'

'Oh, nothing much. Julia's thinking of batting for the other side,' I said sarcastically, shoving the sausages in the oven to keep warm while I put the eggs on to scramble.

'Good 'un!' Rick laughed. 'I'm glad to see you two haven't lost your sense of humour!'

'Unlike you last night,' Julia said, suppressing a smirk. 'I thought you were going to bust a blood vessel.'

'Er, yeah, well. What can I say? I'm sorry about that. It was a bit of a shock, that's all. You know what us blokes are like about our cars.' He scratched his armpit. 'I thought you were bloody havin' me on.'

'That's all right,' I said tetchily. 'Although for future reference, I do not take kindly to being called an effing muppet by you or anyone else, for that matter.' Julia covered her mouth in a poor attempt to stifle her amusement.

'Aw, babe!' Rick dropped his smouldering cigar in the ashtray and insisted on giving me a hug. 'I didn't mean it!'

'It's not my fault Leoni's boys have no respect for other people's property, or indeed that Mario decided to shove half a pint of pistachio ice cream down Frankie's gullet when the kid's not even weaned yet.'

'I said I'm sorry.' I could tell he was trying not to laugh, his chest suddenly tight, betraying him with a slight judder. He pressed me against his shoulder so that I couldn't see him pulling faces at Julia. 'But had I known you were going to cart a bunch of kids around, I would have hired you a Skoda for the day. Now you know why Leoni drives around in a dustbin.'

ALL THAT TALK about sex seemed to have had a startlingly unhousewifely effect on me. After seeing Julia off in a taxi, I returned to the kitchen to clear up the breakfast things, only to find my mind wandering insistently to the pleasures of the flesh. I suppose you could say that I had been a late starter. Of course, I did the sex thing when it was required of me, but it wasn't until I was well into my thirties and free to browse the sweetie counter at my leisure that I discovered what all the fuss was about. Rick had proved himself to be something of a master of the art. He knows exactly where everything is, and he's not afraid to use it. I smiled to myself as I loaded the dishwasher while he finished his cigar, and wished that I'd worn something a little more come-hither. There's nothing sexy about cooking breakfast in a pair of unimaginatively cropped trousers and a green cotton shirt. Giving the oven door a cursory wipe, I checked my reflection in the glass and wondered if I shouldn't make just a little bit more effort. My long-held assumption that women who put themselves through hoops of fire to look great only do it to please men had been unceremoniously debunked. Julia had gone to all that trouble primarily for herself, so that she could stand in front of the mirror every morning and know that she was just plain fabulous.

'Do you have any plans for the day?'

'Yeah.' Rick rustled his newspaper and peered over the top. 'I was gonna try an' isolate the God particle later. Why? What did you have in mind?'

'How about going shopping?'

'What for?' Rick hates shopping. He doesn't under-stand it.

'Who knows?' I said mysteriously. 'Perhaps something a little more attractive for your wife to waft around the house in?'

'Oh yeah?' he put his paper down.

'I wouldn't want you to think I've gone all dowdy on you just because we're married. Perhaps you can help

me pick out something a little more exciting than this?'
I flapped the loose tail of my shirt at him invitingly.

'Come here, you,' he said, patting his lap.

'No.' I flicked my hair aside coquettishly. 'Make me.'

It's a good job we live in the middle of London where
no one gives a flying monkey about the welfare of their
neighbours. In my parents' village, the police would
have been called within thirty seconds of the screaming
dodgeball chase that broke out in our kitchen. Anyone
would have thought that somebody was being mur-
dered. I gripped the edge of the island unit, Rick on the
other side, horns locked as we tried to anticipate which
way the other would go, the pair of us panting hard
from the trivial pursuit that had already had us do six
squealing laps of the kitchen table.

'Your move.' His eyes never left mine. I reached for
the fruit bowl and hurled an apple at his head. 'Right!'
he shouted. 'You asked for it!' I let out another blood-
curdling wail and made a break for the door, only to
catch a glimpse of Helga waiting behind it, pressed flat
against the wall, gripping a chair in her hands.

There was nothing I could do to stop her.

Rick came flying out a split second behind me, the
chair splintering as Helga smashed it over his head. He
went down like a sack of spuds. For a moment, nothing
moved.

'Helga!' I screamed. 'Oh my GOD!'

'Mmmmmph!' After a second that seemed like an

aeon, Rick began to writhe around on the floor, trying to bring himself to his knees before collapsing again. I threw myself to the carpet beside him.

'Rick!'

'*Mudak!*' Helga shook her fist at him. 'You fight Hell-yen? You fight Hell-ga!'

'Shit.' Rick rolled onto his back and attempted to bring his hands to his head, eyes tight shut against the pain.

'*Svoloch!*' Helga kicked him in the ribs.

'Aaaaarrrrgh!'

'Helga!' I grabbed a handful of her thick woollen tights. 'Stop it! We weren't fighting!'

'Jesus Christ,' Rick groaned. 'What the fuck?'

'No fight?' Helga seemed disappointed.

'No!' I tried to lift Rick's head to my lap, but the immediate wave of pain was too much for him to bear. 'For God's sake, Helga! We were just playing!'

'Play?' She scowled at me. 'What play?'

'Go and fetch a towel! Quickly!' Helga muttered under her breath and scuttled off to the downstairs loo. A small trickle of blood made its way through Rick's hair, right on the crown of his head. 'Oh, Rick!' I had a look and tried to assess the extent of the damage. 'You're bleeding!'

'Is that a *chair*?' he slurred, squinting at the shattered remnants scattered around the hall.

'What can I say?' A small hand towel flew into my lap. I picked it up and dabbed gently at the blood.

'Ow!' Rick flinched.

'Sorry. Do you think you can sit up?' I helped him as best I could, given the general disparity of our relative sizes.

'Oh God.' He tried to drop his head to his knees, sinking to the carpet again. 'Babe. I think I'm gonna throw up.'

'Helga!' I shouted. 'Quick! Bring a bucket!' Rick began moaning gently. 'And a phone!' This was serious. 'I think we need to call an ambulance!'

How bad is it?' I jumped to my feet.

'Please.' The doctor said. 'Have a seat.' He perched himself next to me. 'Your husband's suffered quite a nasty trauma to the head. He said something about having been hit with a chair?' I got the distinct impression that the words 'domestic' and 'violence' had probably been bandied around behind closed doors in the last hour or so while I was left to stew in my own juices. It's no wonder nobody had been in to offer me a cup of tea.

'Yes.' What else could I say? 'Although it wasn't me, I hasten to add.'

'There's also the small matter of a couple of bruised ribs.'

'Oh.' I bit my finger and stared at the floor. 'Yes. That would make sense.'

'Do you want to tell me what happened?'

'Our cleaning lady.' If I went for the longer version, we'd be here all day. I mumbled apologetically. 'She's Russian.'

'I see,' he said. 'And have you called the police?'

'Police? No! It wasn't like that! She got the wrong end of the stick, that's all!'

'I see.' He made a note. 'We have a duty to report incidents of violent assault.'

'I appreciate that, but it isn't what you think. Honestly.'

'Then you won't mind if I tell you "that's what they all say"?'

'Ask him yourself,' I suggested defensively.

'I would, except I don't think he's in any fit state to answer questions right now. He had a job to remember his own name and not much idea about how many fingers I was holding up either.'

'Is he going to be all right?'

'Mmm,' the doctor said. 'I think so. He's quite badly concussed at the moment. We've stuck that gash back together. Let's just hope that the old grey matter didn't suffer too much. Swelling can occur when the brain moves inside the skull due to a sudden impact. Most times it has no lasting effects, but we'd like to keep an eye on him for a while all the same. Tell me, did he pass out at all?'

'I'm not sure. I think he may have blacked out for a moment when he hit the floor. And when I tried to get him to sit up he felt dizzy and said that he couldn't see anything.'

'Was he sick?'

'Yes.'

'OK,' he said, flashing a reassuring glimpse of his best bedside manner. 'We'll run a scan just to double-check there's no major damage, but apart from that, I think you can feel confident that he'll make a full recovery. You weren't planning on going on holiday, were you?'

'No. Why?'

'Good. This might take a few weeks, and I wouldn't want him wandering too far from the hospital. Head injuries can be complicated. Time and patience. That's what they need. Do you have any questions?'

My mind went blank.

'No. Thank you, doctor. Can I see him?'

'Of course, but only for a minute.' He stood up. 'But I have to warn you, be gentle with him. He's going to have one hell of a headache.'

Chapter Sixteen

BLOW-UP

'DAVID!' I opened the door wide and invited him in, my heart leaping into my mouth. What the hell was he doing here? 'What a lovely surprise!' Kiss, kiss.

'I was just passing.' He flicked his thumb at the street. 'Thought I'd drop by and look in on the patient,' he said, wiping the rain from his feet on the welcome mat. My face must have given me away. 'I'm not interrupting anything, am I?'

'No!' I trilled. 'Of course not! Come on in!'

'Thanks.' I closed the door behind him. 'Oh, and another thing.'

'What's that?'

'Odene,' he said. 'She's a bloody godsend.'

'Oh!' Phew. Everybody stand down. Panic over. 'Tell you what, David. Nothing could have given me more pleasure. She was obviously destined for you and I'm delighted it's all working out so well.'

'Julia's a changed person. Dare I say it, I've even seen a few glimmers of the woman I once knew.' Hurrumph. 'Sara's been popping in regularly and they've been shutting themselves away in the study for hours. I wouldn't be surprised if she's not thinking about going back to work soon.'

'There, you see? I told you she'd back to her old self in no time, didn't I?'

'You did,' he admitted sheepishly. 'Although I'd forgotten how independent she likes to be. I quite liked the new needy version. Now I suppose we'll go back to the good old days when she spent most of her waking hours chained to her business.' A fleeting vision of Julia shackled to a hotel bed during her lunch break with pink maribou-trimmed handcuffs hurtled through my mind.

'I'm sure things will be different now,' I said, halting my mouth before it could protest too much.

'Where's the invalid?

'Upstairs in the bedroom,' I flicked my eyes to the ceiling.

'And how is he?'

'On the mend, I think, although he remains a bit dazed around the edges, I'm afraid. He's still having trouble remembering things and he's mixing some of his words up. They wanted to keep him in for a few more days, but he'd had enough of that madhouse by Monday night. I can't say that I blame him. Some of those nurses must have been trained by the Gestapo.'

'So I heard.' He shook the rain from his jacket and gave it to me. 'He rang me from the hospital in one of his lucid moments. Said he'd started an escape committee and asked if could I sneak him in a shovel.'

'He's much better off here,' I said. 'His GP has been popping by every day and sending the district nurse over to help keep an eye on his faculties. Come up and see him.' I hung David's jacket on the stand and led the way. 'And try not to take any notice if he says anything weird. Just ignore it. He gets really frustrated if you point out his mistakes and I don't want him getting all worked up over nothing.'

'Sure.'

Rick lay on the bed, propped up on a mountain on pillows, frowning at the television set. 'Who's that?' he pointed at the screen.

'That's Bruce Forsythe.'

'Are you sure?'

'Yes.' I took a long, deliberate look as if to reassure him that I was giving his enquiry my full attention. 'Definitely Bruce Forsythe. That chin's a dead give-away.'

'I knew I recognized him,' Rick said. 'But why's he

wearing a fork round his neck?' I peered at the black bow tie around Brucie's whiter-than-white collar. Rick's brain had obviously not yet made sufficient progress to tell the difference between a tuxedo and a piece of cutlery.

'Who knows?' I said, turning a blind eye to his bizarre error. 'That's prime-time entertainment for you. Guess who's got a visitor?'

'Hi, Rick.' David drew the chair up next to the bed. 'How you doing?'

'Wotcha!' I could tell from Rick's panicked expression that he couldn't quite grasp the name. Don't worry. It was pretty typical of the stuff I'd been warned to expect for a couple of weeks or so. I had a list of the really nail-biting things to look out for, such as seizures, numbness in the limbs, taking a strange liking to day-time American soap operas. Under the guise of re-arranging his pillows, I leaned down to his ear.

'It's David,' I whispered. 'Julia's husband. Your brother-in-law.'

'Of course it's David!' Rick gushed with relief. 'Just because I've had a wallop on the head doesn't mean my brain's fucking fallen out.' I gave David a sly smile.

'Can I bring you anything?'

'Beer,' Rick said. 'Wanna beer?' He pointed at David.

'That'd be good.'

'Back in two shakes,' I said.

Down in the kitchen, I poured Rick a glass of alcohol-free lager. He wasn't allowed any hooch until his brain had regained its bearings, and after kicking up a mighty fuss about it during one of his fits of frustration, I'd resorted to subterfuge and found that in his state he couldn't tell the difference between this and the real thing anyway. Loading up the tray with the drinks and a few snacks, I teetered back up the stairs and pushed the door open with my foot. Rick sat in bed fiddling uncomfortably with the remote control. David sat in grim silence, starting out of the window, ashen-faced. Five minutes. That's all I was gone for. Just five lousy minutes.

'I have to go.' David stood up vacantly. 'Excuse me.'

'David? Whatever's the matter?'

'I'm sorry.' He brushed past blindly, upsetting one of the drinks. The beer flooded the tray, soaking my shirt, cascading to the carpet. 'I can't stay.'

Before I could stop him, his footsteps flew down the stairs and out of the front door. Rick's face twisted with confusion.

'Rick?' I approached him as gently as I could, given that my blood pressure had just gone through the roof. Sliding onto the bed beside him, I took the remote from his hand, my spleen turning somersaults. 'Rick? Can you remember what you said to David?'

'Fuck,' he said. 'I dunno, Hell. Sometimes I open my mouth and I think I'm saying one thing but it just doesn't happen. I can hear sounds – ' his eyes buckled in distress – 'words, but they don't make any sense, and I can tell by the look on people's faces that some other shit came out.'

'Shhh.' I flicked the red button and switched the television off. Take deep breaths, I said to myself. Focus and remember what the doctor said. Don't let him get upset. 'Don't worry about it, darling.' My palms began to sweat. 'It's perfectly normal. The doctor said it might be a little while before you're a hundred per cent.'

'What the fuck did I say to David?' He pressed his hand to his bandage in frustration. I had no idea whether or not he had yet mustered any recollection of the *Whose Baby Are You?* situation, but there was no way I was going to remind him of the big picture he'd been privy to before he'd sustained that blow to the head.

'It's OK.' I kissed his hand. 'Whatever it was, I'm sure it couldn't have been that important.' I tried to dredge up a reassuring smile from the depths of my panic. 'Maybe he suddenly remembered that he was late for an appointment or something. You know how disorganized he can be.'

'Yeah.' Rick began to settle. 'It's probably just me being a bit paranoid. I'm not used to being laid up like this. My mind's starting to play tricks on me. For a minute, I thought I—' He squeezed my hand and seemed suddenly fatigued. 'Nah,' he said. 'I'm probably just hallucinating again.'

'Tired?'

'A bit.' He lay back on the pillows.

'Why don't you take a nice little nap?' I arranged the covers around him, forcing myself to tear my mind's eye from the awful image of David's stricken face. 'Doctor's orders. Plenty of rest. Not too much excitement. Now close your eyes and think of something nice.'

'You in a fur bikini,' he said sleepily. 'Me Tarzan.'

By the time I'd freshened up from the beer spillage and changed my shirt, Rick was fast asleep. I crept out, leaving the door ajar, took myself off down to the sitting room and poured myself a stiff brandy. The telephone stared at me from the table. I stared back at it. *What are you going to do?* it asked. I had absolutely no idea. A few sips. Another ten minutes thinking about it. The telephone waited, arms folded, tapping its foot impatiently. More sips. An empty glass. I put it down, picked up the handset, and stared at the numbers. I should call Julia. *And tell her what, exactly?* Rick said something to David. David was so upset that he fled the house. No, I had no idea what had passed between them, and, what's more, nor did Rick. I put the handset back on the cradle. This whole thing was bound to blow up sooner or later. It seemed that we had been well and truly cornered, like that closing scene in *Butch Cassidy and the Sundance Kid*. They were on to us.

*

256

'I'm sorry,' Sara said. Even though separated by a telephone line, I could feel the unease in her voice. 'She's not taking any calls right now. Not even from you.'

'But it's been three weeks!' I pleaded. 'I'm worrying myself into an early grave here, Sara! She's not replied to any of my messages. I've taken flowers round to the house but Odene wouldn't let me in. How long is she going to keep this up for?'

'Helen.' Sara's exasperation rang out loud and clear. 'Just leave her alone for a while, OK? The shit's really hit the fan around here and she's dealing with it in the only ways she knows how.'

'Is she really bad?'

'Bad in the way you mean? No. Bad as in badass motherfucker? Yup. She fired two people on her first day back, sacked three clients who were late paying their bills and now she's right in the middle of pre-paring for a big pitch on Thursday. Trust me. It's really not a good time. I'd give her a wide berth until she's ready to talk to you.'

'And what about David? He's not answering my calls either.'

'What about him?' I heard her bite into an apple.

'He was pretty upset when I last saw him and I've not heard a whisper from him since.'

'Yeah? Well I can tell you that he was pretty upset when he came home and packed his bags, too.'

'He's *left* her?'

'What did you chuffing expect?' Munch, munch. 'A second honeymoon in Como with a matching spread in *Hello!* magazine?' I fell silent, the distance between us stretching into a cringingly uncomfortable pause. 'Listen,' Sara said. 'I'd really love to stay and chat, but, like I said, I'm up to my eyeballs, so it'll have to wait. Julia's fine. She always knew this could all go tits-up any minute.' Her voice lowered. 'In a way, I think there's a part of her that's relieved it's all over. It was the lying that was really doing her in. If you ask me, she looks like she's had the weight of the world lifted from her shoulders.'

'I know that feeling,' I said softly.

'Don't worry about her, OK? She's a tough biscuit. She can look after herself.'

'Give her my love, won't you?'

'Sure,' she said. 'But you'll understand if I bide my time and wait until she's unarmed before I do it, OK?'

'OK.' I pulled a tissue from my pocket and tried to keep my voice straight.

'And Helen.'

'What?'

'Stop ringing her. There's nothing you can do. Best stay out of it and wait for her to come to you.'

'I'll do that.'

I hung up and allowed myself a good old blub. Everything had unravelled in the blink of an eye, and it was all my fault, just because I couldn't keep my big mouth shut about this one tiny, little thing.

'Hell-yen?' Helga crept towards me, staring in amazement at these strange droplets of water falling out of my eyes. I don't think anyone cries where Helga comes from, unless they're trudging uphill against a biting Siberian wind, carrying logs.

'Hi.' I attempted a weak smile.

'You no, er, *happee*?'

'Oh, I don't know, Helga.' I blew my nose into the soggy tissue and helped myself to another. 'It's my sister.'

'Ah.' Helga nodded and took a seat next to me on the sofa. 'She bin blooding beech?'

'No.' I mopped my face and tried to compose myself. 'She's not speaking to me.'

'Hmph,' Helga said. 'Me sister –' she pointed to herself – 'she blooding beech too. She kill my dog. She fid it somesing. She want it for meat.' She tutted to herself. 'I no like sister. Sister big trouble, eh?'

'Yes, Helga. My sister's in real big trouble.'

'Ta-raaaaaa!' Rick materialized in the doorway, carrying a tray of coffees. His head was pretty much back to normal from a shape and colour point of view, and apart from a couple of Swiss-cheese holes in his short-term memory round about the time of Black Chair Day, his brain had managed to stick itself back together quite nicely these last couple of weeks. Helga jumped up, not wanting to be caught napping on the job.

'I work now,' she said quickly, pulling a duster from her pocket and rubbing it vigorously around the table.

Poor Helga. She still felt terrible about having tried to stove Rick's head in. Once I'd got back from the hospital, it had taken me the best part of two hours (mostly spent with my head stuck in an English–Russian dictionary) to explain to her the nuances of the misunderstanding. As far as she was concerned, she'd walked in to find us in the middle of a full-scale domestic dingdong. Her automatic reaction had been to disable the man, at all costs. Everything else was expendable. Including her job. It was very touching, really. She'd seen a lot of that sort of thing in her time before leaving the motherland. There were only two types of women out there: the ones who took it, and the ones who fought back. No prizes for guessing which camp her family's womenfolk fell into. When the penny finally dropped that Rick and I had been fooling around, as the Americans like to call it, she had cursed herself in a violent display of self-reproach before going off in search of an identical chair and insisting that I should smash it over her head by way of recompense. It was only right, she explained. After all, that was the way they did things in her village. She took some dissuading, and finally accepted that a 'get well soon' card with a couple of words of apology scrawled in pencil would do just fine.

'Sit!' Rick said cheerfully, offering Helga the tray. 'I know the daily routine. It's coffee-break time.'

'*Spasiba.*' She thanked him, taking a mug and sitting down with us, slightly uncomfortable in Rick's presence. In her book, men and women did not sit down and have coffee together, unless they were negotiating a price for sex.

'You know, it's been great hanging out here at home with you girls for the last couple of weeks.' Rick leaned back on the sofa and crossed his legs, unaware that his dressing gown had parted company with itself around the nethers department. Helga's eyes flicked towards mine mischievously. I delivered her a brief smile, the pair of us colluding to say nothing to spoil the comedy of a spontaneous goolie cabaret. 'I had no idea this place was such a hive of activity during the day!'

'A house doesn't run itself, you know.'

Helga muttered *zhopa* under her breath which, I think, means arsehole, or something along those lines. We like to teach each other the odd useful native phrase every now and then.

'I can bloody see that!' He slurped the froth off his cappuccino. 'But I don't think I've ever spent more than a couple of days here in a row, if you know what I mean. People go off on holidays and stuff, when the best thing you can do sometimes is just chill out and enjoy your own gaff!' It was like a revelation to him. He looked around these four walls and seemed quite taken aback.

'Home is what you make it,' I reminded him, biting my lip as his sweetbreads squished around in the fresh air. Helga snuffled into her mug.

'What do you think of the coffee, Helg? Go on! Marks out of ten?'

Since he's been up and about, Rick's kept himself busy with a few regular simple tasks that aren't too taxing on the old grey matter. We promoted him to coffee monitor a few days ago, and like the trooper that he is, he'd confined himself to the kitchen for two whole hours until he'd perfected his frothing technique. Helga and I are now quite spoiled for choice. Latte. Espresso macchiato. Americano. You name it, Rick can rustle it up. And very pleased he is with himself too.

'Coffee?' I asked Helga, tapping my mug. 'Good?'

'Mmm.' She tipped her hand in a so-so gesture. 'Is OK.' She creased her nose. 'But is no, erm . . . *kak eto skazat po angliyski*?'

'She doesn't know the word for it in English,' I explained to Rick. He watched us closely, apparently fascinated by the odd mode of communication that had developed quite comfortably between his two domestics.

'Is no wodka,' Helga said. 'No *wodka*!' she repeated

louder to Rick, pointing at the clock on the mantel-piece.

'Eh?' Rick said. 'You mean to say you drink vodka at eleven o'clock in the morning?'

'Of course not!' I pinched Helga's hand discreetly. 'She must have misunderstood what you meant. Vodka at eleven in the morning?' I chortled with a lift of my eyes. 'What kind of women do you think we are?'

'*Da!*' Helga joined in, mumbling and rolling her eyes to the ceiling. 'Wodka, pah!' Mumble, mumble. '*Zhopha*.'

RICK WAS QUITE right about the home thing. The first few days had been different of course, what with him being on the loony list, but once he was out of the woods and under strict instructions to take it easy, life at home had adapted into an easy, softly-paced routine, with nothing in particular to do except keep the place running and fish the cigar butts out of the waste dis-posal unit twice a week. I imagined that retirement would be a bit like this, the highlight of each day being whether or not there was anything interesting in the post, like a Braille leaflet declaring a special offer on stairlifts for taking laundry baskets upstairs. Astonish-ingly, Rick hadn't uttered a word of protest at having his BlackBerry confiscated, nor had he been anywhere near the study. It was almost as though he was quite content to have been written off for a little while and forced to turn his attentions to the mundane humdrum of those little daily tasks necessary to keep body and soul together. The trolley ground to a halt, yet again.

'Bloody hell!' He picked up a bar of Wright's Coal Tar Soap and held it under his nose. 'Remember this stuff? My old gran used to keep a bar of it in the outside bog at the end of their yard!' He slung it in the trolley. 'Gotta have one a those. Blimey!' He grabbed a pack of Euthymol toothpaste. 'I fucking love this stuff! Tastes like that old cough mix, doesn't it?' A couple of packs of that went in too.

'Rick.'

'Yeah, babe?'

'We've been in here over an hour.'

'I know! It's bloody brilliant, innit? How come I never knew about this place before?'

'What, *Waitrose*?'

'Yeah!' He shuffled the trolley along and started looking at the shaving stuff. 'They've got bloody everything!'

'It's a supermarket, Rick. The concept has been around for quite some time.'

'I'm knocked out!' he beamed, unscrewing a jar of hair gel and giving it a sniff. 'Tell you what, from now on, let's always do the shopping together, eh?'

'Great,' I sighed, wondering how long it would be before he got bored and went back to work. Being married is one thing, but being forced to spend twenty-four hours a day with your husband is an outright breach of the Geneva Convention. Besides, I like doing Waitrose on my own. It's like my personal form of meditation, wandering aimlessly around the wide aisles with an empty trolley, my brain set firmly in neutral while I have a good old feel of the avocados and sneak in a key lime pie while the calorie police aren't looking. By the time we crawled to the checkout, our trolley was groaning under the weight of Rick's impulse purchases.

'Man after my own heart,' smiled the checkout lady as she passed a big bottle of gin over the scanner. 'Oooh! I just love those!' A three-pack of Turkish Delights. Rick grabbed a couple of carrier bags and started indiscriminately stuffing everything in, squashing bread beneath tins, crushing the biscuits under the spuds. I took a deep breath and stopped myself from cuffing him around the head. 'Aren't you lucky?' the lady said to me. 'My husband doesn't even know what a supermarket is!'

'Oh, really?' I sighed sarcastically.

'Thinks our fridge works by magic,' she tutted. 'You know, open sesame and there it all is.'

'Huh.' Rick shook his head. 'That's the trouble with men these days, isn't it?'

'I know!' she agreed, enthusiastically flapping a couple of extra carriers open for him. 'He thinks that just because he goes out to work during the day, he doesn't have to do anything else when he gets home except lie around on the sofa watching the football and reading *Nuts* while I make his dinner!'

'Cheeky bastard,' Rick clucked. 'You should put your feet up, love, and tell him to get in that kitchen and rattle those pots and pans.'

'I should be so lucky! It doesn't even occur to him that I have to work as well!' she simpered at Rick. 'Then I have to come home and do everything else to boot! Oh well. You've got to love them really, eh?'

'Typical.' Rick crushed the fresh cream Victoria sponge under a big bag of carrots. 'It's blokes like that who give us men a bad name. I'll bet he doesn't deserve you, does he? Gorgeous looking lady like you?' She positively preened. 'You can tell him from me, if he's not prepared to look after his wife the way she deserves, then there's plenty of other blokes out there who would.'

I couldn't help but feel that Rick was playing a dangerous game here. For a start, she wasn't a gorgeous-looking lady at all. She weighed more than Rick and me put together, had hit middle age quite some time ago, and appeared to be in dire need of a couple of trips to the dentist. Her hair looked, well, fried. She stopped the belt for a moment and helped us catch up with the packing, tipping me a confidential nod.

'I suppose he's a great cook as well,' she said knowingly. 'My fella's a right useless fart. Couldn't boil an egg if his life depended on it! I'm lucky if he makes me a cup of tea on my birthday!'

'What?' Rick commiserated with her. 'That's terrible, love. Do ya want me to come over and have a quiet word in his shell, like?'

'Don't worry.' She hushed her voice. 'When he's really getting on my nerves, I get my own back by putting laxatives in his tea.'

'What a coincidence,' I smiled sweetly. 'So do I.'

STILL ENJOYING the afterglow of his first supermarket sortie, Rick seemed oblivious to my self-induced coma-tose state as I spent yet another hour of my life decant-ing tins and packets out of carrier bags and putting them into the kitchen cupboards. If I were to tot up all the time I have dedicated to dealing with food in all its variable states, I expect it would amount to the same as a prison sentence for aggravated burglary. The phone rang. Rick picked it up.

'Herro? Chinese raundry!' Oh well. At least it made a change from who's-calling-the-golden-shot. 'Jools! Hello, twinkle! You after the missus?' I dropped the multipack of Jaffa Cakes and raced towards the tele-phone, tearing it from Rick's hand. Between you and me, I had yet to fill Rick in on the nuclear fallout situation that had developed since Black Chair Day. He seemed to have clean forgotten about the episode with

David in the bedroom, and I was in no great rush to tell him that his big mouth had dealt a fatal blow to Julia's teetering marriage. There was no denying that she'd stuck the bullets in the gun herself, but let's face it, he was the one who'd pulled the trigger. His dabs were all over the weapon.

'Julia!' Thank God. She was alive. 'I've been worried sick!' Rick hung around nearby, pulling faces at me, looking all interested. 'Saturday? Yes, of course.' Before I could ask her when, or where, she brought the call to a curt close and hung up.

'Whassup?' Rick hovered around.

'Nothing.'

'Don't gimme that.' He grasped my shoulders and insisted on doing that thing where he looks deep into my eyes and pretends that he can read my mind.

'OK.' I took a deep breath. 'It's Julia.'

'What about her?'

'David's left her.'

'You *what*?' Rick's scalp moved back a full half inch. 'When?'

'Three weeks ago.'

'Why didn't you tell me?'

'You weren't exactly firing on all cylinders. Besides, the doctor said that you mustn't get upset, so I decided not to tell you. I didn't want you to start blaming yourself for—'

'Blaming myself? Why on earth should I go and—'

He stopped dead, his Swiss-cheese memory suddenly plugging one of the holes with a hazy fragment of the last conversation he'd had with David. 'Oh my God.' A glimmer of recognition stirred behind his eyes. 'David. The bloke in the bedroom when I was hallucinating about Bruce bloody Forsythe. Oh, Jeez.' He sat down heavily at the kitchen table. 'Tell me it's nothing to do with—' I held up a hand to stop him.

'Don't even go there.'

'One minute he was fine, and we were talking about . . .' he snapped his fingers and wracked his traumatized brain. 'Cars. We were talking about how you'd trashed the car. And he said something about women being terrible drivers, then I said something about babies throwing up in the back, then he said something about little Frankie, and then I said—' A horrible thought came flooding back to him, his face suddenly laden with doom. He looked up at me. 'Oh *fuck*.'

Chapter Seventeen

HEY, GARÇON

JULIA, svelte in an unforgiving vintage YSL trouser suit, must have shed a good couple of stone since I'd last seen her. Gone were the puffy cheeks – the rise of her sculptural bone structure once again visible beneath perfect make-up. I had been summoned by text message earlier that morning and given the details of her chosen time and venue, invited coolly to the neutral ground of a famous restaurant in Covent Garden that I'd heard of but never visited. It was the kind of place that theatre people frequented, wearing felt hats and elephant corduroy, blowing kisses through the air, aimed loosely here and there. Julia waited languidly at a generous round table near the window, answering messages on her BlackBerry.

'Julia? You look sensational!' I kissed her hello, unsure how to reconnect with her after almost a month of radio silence.

'I know,' she said curtly. I settled myself awkwardly into the seat beside her, arranging my bag on one of the vacant chairs, my mouth suddenly feeling dry.

'How's little Frankie?'

'Fine,' she said. 'We're both fine.'

'Is he with Odene today?' Already I was struggling to find conversation.

'No, Helen. I left him outside in the middle of the road with a packet of razor blades to play with.' So the rapier sarcasm was back with the lipstick and eyeliner.

'Leoni said she drove past your house the other day and saw a For Sale board outside.'

'That's right.' She perused the wine list.

'You're not seriously going to sell up, are you?'

'Why not? I could do with being more central now anyway, so I'm on the lookout for something closer to the office with a decent prep school nearby.'

'Julia?'

'What?'

'Are we going to talk about what happened?'

'Why?'

'It wasn't Rick's fault,' I explained. 'He wasn't well at the time. He's really beating himself up about it.'

'It doesn't matter,' Julia said lightly. 'I'm through with all that marriage crap anyway. At last I feel like I can actually breathe. I can't even begin to tell you how good it feels.'

'You don't mean that.'

'Yes I do,' she said sourly. 'After sixteen years, David and I were merely a habit, that's all. It's only now he's gone that I realize just how dead the whole thing really was. It had run its course, just as everything does. No point in hanging on to old baggage. It just drags you down. We'd had the best out of each other a long time ago, Helen. He's well out of it. We both are.'

'Where is he?'

'Last I heard? Sydney.'

'Australia?'

'No, Helen. Sydney, France.' She gave me one of her looks. 'Of course, Australia, you dunderhead. I think it was the furthest place he could think of.'

'I wonder what on earth he's doing out there?'

'Who knows?' Julia took a sip of water. 'Probably pouring his heart out to whoever will listen to him and doing his best to get off with a twenty-year-old surf babe. Good luck to him.'

'Poor David. He must be in pieces.'

'I really wouldn't know.'

'How can you be so brutal about it? He loves you. Always has done. You know I think the world of you, but I think that maybe it was an unforgivable blow you dealt him. Aren't you even the slightest bit worried about him?'

'No.'

'I don't believe you.'

'Then that's one of those areas in which you and I differ, isn't it? You can't spend your whole life worrying about other people. Nobody will ever thank you for it, and all the worrying in the world won't have any effect on them anyway. Trust me. Worrying gets you nowhere. It's a complete and utter waste of energy.'

'Sixteen years,' I sighed. 'That's a lifetime.'

'No it's not. Forty years is a lifetime, and I'm glad this has happened now rather than when I'm pushing sixty-five and lining up for my free buss pass. David will be fine, in time. And so will I, once I manage to get everything back on an even keel.'

'Did you talk much before he left?'

'Are you kidding?' She emitted a glassy laugh. 'This isn't the Hollywood screenplay version. He barely said two words to me, one of which was *off*, the other beginning with F. Then he marched upstairs, banged around in the bedroom for a while, grabbed a couple of suitcases and left.'

'How awful.' My hand reached for hers. 'I'm so sorry, Julia. If there's anything I can do—'

'Whatever.' Julia picked up the menu and glanced at it vaguely. 'I suppose I should have told him myself, but I don't expect the outcome would have been any different. If anything, Rick did me a favour. There's no good way to break bad news, is there?'

'I suppose not.'

'So tell Rick from me, no hard feelings, and I'll be only too happy to do the same thing for him one day.'

The waiter approached our table, brandishing his pad.

'Are you ready to order?'

'Just a bottle of Meursault for now.' Julia handed him back the wine list and checked her watch. 'We're waiting on a few guests.'

'Guests?' And here was I thinking that we were about to have an intimate sisterly interlude to repair our torn relationship and find a way to move on together. I had expected her to be a wreck, to find her fragile beneath a brave smile, in need of the new strong arm of support I had resolved to offer her. Yet from her impassive expression, I could see that Julia had shed her sensitive skin and shrugged her cast-iron overcoat back on, ready to do battle with the outside world and to sling a hand grenade in the direction of any idiot foolish enough to stand in her way.

'Yoo-hoo!' Paul sashayed through the tables, his manbag raised in a floppy hello. 'Daaaahlings! Mwah! Mwah! My goodness!' He took a dramatic step backwards and held his bag across his chest, gushing at Julia. 'Is it just my imagination or has somebody taken a fabulous pill this morning?'

'It's a work in progress,' Julia said. 'Where's everyone else?'

'They'll be here in a minute.' Paul dropped himself into a chair and let out a happy sigh. 'Leoni saw something in a shop window across the road and insisted on dragging Sally and Sara in for a second opinion. So.' He flapped the napkin into his lap. 'Isn't this nice? I just saw Stephen Fry outside having a sneaky ciggie. I know we'd get on like a house on fire if only he had a chance to meet me properly. I did introduce myself to him once at a TV launch party. We got chatting, but when I went to get another drink, I came back and he'd gone! Apparently he was last seen sprinting for the exit.' He put his finger to his lips. 'Maybe I should go back out there and jog his memory.'

'How could anyone forget you?' I said.

'Huh,' Paul clucked. 'Anyone would think that I didn't exist before Sally came along. If I didn't know better, I'd say the only reason so many people say hello to me is because they're all drooling over my husband.'

'Nonsense.' Julia patted his hand.

Outside on the pavement, Sally administered a sharp tap on the restaurant window and flashed us a winning smile as they walked past. 'Oooh!' Paul bounced in his seat. 'Here they come!'

Working his way through the room, Sally drew the usual gasps of admiration from men and woman alike, mouths agape as he soothed all six-foot-two of his

scorching gorgeousness between the tables before slith-
ering lithely into the seat next to mine. It was all I
could do to prevent myself from breaking into a grin of
epic smugness and pointing at myself, mouthing to the
restaurant, *he's with me*.

'Hey, baby.' Sally kissed me provocatively on the lips.
'Where you been hiding?'

In the mirror opposite, I caught a glimpse of the
dumbfounded blonde woman sitting at the table behind
me, the contents of her forgotten fork falling into her
cleavage.

'Oi! I want to sit there!' Leoni shoved Paul out of the
way and commandeered the chair to Sally's left, shunt-
ing her seat as close to him as physically possible. 'And
if you get the urge to put your hand on my thigh
during lunch, be my guest. I've had a bath and everything.' She stuffed her shopping under the table.

'What have you bought?'

'DIY equipment.'

'Really?' I tried to sneak a glance in the bag.

'I wouldn't go there before lunch if I were you,' Sally
drawled.

Too late. My eager hand had already plunged
through the tissue paper and landed on something soft,
rubberized and frighteningly large.

'Jesus!' My hand jerked back. 'Tell me that's not for
you.'

Sally laughed in that infectious way of his. 'You should have seen the one we made her put back.'

'Panic not,' Leoni said. 'It's merely part of my plan to make Marcus feel inadequate. I'm going to leave it lying around the bedroom accidentally on purpose.'

'Thank God for that.' I could breathe easy. 'My eyes were starting to water just thinking about it.'

'My one's in here,' she said, pushing the other bag along the floor with her foot.

'I don't want to know, thank you.'

'Dare you,' she challenged me. 'It's one of those ones that makes your teeth fall out after ten minutes. It's got a remote control and—'

'*Way* too much information.' I plugged my ears.

'Well, it's all right for you.' Leoni pulled the bag back indignantly. 'You're not having to make do with Mr Richmond Chipolata.'

'Did you see wassername off the telly on the way in?' Sara hissed.

'How could we miss her!' Paul flexed his claws. 'One lick on those lips and you could stick that girl to a window.'

'I was thinking about getting a collagen plump myself, but that's put me right off.' Leoni tired of waiting for someone else to do the honours and helped herself to the wine, dumping the dripping bottle in the middle of the table when she was done with it rather than returning it to the bucket. 'Anyway, it's great to be out with the posse again. It's been much too long. What are we celebrating?'

'We're not,' Julia said archly. 'There's an important reason why I've gathered you all here at the Table of Trust. Usual rules apply.' Everyone murmured their understanding. 'You all know that David has left me, and in order to stamp out any idle chatter, you might as well know why. I've decided to cut you all a slice of the action in the full expectation that I can rely on you to be mature, sensible and helpful in my hour of need. Now, if you'll excuse me, I'm going to hand you over to Sara for a quick PowerPoint presentation while I go and powder my nose.' She rose from the table. 'She'll bring you up to speed – with all the gory details, I'm afraid – and by the time I get back from the ladies' room, I expect you all to have calmed down and stopped screeching or I'm going straight home. Is that clear?'

Julia need not have worried herself. The effect of Sara's potted-version debriefing was to render everyone, except yours truly, speechless. Eyes widened, mouths dropped open, gasps were drawn, but nobody said a word. By the time Julia returned to the table, Leoni was well into her third glass of wine (to counter the shock, you understand), Paul was still shaking his head in mute disbelief, and Sally was chewing erotically on a toothpick, looking Julia up and down thoroughly approvingly with renewed interest and a devilish grin. He offered her a silent high-five as she seated herself.

'Any questions?' Julia said snippily.

Paul managed to gulp a couple of breaths, leaned into the table and lowered his voice.

'Which one is it?' he hissed.

'In there.' Julia tilted her head sideways towards the archway leading to the restaurant's second dining room. 'The tall one with the dark hair.' We all tried not to look. Leoni picked up her knife and angled it over her shoulder, squinting into the hazy reflection.

'Bloody hell,' Leoni said. 'Way to go, girl. He's barely old enough to be out of short trousers.'

'Which is why I've decided I'm going to raise my son on my own.' The table fell quiet. 'It's either him, a high court judge whose name I don't even know, or an incorrigible womanizer who'll expect me to up sticks and move to some draughty old Dracula castle in eastern Europe.'

'Rock 'n' roll.' Leoni banged both elbows on the table and propped her head in her heads. 'Then you can do a big reveal on your death bed and let Frankie take up the quest himself.'

'Never,' Julia vowed, picking up her menu and hiding her sudden flush behind it. We dutifully followed suit, made some pretence of discussing the specials and passed our order to the waiter.

'If I could just play devil's avocado here for a

moment . . .' Paul fiddled with the fringed ends of the sunset-orange skinny scarf knotted casually around his throat. 'What are you planning to do when Frankie's old enough to know that babies aren't really found under gooseberry bushes? I mean, he's going to start asking questions one day.'

'A kid needs a father.' Sally turned a spoon over in his long, sensitive fingers. A gentle wave of sadness passed across the table. Bowed heads and private thoughts silently agreed in a fleeting, ideal world.

'We're going to do this my way, OK?' Julia spoke into her lap. 'You can see perfectly well the scale of the dilemma I'm dealing with. What would I do if it's him?' She bucked her head towards the other room. 'How can I possibly embark on a lifetime's entanglement with a bloody waiter who's half my age? For Christ's sake, when we did it last year he was still living with his parents! It's completely out of the question, and from where I'm standing, none of the other candidates look any better.' I noticed Paul reach tentatively to Sally, squeezing his arm in a moment of quiet condolence. 'This is a tough enough call as it is. I've thought about it long and hard, and it's the only way I can handle it – on my own. And as for Frankie, I'll cross that bridge when I come to it.' Julia took a brief moment. 'It's not like the old days any more. For God's sake, there are stacks of kids out there growing up without knowing who their fathers are. It's yesterday's news. Nobody will bat an eyelid.' From the tone of her voice, it seemed to me that she was more set on convincing herself than us. 'I'm perfectly capable of providing everything my son needs.' Sally raised an eyebrow unsmilingly, rendering his face more gorgeous than ever. 'He'll have the best care, a good education—'

'Love,' Sally interjected, his voice barely audible.

'Drop it,' Sara said, pointing an accusing knife at him. 'If you're not with us, you're against us, *capiche*?'

'I *capiche* more than you could ever know,' Sally levelled at her. Paul rose from his seat to administer a hug.

'You OK?' he whispered. Sally nodded solemnly, and they exchanged a few quiet words before Paul returned to his place.

'Good for you.' Leoni dissipated the emotional tension with a wave of her glass. 'Could be worse, eh? At least he's not a crack baby.'

'I think you're very brave.' I said. 'If it's any consolation, I for one think you're making the right decision.'

'Hear, hear,' Paul added. 'And if little Frankie grows up to be half the man his mother is, I think we can all be very proud.'

Chapter Eighteen

MUTANT NINJA HUSBAND

'WHAT ABOUT THIS ONE?' Rick obligingly held the frou-frou hanger under his chin, the floor-length feather-trimmed chiffon wafting a diaphanous veil in front of his bulky shadow.

'Too green,' I said dismissively, flicking it away with my hand. 'Makes me look sallow.'

''Scuse me!' Rick bawled at the assistant. 'You got this in any other colours, love?' She gave him a funny look and fled to the stock room.

'Shouldn't you be thinking about getting back to

work soon?' I suggested conversationally, while browsing a rail of fussy knickers, each pair looking about as comfortable as a bag of angry wasps. I'd been trying to pin Rick down about it all week to no avail, and my patience was beginning to wear wafer-thin. I crossed my fingers. Third time lucky.

'Why?' Eagerly joining in the rummage on the reduced rail, he picked out a hideous red-ribbon suspender belt and waggled it in front of me. 'I've never had so much fun in my life!'

I pulled a face at the hanger and ferociously shook my head.

'Nobody wears those things any more.'

'Really?' He looked at it. 'That's a shame.' Putting the hanger back on the rail, he sidled up to me, real close. 'You know what, babe? That bang on the head's really got me thinking.'

'Oh yes?' Oh no, you mean. With Rick hanging around under my feet morning noon and night, I'd been subjected to a never-ending stream of semi-consciousness, covering every topic from sushi rice to dogshit bins. I think it's what they call too-much-time-on-your-hands. I've seen him sitting out in the courtyard for hours, rubbing his chin and mulling over all sorts of rubbish, which he then shares with me in tedious detail over dinner. Like how to avoid getting frost monsters in the freezer. Why a slice of bread always lands jam-side down. Whether there really *is* a margarine somewhere in the world that tastes like butter. I braced myself for another shaggy-dog lecture on the daily minutiae of life.

'I never really thought much about the future before. You know, too young an' all that guff about what-else-would-I-do-with-my-time. But now that I've got you, I'm seriously thinking about packing it all in and enjoying the fruits of my hardly-earned dosh.' Before I had a moment to freeze-frame my face and cover my tell, there it was. I felt my bottom lip pull tight. Rick winked at me. 'I knew you'd be pleased,' he smiled. 'We can have lie-ins every day, go travelling and see some of those places everybody's supposed to see before they die.' How reassuring. 'Look!' he gestured around. 'You've even taught me how to enjoy shopping!'

A deafening alarm bell went off in my head. I looked at Rick and realized in that moment that he had somehow morphed into some kind of mutant while I wasn't looking. Half man, half shopa-longa-girlfriend, he even knew the difference between mousse and serum. How could I not have read the danger signs? The perfectly stacked dishwasher. The stubble shavings so considerately rinsed from the washbasin. The frothy coffee with chocolate sprinkles on top. Shit, I thought. I've created a monster.

'Retire?' I tried to make it sound silly, rather than petrifying. 'At your age?' I began to walk nonchalantly, unsteady legs heading towards the exit in the hope that a little fresh air might bring him to his senses. He caught up with me in two easy strides and opened the door for us.

We strolled for a while in the early September sunshine, sensing the first subtle hints of autumn in the occasional chilly breeze. 'I'll be fifty-four next year,' Rick said, patting the hand I'd tucked into his arm. 'Then sixty. Then seventy, if I'm lucky.'

'That's a long way away,' I said.

'Yeah, babe. That's what everyone says until they wake up old one morning or keel over after a fried breakfast.'

'Don't be maudlin. You're not going anywhere just yet.'

'But that's the point, innit?' He stopped walking and turned to me. 'How do we know how long we've got? My old man dropped dead of a heart attack by the time he was my age. Sure, the fact that he was running away from the Old Bill at the time carrying a television set while severely pissed probably had something to do with it, but still,' he sighed. 'It don't bode particularly well on the longevity front, does it? And what more do I want out of life?' His face searched mine. 'What do *you* want out of life, Hell?' We stood there on the pavement, quite still amid the constant footfall of passing shoppers, silent beside the lanes of frustrated traffic, airbrakes hissing from queuing buses. I stared back at him vacantly. I stopped asking myself what I wanted out of life a long time ago. Frankly, these days I'm happy if I can make it through to suppertime without any major incidents. 'I've got everything a man could possibly want. And I've never been happier in my whole life than I am right now this very second. I've been asking myself just one question this last month or so, babe. I've spent hours thinking about it. If not days.'

'What's that?'

'How much?' he asked with a disarming smile. 'It's that simple, isn't it?'

'Eh?'

'How much is enough, babe?'

I wasn't sure I knew what he meant. 'What, money?'

'Nah!' He pulled a fresh cigar from his pocket, bit the end off and stuck it in his mouth. 'It's not just about the readies, Hell, is it? It's about everything. Life, family, the people you meet who change everything.' Rick lit up, taking his time, enjoying those first few puffs, dispensing an aromatic cloud that perfumed the pavement around us. 'Money doesn't really mean anything at the end of the day, does it? I mean, you can't have a meaningful relationship with a wad of cash, can you?' I stared at him, slightly incredulously. 'Don't get me wrong,' he said quickly. 'I know there's a lot of people out there worrying about where their next McDonald's is coming from, but you know what I mean. I don't want to be one of those twats who missed out on life because he was busy making plans for a future that never came. It's not about the future, babe. It's about the now.'

'Wow,' I said, because it was the only response I could think of. So his bruised brain hadn't been quite as idle as I'd assumed. The thought of Rick as a retiree conjured up a slideshow of hideous pictures in my mind. Wrinkly old codgers shuffling around a decaying nursing home. Brown flannel dressing gowns. Trying to eat toast with no teeth. He couldn't retire. Retirement is for old people, and I'm not ready to be married to an old duffer. God knows, I'm still not sure if I'm ready to be married at all. This has all been very stressful.

'You OK?' Rick asked. 'You look a bit peaky all of a sudden.'

'Yes,' I said. 'It's just . . .' I couldn't think straight. 'Don't you think you'd get bored in a couple of months?'

'Why? We've got each other, haven't we?' I wondered how long it would be before I started feeling like the Prisoner of Zenda. 'Think about it. No ties. No commitments. Just empty days to fill with whatever takes our fancy.' And a small vial of arsenic secreted behind the bread bin. He held my hands and gave me a big smile, cigar stuck firmly between grinning teeth. 'We could have a lot of fun together, you an' me, babe.'

'I know.'

'Then why not let's start now? Fuck all this work

stuff. That's just about a man feeding his ego. I've done it for long enough. There's plenny of cash to last us, so long as we don't do anything stupid with it.'

'Like putting it in the bank.'

'You know me, babe.' In that moment, I began to suspect that I didn't really know him at all, confirming my suspicion that marriage really is like a watermelon – you don't know if it's any good until you get inside. Rick misunderstood my blanching expression and sought to reassure me. 'I've never invested a penny in anything I didn't understand, and that's the only reason I'm still standing here instead of sticking my head in an oven like that geezer who bought the restaurant chain off me last year.' I remembered the article in the newspaper. The whole operation had gone belly-up less than three months after Rick sold out, and the bloke had topped himself. We began to walk again.

'Don't you ever feel bad about that?'

'Nope,' Rick said. 'Business is business. He wanted it. He bought it. Everybody knew the economy was going to the dogs. I assumed he'd do the smart thing by breaking it up and selling it on instead of spending a fortune and opening up a string of Robin Hood theme restaurants specializing in venison burgers when nobody could afford to eat out anyway. Bloody nutter. Can you imagine telling a kid that he's eating minced Bambi? The man had to be a lunatic in the first place.

He'd have been better off investing his money in Woolies.'

'I forgot you were in the restaurant business,' I said, feeling slightly shame-faced.

'I wasn't. It was just part of an investment portfolio, that's all. I don't have anything to do with any of it. Just the bankroll and the bottom line. The trick is not to hang on to anything for longer than you have to. Pick smart partners who know what they're doing, turn a profit, line up the lawyers and get out fast.'

'It sounds so ruthless.'

'That's because it is. But three weeks of lying in bed staring at the ceiling and dribbling was just the wake-up call I needed. It's just not me any more, babe. I'm done with all that. I should be bloody grateful for everything I've got, not looking for more, so that's it, the end of the road. Goodnight, *muchachos*.'

'You're really serious about this, aren't you?'

'Yep.'

'So you won't be going back to work at all?'

'Nope.'

'But what about the office?'

'Angela can sort that out. She's been running it for years anyway.'

'And what about your employees?'

'Employees?' He looked at me. 'What makes you think I employ people?'

'Well, don't you?'

'Only when I need them.'

'Then who are all those people in your office?'

'What people?'

'The ones I saw when I came for that interview a million years ago!'

'Nothing to do with me, gorgeous. I just rent enough space to do what I need to do. The rest is occupied by other businesses.'

'So the office isn't yours, then?'

'Nope.'

'Furniture?'

'Uh-uh.'

'Pens and pencils?'

'Rented.'

'Well, bugger me,' I said. 'And all this time you let me believe that you owned a massive great conglomerate in Mayfair.'

'No I didn't.' He took a good long drag. 'You leapt to your own conclusions and never bothered to ask. Nobody like me really needs an office these days. It's just handy for show now and again. You can run a small country from a satellite laptop in the middle of the Med if you want to.'

'What about the house?'

'What about it?'

'Is that rented too?'

'Course not!' He pulled me in for a hug. 'You've got

nothing to worry about, babe. From now on, I'll never leave your side.'

I fell into step beside him, dodging the cracks in the pavement.

HALF PAST NINE in the morning. I'd barely digested my croissant and was planning on spending the next few hours curled up with an unsuitable novel while Rick tackled his first solo attempt at making us something edible for lunch. Fifteen bodice-ripping pages in, the scullery maid was just about to have her rhubarb tarts crushed by the rampant gamekeeper when the phone rang.

'Helen?' Had Mum's voice been any more shrill it would have melted the red-hot receiver in my hand. 'What on earth's going on down there?'

'Mum?'

'Don't you play all innocent with me!' Here we go. I put the book down. 'We've received a very alarming letter from David this morning, and Julia seems to have conveniently disappeared off the face of the earth.' My heart sank. Clearly, it was going to be one of those days.

'What are you talking about?' When it comes to spilling beans, I learned long ago that when Mum's involved, it's best to keep the clothes peg on the bag.

'I think you know very well what I'm talking about, young lady.'

'Mum, just calm down and tell me.'

'He's in Australia, you know.'

'Yes,' I said. 'I had heard.'

'So you *do* know.'

'Mum, I'm not pretending to know anything. This is nobody's business except Julia's.'

'Nonsense!' she puffed. 'I always knew this would happen! A baby comes along and the wife then ignores the husband, pouring all her attentions on the new arrival instead. And what happens?' Huge sigh. 'Men aren't sophisticated creatures, you know. They're just little boys who need lots of love and reassurance. Of course he's had his nose put out of joint, but really, she's gone too far this time.'

'You don't say,' I said dryly.

'This is all Julia's fault. She's taken that husband of hers for granted ever since I can remember. And fancy allowing yourself to get into such an unattractive state after giving birth! There's no excuse for it. Nobody wants a wife who looks like a dumpling and can't be bothered to brush her hair and put a little bit of lipstick on.' I glanced at my reflection in the mirror above the fireplace and shuffled my hair around with my free hand. 'She doesn't even cook for him. Is it any wonder that he's upped and left?'

'Mum, if you could just—'

'Of course it isn't. I expect he's going to teach her a lesson she won't forget in a hurry. Leave her to stew in her own juices while he does his own thing and gives her a taste of her own medicine. That will show her. I told her, "Just because there's a new baby in the house, that's no excuse to neglect your husband," but would she listen to me? Oh, no. You young women think you know everything. In my day—'

'Mum—'

'—we made sure we did our exercises, took a little nap so that we wouldn't be too tired in the evening when our husband got home—'

'MUM!' I shouted. 'Just shut up for five seconds, will you?'

'Helen! How dare you speak to me like—'

'Like what? Like if I wait for you to come up for breath it'll be dark outside? For heaven's sake, mother. A telephone is a two-way invention, OK?'

'Hmph,' she sniffed. 'I don't know what the world's coming—'

'What did David say?'

'I haven't spoken to him.'

'The letter, mother.' Give me strength. 'What did he say in the letter?'

'Well, it wasn't a proper letter. More of a note, really, on hotel paper, just telling us where he is and saying that he and Julia are spending some time apart.'

'Is that it?'

'Hold on a minute.' I heard her put the receiver down, then some rustling noises. 'Here it is. He's in

293

Brisbane and is planning on staying for three months, then he gives the address of a friend where he can be contacted. Then – ' she began to read – '*Julia and I have had some difficulties and we thought it best if we spend some time apart*. Then he says, and this is just so sweet, *you have both been wonderful in-laws and I wanted to thank you for that*. Isn't that nice?'

'Does Julia know?'

'What? That he's in Australia?'

'No, Mum.' I stifled an intense urge to scream. 'About the letter. Does Julia know about the letter?'

'I've left a string of messages for her, but she hasn't returned my calls, as usual. She probably thinks we have no idea what's going on. Huh. How can a mother not know what her own daughter is doing?' I heard her take a self-satisfied sip of tea. 'I expect she thought she could keep us in the dark until he comes back and that nobody would know. She's bound to be feeling thoroughly ashamed of herself and was probably too proud and embarrassed to say anything.'

'Mum, this really is a private matter. Please don't go upsetting the apple cart. Julia has quite enough to deal with right now.'

'And who's fault is that? I warned her, but would she listen?'

'What does Dad think about it?'

'Oh, you know your father. Typical man. Sits around and flaps his newspaper without saying a word.' Wise move. 'When I ask his opinion, he just says, "Whatever you say, dear".'

'Is he around?' I asked. 'Maybe I should talk to him.'

'No,' said Mum. 'I packed him off in the car and told him to go and find Julia and talk some sense into her.'

'*What?*'

'What else is a father for, dear? Julia needs a firm hand. Your father will know how to deal with her.'

'Oh, *Mum!*'

THE SHEPHERD'S PIE was about perfect. I was just admiring the crisp little golden cheesy peaks and the delicious curl of savoury steam rising from the hole in the middle when the doorbell went.

'I'll get it!' yelled Rick. I had a sneaky shufti in the oven while he was gone. If that thing tasted as good as it looked, it might well give my own pie a run for its money. Like I say, if you can read, you can cook, and it seemed that Rick had followed Delia's every word. I turned the oven down low and put the peas on the hob to simmer in their own good time. A few minutes later, Rick brought the visitor trailing forlornly into the kitchen. 'You were spot on, babe,' he said.

'Hi, Dad.' I slouched towards him for a hug.

'Hey, darling.' He kissed my hair. 'I hear you were expecting me.'

'Had Mum on the phone this morning.' I gave him a wry smile. 'I guessed it was only a matter of time.'

'Make yourself at home,' Rick insisted, offering him a chair.

'Thanks.' Dad raised his hand in polite refusal. 'But I've been sitting in that car for the best part of three hours thanks to the twit who overturned their lorry on the motorway. I'd better stand up for a while and get my circulation back to normal.'

'Course.' Rick stood too and kept him company.

'We had a rather cryptic letter from David this morning. Your mother seems to think it's nothing more than a tantrum, but if you ask me, it looked more like a big, loud thank-you-and-goodnight. Julia's quite clearly avoiding the phone, which is probably just as well with your mother on the war path.'

'So we heard,' I said. Bloody Norah. I just said *we* without thinking about it. Shock horror. I checked the backs of my hands for werewolf hairs.

'I told your mother it's none of our business, but you know what she's like. She won't have it. Now I'm under strict instructions to give your sister a stern talking-to and effect a full reconciliation before I show my face back at home.' He shook his head at me. 'I'm armed with a pair of pyjamas, two fresh shirts and a toothbrush. What the hell do I know about marriage? I just do as I'm told and try not to breathe too loudly the rest of the time.'

'Did you manage to track Julia down and speak to her?'

'Not likely.' Dad shrugged his jacket off and hung it on the back of a chair. 'I have absolutely no intention of meddling in your sister's life. Or yours, for that matter. I'll just hide out here until the sabre-rattling stops, if that's all right with you.'

'Scotch?' Rick said.

'You know what, Rick? That's the first sensible word I've heard for days. Joyce's nagging is like tinnitus. You become so used to it that, when it stops, you think there must be something wrong with your ears.' Rick went to fetch the decanter, leaving Dad and me alone. 'What's going on, love?' he asked gently.

'They've separated,' I said.

'I'd already deduced that for myself. Are you going to tell me why?'

'No. That's up to Julia.'

'Here we go!' Rick bounded back in, glugged two good European measures into a pair of thick-bottomed whisky glasses and pushed one towards the old man. 'Get your tackle around that. I think you might be impressed.' Dad took a small sip, rolled it around his mouth and nodded appreciatively. 'Good, huh?'

'Very good.'

'It's a twenny-five-year-old Longmorn. A bit spesh, dontcha think?'

'I could certainly get used to it.'

I left them to their whisky talk, discreetly took my leave and slipped away to the study.

'SHE'S BUSY.' Sara answered Julia's mobile. 'I'll get her to call you back, but it might not be today.'

'It had bloody well better be,' I said. 'Because I've got a major situation unfolding in my kitchen. So you just tell her from me to drop whatever she's pretending to do and get over here on the double. Or else.'

'Or else what?'

'Look, Sara. Just tell her that Dad's turned up and he's looking for her.'

The phone went quiet, muffled into her chest, no doubt, then Julia came on the line. 'Helen? Is Dad there?'

'Yep.'

'Why?'

'Oh, don't give me that shit, Julia. How many messages has Mum left for you?'

'Thousands. I stopped listening to them long ago.'

'So you don't know about the letter they got from David, then.'

'You *what*?'

'Mum's completely doing her marbles and has sent Dad to smoke you out from wherever it is you're hiding.'

'*Fuck!* What did he tell them?'

'How the hell am I supposed to know? The general gist I got from Mum goes something along the lines of "you're spending some time apart".'

'Is that all?'

'I think so.'

'And what have you told the old man?'

'Nothing! He's in the kitchen drinking whisky with Rick and I reckon I can stall him for another hour with a big lump of shepherd's pie, but that's about as far as it goes, right?'

'*Shit!*'

'So you'd better get your arse over here pronto, because I'm not standing with my finger in the dike indefinitely, understand?'

'You've got to be joking. I'm not coming anywhere near the place. You deal with it.'

'What?'

'This would never have happened if you hadn't opened your big mouth and blabbed.'

'Excuse me? I wasn't the one who went off and got herself knocked-up by a bloody waiter. Oh, wait a minute. He's just one of the potential fathers. The baby could be anybody's. Of course. How silly of me.'

'Oh, shut up. What would you know anyway, goody two-shoes? I suppose you have to have all the lights off and do it through a hole in the sheet.'

'You get over here right now and clear your own mess up.'

'Bollocks,' Julia said. 'You do it.'

And on that elegant note, she hung up.

Chapter Nineteen

THE TRUTH, THE WHOLE TRUTH...

'YOU CHOSE yourself a good man, there,' Dad said, carefully picking his way through the fragrant honeysuckle, pinching out the spent flowers and casting them aside. The courtyard was an easy garden to handle, planted with slow climbers and a yellow rambling rose that didn't mind the high, shady walls and poor soil. Everything else was imprisoned in pots, most of which were liberally adorned with crumpled dog-ends. Although the space was a good deal bigger than the usual postage stamp allocations round here, the enclosed cobbles felt almost claustrophobic when compared with Dad's freestyle plot at home, with its untidy rows of salad vegetables and rattling Heath Robinson bird-botherers.

'I did indeed,' I smiled. 'We're very happy.'

'Glad to see it, love. Glad to see it.' I set about the rose with my trusty old secateurs, cutting out the dead wood, trimming the stems back to the second bud. 'All I ever wanted was to see you girls happy.'

'I know.'

'So are you going to tell your old man what happened or are you going to let me suffer the awful penance of not knowing?'

'Suffer?' I stopped pruning. It never occurred to me that he might be torturing himself. I thought that was strictly women's territory. 'Oh, Dad! You really mustn't worry about either of us. We're fine.' Dad hung his head for a moment, wiping his green fingers on his trousers, unconcerned by the grubby marks they left. He moved slowly to the patio set and sat himself wearily on one of the wrought-iron chairs.

'No matter how old I get, or how grown-up you girls think you might be, let me tell you something. I've never once stopped worrying about either of you. It comes with the job description. I'm your Dad, and that's never going to change. I was there when you spoke your first words and took your first steps.' He smiled to himself. 'Remember when you lost that daft rabbit you used to carry around with you everywhere? I drove all the way back to the campsite to get it. Remember that?'

'Yes.' I came and sat next to him.

'You might think that things are different now, just because you're all grown up and have your own lives. But what you have to understand is that, to your mother and me, well, you girls *are* our lives. God knows, there's nothing else going on of any interest. Your mother's got her gruesome little coven at the WI. I've got my runner beans. But it's you kids that hold everything together. Can you understand that?'

'Yes,' I said, feeling suddenly selfish.

'Now. Are you going to tell your old man what went on between Julia and David? You don't have to. But I'd appreciate it if you did.'

The way he asked the question, the way he made me remember that summer when I'd left Mister Buttons at the campsite, hidden under a nice little bush in which I'd made a home for him, then promptly forgotten where it was ... It was all such a long time ago, in a different world with pink sugar-mice, where you had to get up and walk to the television set in order to change channels and there was never anything on anyway. Dad was the one man I had always been able to rely on. Always there, through thick and thin, in his own quiet way. Always ready to take my side without explanation or argument. He'd asked me a direct question, which was rare indeed. For me to lie to him would have been unconscionable.

'The truth?' I said tentatively, suggesting that he should prepare himself for the worst. 'And you promise you won't freak out?'

'Scout's honour,' Dad nodded.

'OK.' I said. 'It was about Frankie.'

'I see.' Dad seemed instantly relieved. 'Mmm.' He rubbed his cheek for a while. 'Your mother suspected as much. Looks like the old dear was right. That'll make her day.'

'I very much doubt it.' I gritted my teeth. 'You see, Dad, Frankie's not David's.'

In all my days, I have never seen anyone look quite so shocked. Dad's face went through about six hundred different expressions in the space of a millisecond. His ears went white, then glowed bright red. His eyes widened, narrowed to tiny slits, then widened again. I imagined his whole life was passing in front of his face, or at least Julia's. New baby going *waaaah*. Little girl riding a bike. Smiling graduate. Proud bride. Successful businesswoman. Shameless adulterer. Single parent.

'Dad? Are you all right?'

'Yes.' He nodded quickly, trying to snap himself out of it. 'Yes. Er. Right. Crikey.'

'I'm sorry,' I said. 'But there's no point in beating about the bush, is there? Although heaven only knows what we're going to tell Mum.' His ears were nearing purple. I hoped to God that he wasn't planning on having a seizure. Then I'd really be in trouble with the old dear. 'It's a real shocker, isn't it?' He shook his head slowly.

'Bloody hell's teeth.'

'You can say that again.'

'Who's the father?'

'Ah,' I said. 'Well, that's the other thing.' At that moment, I realized that I had imparted sufficient information to do the job. To colour in the details would serve no purpose at all other than to cause more pain. Perhaps Julia's blushes could be spared. If only for a little while. 'She hasn't disclosed to anyone who the father is. He doesn't know about it either, and she's decided to bring up Frankie on her own.' Dad pressed his hands to his face, rumpling his rosy cheeks. 'You know, Dad, I think it was just one of those things. It could have happened to anyone. You mustn't think badly of her. She's doing enough of that without any help from us.'

'I must be getting old,' Dad said. 'There was a time when a situation like this would be considered the worst thing in the world, a woman having a baby on her own.'

'It's not so bad.' I smiled and touched his hand. 'Julia's happy with her decision, if happy is the right word. She's got a full-time live-in nanny and she's gone back to work, which was probably the best thing for her. You know, help keep her mind off it. So you're not to go worrying yourself. She'll be OK. Just you wait and see.'

'I don't doubt it,' he said sagely. 'She's always been very strong-willed.'

'She just wants to lie low for a while and let the dust settle.'

'When did all this happen?'

'A few weeks ago,' I said.

'And she told David herself?' Dad almost winced at the thought.

'More or less.' I wobbled my hand. 'He was out of there like a shot. Can't say that I blame him. I expect there'll be a divorce somewhere down the line and all the mess that goes with it.' I found myself picking grimly at a loose flake of paint on the table. 'Mum's going to go ape, isn't she?' Dad raised a cool eyebrow and sucked his breath through his teeth. 'I thought so,' I said. 'Oh well. Can't make an omelette, I suppose. I was thinking, Dad. I know it's a lot to ask, but maybe you could stall her for a while? And if you can't bring yourself to do that, then break it to her gently, you know, ask her to go easy on Julia rather than having one of her meltdowns. I can imagine her flying straight off the handle, and right now that just wouldn't be helpful.'

'She'd have no right to,' Dad said, pulling a small penknife from his pocket and easing a splinter of plant life from his thumbnail. 'Everyone has a skeleton or two in their closet, Helen. You of all people should know that.' I dropped my face, hiding its sudden blush. 'Your mother's been no saint either.'

A creeping sensation slithered down my spine.

'You mean . . .' I looked around quickly and hushed my voice. 'She had *affairs?*'

'Good heavens, no!' Dad said. 'At least, I bloody well hope not. By the time we were married, I think she'd more than got all that out of her system.'

'What do you mean?'

'Oh,' he sighed. 'Nothing. It doesn't matter.' His shoulders drooped a little. 'Water under the bridge.'

'Dad?' Something had come over him, dark and distant. A passing cloud stole the sun for a moment, bringing a pale shiver to my sleeveless arms. 'Hey.' I rested my hand on his. 'What's the matter?'

Before he could answer, Rick's voiced boomed out from the kitchen door.

'Hey, Frank! You fancy nipping out with me for a while? I've got to go and pick up the jalopy from the repair shop.'

'Sure.' Dad patted my hand briefly.

'Oh!' I said, resentful of the intrusion. Dad and I so rarely had the chance to sit and talk together, and when we did, the time seemed to fly by in a matter of moments. 'Can't you get them to deliver it?'

'Nonsense.' Dad stood up and shook off the shadow

of whatever it was that had bothered him a few moments ago. 'I've spent far too much of my life in the company of whingeing women, and seeing as I'm down to just one son-in-law, I might as well grab every macho moment I can get.'

EVENING SETTLED IN, and the last of the flowers disappeared into the dusk as the light faded from the courtyard. It looked like rain, so I closed the back door, lowered the windows and wondered where on earth Rick and Dad had got to. Rick had forgotten to take his phone, and although Dad learned how to carry a mobile some time ago, he never switches it on unless he's making a call, lest the battery should run down. I've given up trying to explain to him that the whole point of carrying a phone is so that people can get hold of him, but he says he doesn't know anybody that he wants to hear from anyway, and obstinately sticks to his guns.

The phone rang. Thank God for that.

'Hello?'

'Helen?' Great. That's all I need.

'Hi, Mum.'

'Have you heard from your father or Julia yet?'

'No, Mum.'

'Good,' she said. 'I don't mind telling you, I thought your father would head straight for your house rather than taking the bull by the horns and doing what he's supposed to do. If he turns up there, you just turf him out, you hear me?'

'Oh ye of little faith,' I mumbled.

'If he's not with you, he's bound to have caught up with Julia by now, although I do wish he would telephone me and keep me informed of what's going on. It's very difficult just sitting here and waiting around.'

'Maybe if he turned his phone on—'

'Runs the batteries down, dear. They're only supposed to be used in an emergency.'

'Whatever.'

'So I thought I had better ring round and tell everybody not to phone me because I need to keep the line clear.'

'Good idea.'

'But I don't mind telling you, it's very frustrating.'

'Then why didn't you go with him?'

'Me? Go on a wild goose chase like that? Don't be so ridiculous, dear. Somebody has to stay here in case David telephones. Or Julia, for that matter. For all I know, I could have one or both of them turning up on my doorstep looking for tea and sympathy at any moment.'

'I wouldn't hold your breath.'

'Never mind. Your father will sort it out.'

'Mum?'

'Yes, dear?'

'Are you happy, you know, married to Dad?'

'What on earth kind of a question is that, dear?'

'I mean, would you say that you've had a good marriage together? You know, that you chose the right man to be with for the rest of your life?'

'What a silly thing to ask!' she snorted. 'I've never heard such a load of nonsense in my life. What's got in to you? Have you been taking those funny hormone supplements I've been reading about in all the magazines? You're still rather young for all that, dear.'

'Mum—'

'I remember when I went through The Change.' She rolled out a painful sigh. 'It's a terrible thing to happen to a woman, but you'll get through it, just like we all have to eventually.'

'Oh, forget it,' I muttered. 'Look, Mum. I've got to go. I've got something in the oven.' Like my head. 'I'm sure Dad will call you soon.'

'He had better. My nerves really are quite tattered today.'

'Bye, Mum.'

No sooner had I replaced the receiver than the phone started ringing again.

'What now?' I said wearily.

'Well, that's nice, isn't it?' Sara said. 'Remind me to send our next receptionist over to you for training.'

'Sara! Sorry about that. I just had the gorgon on the phone again chewing my ears off. What's occurring?'

'I thought I'd better call you and give you some forewarning about what's heading your way.'

'Let me guess,' I said. 'Hurricane Death? A swarm of man-eating bees? That massive lump of comet out of Armageddon?'

'Rick and Frank turned up here about twenty minutes ago, pissed as newts the pair of them, demanding to see Julia.'

'Oh God.' I slapped my hand across my eyes.

'Don't worry. She wasn't here. I shoved them both in a taxi and sent them on their way.'

'Lying bastard. He told me they were going out to pick up the Bentley.'

'They did,' she said. 'But now it's back in the repair shop. Rick insisted your dad have a go and he backed it into a pair of steel bollards.'

'Before or after they'd been out on the lash?'

'I didn't ask, and from the state they were in, I very much doubt that they'd be able to remember.'

Chapter Twenty

THE BLACK DOG

'GOOT MONGING!' Helga slammed the front door, rattling the windows, and came scampering into the kitchen.

'Morning, Helga. I hate to ask you this, but would you mind changing a couple of beds again today?'

'Bids?' She shook her head furiously. '*Nyet*. Me do bids yesterday.'

'I know, but two of them are going to need doing again, I'm afraid.'

After sucking the Anglesey Arms dry, Rick and Dad had spent most of the night sweating several gallons of second-hand hops, judging by the revolting smell upstairs. At least Rick had had the courtesy to go and sleep in one of the spare rooms, although his drunken snoring rumbled straight through the floorboards and kept me up half the night. As soon as I'd got up, I'd opened a few windows in an attempt to dissipate the fug of brewery fumes, only to find my highly sensitive nose twitching against the aroma of something all the more grotesque coming from downstairs. The remains of a half-mauled doner kebab lay abandoned on the arm of one of the sofas, leaking a vile juice of grease and chilli sauce into the suede. After scraping the worst of it off with a fish slice and dumping it in the outside bin, the place still stank to high heaven. Half an hour later, I found the other one squelched down the back of a radiator.

Helga dumped her crumpled Tesco bag-for-life on the table, pulled on her overall, then stopped, sniffing suspiciously at the air.

'You cook dog?' she asked.

'No, Helga. My Dad turned up yesterday. He and Rick tried to redecorate the house last night with a couple of kebabs.'

'Ah,' she said. 'Smell like dog.'

'Maybe it was,' I conceded. One does hear all kinds of rumours about what they put in those things. 'Not that either of them would have been able to tell the difference. Goodness me!' I looked towards the shady movement at the kitchen door. 'It's the creature from the black lagoon!'

'Morning, love.' Dad shuffled in, looking like a clothing recycling bin.

'Dad, this is Helga. Helga, Dad.' Helga bobbed up and down.

'Frank,' Dad said, introducing himself. 'Forgive my rather dishevelled appearance.'

'*Da.*' Helga looked him up and down. 'You make piss?'

'I beg your pardon?' Dad blanched.

'You.' Helga pointed at him. 'You and Reek make piss!' Dad opened his mouth at me.

'I think she means you and Rick were out on the piss last night.'

'Oh!' He nodded politely. 'Yes. I suppose we were.'

'Now bid stink,' Helga tutted as she picked up her cleaning bucket and headed for the stairs. 'I make bid yesterday. Now make again today. Pah. *Zhopa.*'

'Don't take any notice of her,' I whispered at Dad, winding a finger at my temple. 'She'll be all right after she's had her elevenses.'

'Hope we didn't disturb you when we came in last night?'

'No chance,' I said. 'I took a sleeping pill and shoved a couple of British Airways ear plugs in about half an hour before last orders. Did you have a nice time?'

'Who knows? I think so.' He sat at the table and stifled a yawn. 'Although I've woken up with the most horrible taste in my mouth. Any chance of a cup of tea?'

'Coming right up.'

'Blimey,' Dad mumbled. 'It's been a long time since I did anything like that.'

'It's good for you,' I said.

'I'm not sure your mother would agree.'

'Then it's just as well she doesn't know, isn't it?' He smiled into the table. 'By the way, she rang yesterday afternoon wanting to know if I'd heard from you. I said no, of course, but you might want to think about giving her a call.' I plonked a steaming mug in front of him.

'Thanks. Better have a couple of these first, eh? Then we'll see about getting our story straight before I ring her.'

The doorbell went.

'Helga!' I shouted. 'Can you get that? Probably the postman,' I said to Dad. 'He's one of those irritating people who'll keep you talking on the doorstep for half an hour moaning about his job if you let him. Helga will sort him out. He's scared shitless of her.'

'I'm not bloody surprised.' Dad picked up his tea and drank most of it down in one go. He has an asbestos tongue and could probably imbibe boiling water straight from the kettle.

'Hi.' Julia wandered in. 'Got another one in the pot for me?'

'Julia!' Dad was on his feet in an instant. 'Oh, thank heavens! Are you all right, love?'

'Hey, Dad.' Julia said between kisses. 'Sorry about giving you and Mum the runaround yesterday. I wasn't thinking straight.'

'That's OK, love.' Julia pulled up a seat at the table next to him. 'I expect speaking to your mother is about the last thing on your mind right now.'

'So you've heard from David, then?'

'Yes, love.'

'I'm afraid it's all a bit of a mess, Dad.' Julia put on her brave face, loosened her shoulders and sighed. 'I don't really know what to say to make it sound any better than it is.'

'It's OK, love. You don't need to explain. Helen told me what happened.' Julia's head jerked towards me.

'Dad knows it was just one of those things.' I said quickly. 'You know, an accidental one-night stand in a moment of madness.'

'Unlucky,' Dad sympathized. 'And very honest of you to own up and face the music. I expect there are a lot of women out there who wouldn't have.'

'With hindsight, I think they're probably right,' Julia said.

'Do you think there's any chance David will—'

'No,' Julia interrupted tersely. 'And there's no point in any of us pretending otherwise. No man in his right mind would have stuck around.'

'Have you spoken to him?'

'What is there to say?'

'I suppose.' Dad gave a small, sad shake of his head. 'What a terrible shame. We were all very fond of him.'

'It's over, Dad. I just want to move on as quickly as possible, because if I stop to think about it, I . . .' Her face reddened. 'I don't think I could . . .' She paused, hung her head and began to weep. 'I've been such an idiot.'

'Hey!' Dad moved in closer and put his arm around her shoulders. 'Come here!' he said, pulling her towards him. 'Go on, love. That's right. You just have a good old cry and let it all out.'

'I can't face Mum,' Julia sobbed.

'You won't have to.' Dad stroked her hair. 'I'll speak to her. And if she dares utter one word out of turn, I'll tell everyone in the post office that she's been faking her award-winning strawberry jam for years. She buys it from a farm shop near Bicester and puts it in her own jars. Bet you didn't know that, did you?' Julia pulled herself together, summoned a watery smile and blew her nose. 'That's better now, isn't it?' Dad patted her hand.

'Thanks, Dad.'

'No sweat. That's what I'm here for.'

There came a small knock-knock. Rick hovered in the doorway, looking like a train wreck. 'Family only or am I OK to come in?' he said.

'You are family.' I went to give him a kiss, pressing my mouth close to his ear to give him the Official Version. He rummaged in the pocket of his bathrobe for a cigar.

'Morning, Frank! Feeling bright and breezy? How many d'ya reckon we sank last night?'

'I wish I knew,' said Dad. 'I'd have it printed on a T-shirt just to annoy my wife.'

'Jools.' Rick gave her a thumbs-up. 'Bearing up, treacle?'

'Kind of,' Julia said. 'I just wish I could hit the fast-forward button and zap through the next six months without waking up.'

'Well, if it's any consolation, you're looking fucking great. If I hadn't already gone and married your sister, I'd be first in line to woo you.'

'Thanks,' Julia said, smiling.

'Is that tea?' Rick pulled up a chair. 'Do us a cuppa wouldya, babe? My gob feels like it's eaten a dead dog.'

I'M NO STRANGER to depression. I can usually feel it creeping over the crest of the hill and manage to snap myself out of it with the help of a brisk walk and a handful of herbal pick-me-ups. Valerian's pretty good, so long as you don't overdo it. I tried Prozac once, but it made me feel worse than I did in the first place and I started having weird episodes (like finding myself in the middle of Sainsbury's weeping over a packet of cream crackers). On the upside, no one seems to get embarrassed about it these days. In fact, it's quite the In Thing in certain circles. You're nobody unless you've had a couple of close encounters of the mental kind. I found myself sitting in bed, endlessly staring at the wall as if it would yield an answer to all my troubles.

'You all right, babe?' asked Rick, clearing away the stone-cold cup of tea that he'd brought me an hour ago.

'Yes,' I said, unconvinced.

'You sure?'

'No.' I felt my nostrils flaring.

'Anything I can do to help?'

'I doubt it, unless you happen to have a time machine tucked up your sleeve.'

He sat down on the bed with me. 'And if I did, where would you want it to take you?'

'Back to the beginning,' I said. 'Back to a time when everything was a lot less complicated than it is now.'

'What's complicated?'

'Everything.'

'This is about Julia, isn't it?'

'Is it?' Fucked if I knew.

'She'll be fine.'

'I thought she and David would be together for ever,' I said. 'They were that kind of couple.'

'You never know what goes on behind closed doors, babe.'

'Tell me about it.' I raised an eyebrow. 'Rick?'

'What?'

'Do you think we'll ever be like that?'

'Like what?'

'You know.' I shrugged. 'Conducting separate lives while living under the same roof.'

'I wasn't planning on it.'

'Marriage is too hard,' I said. 'It's just a ridiculous, unfair contract that goes against the very grain of human nature.'

'Is it?'

'Of course it is. People only ever do it out of fear. Fear of ending up alone. Fear of losing the person they think they love. Fear of the unknown. How many married couples do you know that definitely shouldn't be together?'

'A few, I guess.'

'Huh,' I scoffed. 'It's more than a bloody few.' I pulled my knees up under my chin. 'They start out with a string of absurd promises and a slice of cake, and the next thing you know, they're rigging the garage doors up to a pound of high explosives or poisoning each other's curry.'

'Is there something you want to tell me, babe?'

'Like what? We've bloody gone and done it now,

haven't we? Now all we have to do is sit around and wait for the contempt to start breeding.'

'I know what you need.' He scooched up beside me.

'Oh, for God's sake. Put it away will you?'

'What? I was only looking for a light!' Stretching himself out, he sparked up what remained of his Cohiba and sucked on it thoughtfully. 'How do you fancy getting out of here for a few days?'

'And what good will that do?'

'Oh, come on, babe! Whatever's going through your head at the moment, it ain't the end of the world. Trust me.' I supposed he was right, even though it didn't feel like it. 'Let's just chuck a few things in a bag, jump in the car and see where it takes us, eh?'

'But I thought it had gone back in for repair?'

'S'all right,' Rick said. 'Just a little ding on the back bumper. The bloke at the garage said it was only superficial.'

I HAD FORGOTTEN just how beautiful this England is. We had been in the car no more than an hour before the countryside opened up around us, fields of green dotted with cotton-wool sheep, dense copses of woodland clinging to rolling hillsides. Rick eased the Bentley off the main drag, carefully curling us along the winding country lanes, switching the headlights on as we disappeared down gladed tracks where the sun barely glimpsed through the trees. A rickety sign pitched beside the road proudly proclaimed *Holly Ridge Country House Hotel*.

'Look,' Rick pointed. 'It's a sign.'

'I can see that.'

'Wanna give it a try?'

'Why not?' My tummy was rumbling anyway.

Although the sign had said to take the next right, there was a point at which we wondered if we hadn't made a mistake – the narrow track was little more than a series of waist-deep pot holes interspersed with the occasional worn patch of tarmac. Just as we were about to give up, a gloomy Victorian red-brick monstrosity curved into view. Rick and I exchanged a glance.

'What do you think?' I said. Rick leaned over the steering wheel and peered up at the building.

'It's the bloody Munsters.'

Inside, the heavy oak-panelled walls seemed to suck all the light from the diminutive overhead chandelier – a cheap Homebase replacement of the likely original which had probably ended up on eBay. We crept along past a row of spooky, scowling portraits, our feet silenced by the swirling wall-to-wall pub carpet. The reception desk was deserted. Rick hit the bell, and his hand landed with a dull thud as the spring inside collapsed. We hung around for a while, waiting for someone to make an appearance.

'There's nobody here,' I whispered. 'It's like the *Marie Celeste*.'

'Hello!' Rick shouted. 'Anybody home?'

A couple of dogs started barking, one irritatingly yappy and another that sounded seriously big. I clung to Rick's arm.

'Won't be a minute!' came a disembodied voice. 'Bosun! Shut up, you daft animal!' The barking became more frantic. 'Get off! Brenda! BREN-DA! There's people at the desk!'

Some sort of commotion broke out a couple of rooms away and made its way towards us. Suddenly a door burst open, unleashing a beast of a dog, head like a bucket of concrete with slavering jowels, dragging a man from his belt-sized collar. 'Hello!' the man tried to appear casual. 'Just give me a couple of—' The dog saw us and went nuts. 'Bosun! For Christ's sake!' He tried to haul the dog back, wedging his heels into the carpet and straining with all his might. 'Quick!' he shouted at Rick. 'Pass me that newspaper!' Rick edged forward and handed the man the day-old copy of *The Times* that had been lying on a nearby seat. 'Thanks,' the man said, folding it into a brick and whacking the dog over the head with it. 'Sit!' he yelled. 'Down! Down boy!' The dog started snarling as the man opened the door from which he had come. A few more swipes around the bucket-head and the man threw the newspaper into the room. The dog pounded after it, barking and growling. He slammed the door shut, leaned against it for a moment, and smoothed his grey, unruly hair while the dog went bananas, tearing the newspaper to shreds and, from the sound of it, making a start on the furniture.

'Sorry about that.' He looked at his watch. 'BREN-DAAAA!' He listened out for a while, gave up and offered us an apologetic shrug. 'We're a bit short-staffed,' he explained. 'What can I do for you?'

'We want the best room you've got,' said Rick.

'Really?' The man seemed taken aback.

'I'm thinking along the lines of your bridal suite.'

'Bridal suite?' He straightened himself untidily. 'Er, yes. Of course.' He began flicking through the blank bookings diary. 'Now, let's see.'

'You busy at the moment?' Rick cocked his head at the empty pages.

'Er . . .' The man smiled nervously. 'To be honest, we've only just taken the place over. It's taking us a little while longer to find our feet than we'd hoped.' He turned to the pigeonholes behind the desk and selected a tasselled key. 'I'm not sure what the procedure is for checking in.' He frowned at the mess of papers on the desk. 'I'll take you up and ask Brenda to sort that out with you later. She's my wife. If you think Boson's fierce, well . . .' He pulled at his ear. 'Always wanted us to run a little country hotel. Any luggage?'

'In the motor.' Rick said, thumbing over his shoulder. 'But don't worry,' he smiled. 'I'll grab it in a minute.'

'I'm Vic,' the man said, showing us towards the wide staircase. 'Have you come far?'

'London.' Rick trudged up the stairs behind him. 'Thought we'd escape the smog and see if our lungs are still able to cope with a bit of fresh air for a few days.'

'Well, you've come to the right place,' Vic said. 'There are some lovely walks round here, and a nice pub in the next village that isn't too far to stagger. Just let me know when you're going out and I'll tie the dogs up. They haven't learned to distinguish between a guest and a burglar yet.' He paused at a wide oak door on the first landing. 'Here we are. This is you.'

A small panelled vestibule opened out into a room of palatial proportions dominated by an enormous four-poster bed with a huge, lumpy mattress. Old rugs did their best to cover the threadbare nature of the worn carpet, and the slumbering furniture stood to attention, trying to put its best foot forward. It was at once grand and charmingly shabby. A bit like Rick.

'It's lovely.' I put my handbag down and went to the window; a deep-buttoned seat ran along the curve of its bay. Opening the latch and leaning out, I looked out over an uninterrupted view of the tree-lined valley and grazing pastures beyond. The leaves of the nearby trees shimmered and sighed in the breeze, birds chattering in their boughs. I filled my lungs, took a seat and gazed out.

'Thanks, Vic.' I heard Rick fumble a note out of his wallet.

'Isn't this beautiful?' I sighed.

Rick came to the window and shared my vista.

'What's that funny smell?'

'Leaves and rain,' I said. 'Leaves and rain and flowers and all those things that we don't have at home.'

'Smells like rising damp to me.'

'Philistine.'

'So, now that we're here, waddya wanna do first, babe?' He flicked his eyes towards the bed.

'Eat,' I said. 'And if you carry on like that, there'll be nothing for dessert either.'

'IS EVERYTHING all right for you here?' Brenda peered at our plates. Rick gamely had another go at hacking into his hobnailed dinosaur steak.

'Great,' he said politely, slipping me a glance.

'Not enjoying the fish pie?' She pointed accusingly at my abandoned dish.

'It's lovely,' I lied. 'I'm just not particularly hungry.'

'Chef's speciality,' she said proudly. 'Freshly made yesterday.' I felt my stomach turn over. We were the only ones in the restaurant, bereft amid a sea of empty tables, the clock ticking loudly above the cold fireplace.

'Everything's fine,' Rick said, hoping she'd go away.

'My husband tells me you're escaping the noise of the city for a couple of days.'

'Yes.'

'Excellent,' she said. 'You're precisely the kind of customer we're hoping to attract. Perhaps you'll tell all your friends about us.'

'You can count on it.'

She stood easy and settled in. 'We have all sorts of plans for this place, you know. I keep telling Vic that we should do special events and group house parties rather than faffing around with the odd unexpected guest here and there.' We smiled at her grimly. 'Murder-mystery weekends are all the rage, but you have to get actors involved, and you know what they're like. Vic used to dabble in a bit of amateur dramatics. Drunkards, the lots of them.'

'Right.' Rick put his cutlery down and sighed patiently.

'Weddings is where the real money is, mind you,' she confided. 'But we've got a few health and safety issues. You wouldn't believe what they expect us to do just to get past the basic fire regulations. I said to Vic we'd be better off spending the money on a decent chef.'

'Good idea,' I mumbled.

'He's worth every penny! Don't you think?' She rearranged the salt and pepper pots. 'Let's just hope the inspectors don't turn up asking to see our safety certificate.'

'And what do we do if a fire breaks out?'

'Tie your bedsheets together and climb out of the window, of course!'

After suffering an insisted-on slice of apple pie with cardboard pastry courtesy of the dessert trolley from hell, Rick and I decided to brave the fresh air and stroll the damage off.

'Bloody hell, babe.' Rick puffed his way over a stile, dropping with a squelch into half an inch of soggy mud on the other side. 'When you said you wanted to go for a walk, I didn't realize you meant a bloody Blue Peter expedition. Look at all this shit!'

'Stop complaining, city boy. It's good for you.' I caught my breath for a moment. 'Come on. There's the village over there. Maybe there'll be somewhere we can get a cup of tea.'

'I don't understand what people see in the countryside.'

'That's because you're a street rat.'

'It's just a load of muck and cow farts, innit?'

'Right.' I pulled on his sleeve, forcing him to stop. 'What kind of tree is that?' I pointed into the branches of an enormous spreading beech, its leaves beginning to hint at the first flush of autumn copper.

'Dunno,' he said.

'It's a beech. What about that one?'

'Oak?' he shrugged.

'No. Maple.'

'Well, how the fuck am I supposed to know that?'

'It's the English countryside! Everybody's supposed to know a few trees and birds!'

'I do.' He fished around in his pocket, came out with a book of matches and a crumpled dog-end and sparked it up. 'Sparrows. Pigeons. Trees riddled with Dutch elm disease. What more do you want?'

His throwaway question hit me like a rock. What more did I want? When he'd asked me that a while ago, standing on the pavement in the middle of Knightsbridge amid the throng of shoppers, I hadn't had the faintest idea. Now I had never been so sure about anything in my life.

'A fresh start,' I said, lifting my face to the rushing leaves.

THE BED WAS EVERY BIT as lumpy as it looked, with springs digging their way out of the mattress and a huge dip on Rick's side where a buffalo had slept for a year or two. I didn't feel much like sleeping anyway.

'Rick?'

'Mmmph.'

'Are you awake?'

329

'Dunno,' he said. 'I seem to have lost all feeling in my legs.'

'I need to tell you something.'

'What?'

'A couple of months ago – ' I fiddled with the edge of the sheet – 'I was clearing out one of the cupboards and I found some things of yours.' His bedside light snapped on. He propped himself up on one elbow and looked at me knowingly. 'I realize it was none of my business and I know I shouldn't have looked.'

'Which cupboard?'

'Your wardrobe,' I admitted. Rick gallantly chose to say nothing. 'I don't know what came over me. I think I must have been having a brainstorm.'

'And did you find what you were looking for?'

'I'm sorry,' I said. 'I feel really bad about it.'

'Then why did you do it?'

'Insecurity, I suppose. That feng shui woman started asking all kinds of questions and I suddenly realized just how little I knew about you. You know what it's like. You marry somebody, then you wake up one morning and realize that you have no idea who they actually are.'

'Is that so?'

'Surely you must have felt it too?'

'Nope.' He sat up, winced at the sudden twinge from his back and gave it a rub. 'I thought that was half the fun of getting married, you know, learning about each other over the years, taking each day as it comes.'

'I didn't mean to pry.'

'Yes you did.' He flicked the covers back, got up and went in search of a cigar, rummaging through the pockets of his clothes, entirely unconcerned about being bollock naked. His lily-white buttocks glowed in the moonlight.

'You can't smoke in here,' I reminded him.

'What? In case a fire breaks out?' He lit up. 'Let's just hope they've left us a couple of extra bedsheets.'

'I found a photograph album,' I said. Rick chewed on his cigar thoughtfully, staring into the darkness. 'It was a wedding album, Rick.'

'You know very well I've been married before.' He took a glass from the nightstand to use as an ashtray.

'Twice, you said. You told me that you had been married twice.'

'No I didn't. That was you jumping to conclusions again.'

'And you never thought to put me straight?'

'Oh, for Christ's sake.' He took a long drag.

'Why didn't you tell me about her?'

'It's no big deal.'

'No big deal? A wife that you forgot to mention?'

'We were kids, Hell. Neither of us knew what we were doing. Just leave it, eh?'

'But why keep the photographs hidden away like that?'

'Hidden away? Why the fuck would I want to hide stuff in my own house?'

I watched the tip of his cigar glow bright. 'That thing must have been up there gathering dust for years. I've never even looked at it.'

'Have you any idea how it made me feel? It's not as though you and I have a single picture from our wedding.'

'Is that what this is all about?'

'No! Of course not!'

'Blimey. All you had to do was ask, babe. I know it wasn't exactly the big day you were hoping for.'

'I told you. It's nothing to do with that,' I said decisively, denying my bitter disappointment. I didn't have the heart to tell Rick how much I regretted our moonlight flit. The Vegas drive-thru experience had felt positively tawdry to an old-fashioned girl like me, and I had burned with envy at the sight of the unknown girl with the white ribbons in her hair. 'It doesn't matter about the wedding,' I said.

'Are you sure?' He pulled the cigar from his mouth and seemed anxious. 'Because I know what you women are like, and the last thing I need is for you to hold it against me for the rest of our lives.'

'I wish you had told me,' I said. 'Then maybe I wouldn't have felt like such a fool.'

'I was twenty-three.' Rick took my hand and looked me straight in the eye. 'I loved her, you know. Only I loved her a lot more than she loved me. Do you have any idea how crap that is? Looking over your shoulder and waiting for the day your wife decides she can do a whole lot better? Three months it lasted. Three agonizing months before she walked out without so much as a note left on the kitchen table. I was devastated.' He ground his cigar out in the bottom of the glass and let out a painful sigh. 'It took me years to accept she would have gone sooner or later anyway.'

'I'm sorry.' I hung my head in shame. 'I didn't realize.'

'Course you didn't. That's the kind of stuff that a person chooses to share when they're ready, or not, as the case may be. Still, I see you've beaten me to it. I'll burn it all when we get back, if that'll make you happy. I'd forgotten it was even there.' I slid down beneath the covers, pulling the sheet up to my chin, covering my disgrace. 'You know what, Hell? I've done some things in my life that I'm not proud of, but that's my business and I hope I've learned from my mistakes. If you want out, babe, you just say the word. But I'm in this for keeps, if you'll have me.' His hand squeezed mine. 'Let's not fuck it up, eh?'

'You're right.' I threw Leoni's instruction manual out of the window. God knows, she's hardly forged the kind of marriage anyone would want to duplicate. 'I'm sorry

I doubted you,' I said. 'No more secrets. I've seen what that did to Julia.'

'Julia.' Rick repeated her name softly. 'Oh, what a tangled web we weave.' He squeezed my hand. 'So from now on, we're gonna tell each other everything, right?'

'Right.'

'No matter what it is?'

'No matter what it is.'

Rick leaned back on the pillows and seemed pensive. 'That's the thing, you see,' he said cautiously. 'Because sometimes, babe, the truth is kinda hard for someone to hear. Especially if you love that person. Do you understand what I'm saying?' The tone of his voice had changed almost imperceptibly. A cold feeling crept up inside me.

'Rick?'

'Yeah, babe.' He set the glass down on the bedside table.

'Is there something that you want to tell me?'

'Not really.' He slipped his arm around me and pulled me close into his chest before switching his light off. 'But I think I probably should anyway.'

Chapter Twenty-one

DIVINE INTERVENTION

'RICHARD!' Mum answered the door in her best regatta dress, a navy blue imitation silk scarf tied jauntily around her throat. 'You're right on time! I've just taken one of your favourite cakes out of the oven and popped in a nice batch of scones! I thought you might like to try some of my home-made strawberry jam. I get a prize for it every year without fail at the horticultural show!'

'Joyce!' Rick showered her with kisses, then presented her with an ostentatiously huge bouquet of flowers.

'Oh!' she gushed, hoping to be overheard by Mrs Critchley next door but one, nosily snipping at her privet, peering through the gaps in the hedge. 'You really shouldn't have! Gosh!' Volume going up a little. 'Long-stemmed roses! There must be three dozen here!'

'Hi, Mum.' I waved over Rick's shoulder. She tore her eyes from the velvety blood-red blooms.

'Hello, dear!' Then her eyes landed on Julia, a sleeping Frankie slung quietly over her shoulder. 'Julia!' she almost shrieked, her face flushing. 'What are you doing here?' Rick quickly guided Mum inside.

'We thought you might like to show your grandson off to the neighbours,' he said cheerfully. 'Now, why don't you go and tell Frank I'm expecting a swift visit to his local hostelry. I could bloody murder a pint.'

'Fraa-aaaaaaaank!' Her voice tore through the cottage. Dad appeared. 'Oh no!' Mum pulled at him. 'You're not wearing that old jumper with the hole in the sleeve, are you? Go and get changed at once, dear.' Dad sighed at us and loped back upstairs.

MUM, JULIA AND I sat at the kitchen table, sipping tea from Mum's best Minton, passing occasional platitudes through the brittle atmosphere.

'I expect they'll be back in a few minutes.' Mum worried at the clock. 'Your father never goes to the pub for more than half an hour. Their beer really doesn't agree with him.'

'Is that what he says?'

'No, of course not! Men can't be expected to know what's good for them.'

'You should pop out with him for a sherry now and then.'

'Me? In a pub?' She perished the thought. 'No thank you. I prefer not to mix with the kind of people who have nothing better to do with their lives than spend money on beer and talk a lot of hot air all evening.'

Julia could stand it no longer.

'Aren't you going to say anything about what's happened?' Mum twitched uncomfortably in her chair. 'Because if you are, I'd rather you got it off your chest now.'

'It's your life, dear.' She fiddled uncomfortably with the cake doily. 'Your father has said that it's none of our business and that's that. Only – ' she toyed with her teacup – 'you'll forgive me if I don't mention it around the village.'

'Whatever you want, Mum,' Julia said.

'Mrs Cole's daughter got into trouble by her own brother-in-law then ran off with his best friend, so I suppose this is light by comparison, but still,' she sighed. 'One doesn't like other people knowing one's business. And we can hardly be compared to the Coles, can we? I mean, they've been showing themselves up for years. Bad apples, all of them.' She folded her hands in her lap. 'But I won't pretend that I'm not sad about your failed marriage.' She stressed the words *failed marriage* distastefully. 'It's not as though he was a bad husband.'

'I know,' Julia said. 'And I deeply regret having caused him such anguish. He didn't deserve it, but what's done is done.'

'Then we'll say no more about it,' Mum concluded. 'Least said, soonest mended.'

I watched Mum and Julia, feeling like an outsider, knowing what I now knew.

Two weeks ago, lying in the lumpy old bed at The Munsters, Rick and I chose to impart our deepest, darkest secrets, talking until the early dawn pressed its golden fingers through the chink in the moth-eaten curtains. Julia looked up and caught my eye, her weary smile showing a certain relief, a certain strength. I smiled back at her. The beautiful face I knew so well. The strong, straight nose. The thick mane of shining, dark hair. The naturally graceful repose. Only now it all made sense.

You see, Julia is not my sister. Not in the full sense of a true sibling made from the same pantry ingredients. No. Julia had been cooked up before my mother and father had shared so much as a kiss. And my father had offered to marry her, simply because he was that kind of man. The funny thing was that, as Rick had begun to tell me the big secret that my father had unburdened himself of that night in the Anglesey Arms after a skinful of beer, I felt as though a hundred missing pieces of my own personal jigsaw had suddenly dropped into place. The differences between us. The inadequacies I had felt as we grew into two disparate beings who shared little more than a bedroom and a handful of family expressions. I watched Julia get up from the table to attend to her infant son, the beginnings of his wakefulness rising from the bed we had made for him on the sofa in the sitting room. Inside, something detached, like a tiny thread giving and floating away. The sister I had loved all these years, looked up to and admired so blindly, was now revealed to me as the turning point of the two lives that were my parents. Dad had never said a word. Never shown a sliver of favouritism. Never let her down. And Julia had no idea.

'Let me.' Mum got up. 'We see little enough of you as it is.'

'Thanks.' Julia smiled at her gratefully. 'He'll want changing and feeding.'

'I know!' Mum raised her eyes to the ceiling. 'Goodness me! Once a mother, always a mother!' She averted her face, and reached a tissue from her sleeve.

'THE LEAVES ARE TURNING,' Rick noticed as we weaved our way along the scenic route home. Julia had decided to stay on with the parents for a couple of days, despite not having taken a thing with her. Mum had promptly gone off to find her a floor-to-ceiling Sergeant Major nightie to borrow and insisted that Julia should help herself to anything she wanted out of her wardrobe.

'It's my favourite time of year,' I said, relaxing into the passenger seat, gazing out of the car window at the passing scenery. 'Give it a few weeks and the trees will be just breathtaking. Gosh, I miss the countryside some- times. London's so stressful.' I sighed heavily. 'The thing is, we live there and we get used to it, and we forget that there are other ways to beat an existence, that there are places where people smile at each other and say good morning and know your name.'

'The East End used to be like that,' Rick said. 'You didn't dare get caught nicking coal or letting tyres down because every bugger knew who you were and where you lived.'

'Some days I feel like I can't breathe,' I said. 'And I open the window and I still can't breathe. I miss the trees, and the air, and the smell of wet hedgerows. All the things that remind me of my childhood. Don't you ever yearn for a bit of wide open space?'

'Dunno,' he said. 'I never lived more than a couple of feet away from a brick wall.'

'It's wonderful,' I said wistfully. 'You should try it some time.'

'Maybe we should do another weekend at The Munsters and find ourselves a decent conker tree. Not that I'd know what one looks like.'

'Big thing,' I said. 'Small green landmines hanging off the branches. There's a really good one outside the village post office, but you have to get in quick because all the kids strip it bare the minute the first one hits the ground in October. Soak them in vinegar overnight, stick them in the oven for a while and they turn into rocks. I was brilliant at conkers. '

'See?'

'What?'

'I've just learned something about you.'

He glanced at me with a tender smile, taking his eyes off the road for one, crucial moment.

'Look out!' I screamed.

Too late. As Rick hit the brake, the back end of the Bentley slid on a puddle of mud, flicking itself sideways, sending us hurtling towards the steep verge.

'Shit!' Rick shouted, grappling with the wheel while I covered my eyes and wished that I'd made peace with God and gone to confession once in a while. 'Hang on!' he yelled. The car continued its purchase, mounting a grassy bank and leaping head first into a ditch. Before I knew what was happening, Rick had abandoned the wheel, flinging his left arm into my chest to protect me from the imminent impact.

BANG!

Wooden post puncturing the radiator.

Steam hissing from the engine. Then a crude, juddering halt.

'Are you all right?' Rick grabbed hold of me.

'Urrgh.' I tried to steady my rattling brain. 'I think so.'

'Bollocks!' He undid his seatbelt and pushed his door open. 'I don't fucking believe it! Hang on there, babe. I'll come round and get you out.' The angle of the car meant Rick had to haul me unceremoniously out of the passenger side by my armpits, my feet pedalling air as he lifted me out of the ditch. He pulled his phone out of his pocket. 'It's all right.' He settled me on the damp verge. 'Don't panic. I'll call the AA.' He gave it a try, then frowned at the screen. 'Bloody brilliant. No signal.' He held his handset up as if trying to charm a signal from the trees. No luck. 'Wait here,' he said. 'I'll walk up the hill a bit.'

'No chance.' I pulled myself up. 'I'm not waiting here on my own for some mad axe murderer to stroll past and hack my head off. I'll come with you.'

We trudged along for ten minutes or more, Rick stopping sporadically to check his phone. 'What's the matter with people round here?' he grumbled at the handset. 'Doesn't anyone have a fucking phone that works?'

'Look.' I pointed through a small gap in the trees. 'There's a house down there. Maybe they'll have a phone we can use.'

We pressed on, taking a short cut through a thicket of brambles that clung to my skirt, leaving hundreds of snags in their wake. Rick held my hand tightly, clumsily stamping thistles out of the way and guiding me over the odd fallen branch.

'Shit . . .' He began wobbling, his foot well and truly stuck in a soggy patch. 'Hang on.' He gripped my hand harder. The mud made squelching, sucking sounds as he pulled hard, and his shoe came clean off. 'Whooooooaaa!' His free arm flailed over his head before his body wrenched itself backwards, taking me with him, and the pair of us fell into a vicious thatch of stinging nettles. 'Aaaarrrrrghh!' he yelled, swiping them out of his face. I tried to scrabble to my knees.

'Ow!' Sting sting, fizzle fizzle. 'Ow! Ow! Ow!'

'Fuck!' Rick yanked me out of the evil weeds, his sock covered in muck, and went to retrieve his shoe, bending down and tugging away, muttering under his breath. The shoe was stuck fast, so he employed that favourite male tactic and started shouting at it. 'Right! I've just about had enough of this!' Suddenly the shoe came free, sending him flying back into the mud, where he sat and swore at the top of his voice. 'And what are you laughing at?' I couldn't help it – the sight of him planted in the middle of a bog, his clothes ruined, his shoe now just a big claggy lump in his hand. 'Don't just stand there! Gimme a hand out of here!'

'Sorry.' I reached out.

'Gotcha!' He pulled hard, landing me right beside him, and slid a muddy hand around my waist. 'Give us a kiss, missus!'

'Get off!'

BY THE TIME we got to the front door, we looked like we'd spent the afternoon mud-wrestling. I don't think it would have mattered so much had it not been such a posh gaff. Georgian probably. Big, square, perfectly symmetrical windows, the whole thing painted dove grey and surrounded by formal gardens that had softly matured over the years and needed no more than a regular lick with a lawnmower. A red Virginia creeper clung to the stonework, its tendrils spreading unchecked, touching the windowpanes. Rick pulled on the old-fashioned doorbell and we heard a distant tinkling somewhere at the back of the house.

'How do we look?' I whispered, trying to smooth the worst of the damage out of my clothes.

'Fucking ace,' he said, the muddy shoe still dangling from his hand. There was no answer.

'Give it another try,' I told him. 'In a place like this it probably takes them ten minutes to get to the door.'

We hung around for all of that and more before realizing there might not be anyone at home. 'Let's go and have a shufti round the back,' Rick suggested. 'Maybe somebody's outside in the garden.'

'Good idea.'

But there was nobody there either. Rick pressed his face up against a couple of the windows, cupping his hands against the glass to cut out the reflection of the burnished evening sun slicing through the trees. 'Blimey,' he said. 'Come an' have a butchers at this, babe.' I had a quick check round to make sure no one could see us before joining him for a good old nose. Inside, it looked like one of those houses that hadn't been touched in years, stern portraits on the walls, neglected aspidistras cascading from elegant porcelain jardinières, huge pieces of furniture that nobody would know what to do with these days.

'I can't see any lights on,' I said. 'Looks like we've had our chips.'

Rick checked his phone again. 'Still no signal. What now?' I put my hands on my hips and looked around.

'The village, I guess. We're just about there anyway.'

'Right,' Rick said. 'Only this time we'll go down the drive and walk on the road like normal people, if that's OK with you.'

'Done,' I said, laughing. Looking down at his feet, Rick pulled his other shoe off and threw both of them in the bushes.

'Never liked them anyway.'

At the bottom of the tree-lined driveway, we found our path blocked by a pair of high, locked gates with a heavy chain wound around the innermost railings and secured with a big, rusted padlock. Rick gave them an impotent rattle.

'Bloody typical,' he said, his eyes following the boundary. 'Hang on a mo. There's a gap in the fence over there. Come on.' He grabbed my hand.

Easing ahead of him, I squeezed through without any trouble and held on to my hysteria as Rick puffed and griped, tearing his shirt as he squashed his way through, snapping a couple of planks and rendering the gap a whole lot bigger. Turning towards the village, we passed in front of the big gates again, this time road-side, and slowed simultaneously to stare up at the big red sign hammered to the wooden fence post.

FOR SALE BY AUCTION. SEPTEMBER 15TH

We stood there for a moment, just gawping at it. I turned to Rick, my mouth opening mutely. He let go of my hand, rummaged in his pockets, found a dented cigar and stuck it in his mouth. 'Well, well.' He rocked on his heels. 'Waddya know?' He produced a match and struck it between finger and thumb, held it against his Cohiba and drew the yellow flame into the cigar, puffing along casually. The rich smoke mingled with the sweet perfume of the wet hedgerows, and somehow, it smelled just right.

Chapter Twenty-two

TWO MONTHS LATER

'LADIES AND GENNELMEN!' The red-coated master of ceremonies tapped his rod on the temporary floor. 'Pray be upstanding for the father of the bride!'

Every table in the marquee stood rowdily to attention, a loud cheer rising from the feasted rabble. Dad, instantly embarrassed by the applause, placated the crowd with a humble nod and motioned everyone to sit down. Reaching into his pocket, he drew out the speech he had been fretting over since Rick and I had announced our intention to effect a Crimewatch re-enactment of the wedding that everyone had missed in May. Sure, the old man had prepared a speech for the first, bungled, attempt, but it had somehow got lost in

347

the afternoon's affray and, being a man, he hadn't made a copy and couldn't remember what he'd said anyway. So here we were again. Only this time, as Rick had insisted to Mum's screeching delight, we were going to do it properly. A church filled with scented freesias and stargazer lilies. A vicar who suspected he'd never see us in there again once the ceremony was over unless somebody died. A half-blind octogenarian organist who hadn't been able to get her arthritic fingers round the *Wedding March* for about fifteen years. An enormous marquee set with twenty-two tables, a big dance floor in the middle and a wobbly stage hidden behind a spangly curtain for a mediocre but enthusiastic band to belt out the usual post-wedding repertoire for a spot of drunken floor-staggering afterwards.

The whole caboodle had arrived last Tuesday in two heaving great pantechnicons, and it had taken the best part of a week to put everything together with Angela firmly at the helm, shotgun in hand, barking orders at the events staff while Rick and I remained at a safe distance. Despite her ferocious manner, I could see why Rick had held on to her for all these years, and she came to view our renewal-of-vows-cum-blessing ceremony as her swansong, having gracefully accepted Rick's generous severance package in view of his impending retirement. Angela had been permanently red-eyed ever since the news broke and made no attempt to mask her firm opinion that I was to blame for the leopard's sudden change of spots. Still, office politics aside, I had my hands full anyway. One of the lorries had nicked the corner of the village churchyard wall and knocked a couple of stones out, and the last thing we wanted was to be lynched by an angry mob from the parish council before we'd even set foot in the place.

Once the hammer came down, Rick and I had found ourselves the proud owners of Hanwick Grange, lock, stock and two smoking squirrels, complete with leaking roof, condemned plumbing and crumbling plasterwork in half of the dozen bedrooms. The lady who had lived there in her dotage had eventually confined herself to one dusty corner of the draughty old house, leaving the rest to fend for itself until the next generation came along and breathed new life into the place. And those people just happened to be us, caked in mud, pressing our noses up against the windows one soggy afternoon as the leaves were starting to turn.

Dad fumbled the sheet of paper open, smoothed out the wrinkles and tried to pull it into focus. Rick sat back in his chair and fired up a cigar, sending a great cloud of smoke curling around Mum's pantomime hat while she tried not to gag. He reached out and took my hand.

'This is gonna be good,' he winked.

'Ahem.' Dad cleared his throat and took a sip of water as though it might somehow help him navigate his way round the three large gin and tonics he had

had before the church service, the champagne he'd quaffed afterwards, and the four different wines that had done the rounds of the tables while we all ate ourselves into a celebratory stupor. He squinted at the page, trying to make sense of his unintelligible scrawl while loaded whispers passed from table to table, then gave up. Casting the sheet aside, Dad engaged his audience with the proud and slightly ruddy smile of any man marrying off his daughter that day.

'The best thing about being Helen's father,' he began, 'is that I get to go to all her weddings!' Mum spluttered on her wine and stared up at him in wide-eyed disbelief. 'Although, thankfully, this one isn't costing me anything, which is just as well because my wife spent every last penny we have on that ridiculous hat.' Oh God. He's going off-piste. 'Now, I suppose I ought to say something nice about my new son-in-law, especially seeing as we've gone and lost the other one due to circumstances beyond our control.' A smattering of tense tittering crackled through the marquee. 'But the only time I ever spent more than a couple of hours in Rick's company, we got so blind drunk that I can't say I remember anything about it.'

'Frank!' Mum hissed.

'Not now, dear,' Dad slurred at her. 'I'm trying to make a sshpeech.'

Dad picked up his water glass and waved it around, spilling most of it. 'Still, he seems sound enough to me from the little I know of him.' He paused to stifle a rogue belch. 'Anyone who's got the courage to wade through a slice of Joyce's cake without calling for an emergency dentist can't be all bad.' His eyes wandered to the towering six-tier wedding confection perched precariously on a fancy stand a few feet away. 'Don't worry,' a small hiccup escaped from him. 'That one's edible.'

Mum sat rigid, face set with a rictus smile, pretending to join in with the delighted amusement of the dismayed congregation.

'So, marriage, eh?' Dad placed an unsteady hand on Mum's shoulder. 'What can I say about that? It's not easy, is it, dear?' Mum peeled his hand off. 'See what I mean?' He shot a brief, knowing glance at Rick. 'So my advice to you would be – ' he tried to concentrate on his hand, counting off his fingers – 'don't enter into any conversation that you don't fully understand. Stick to yes and no answers whenever you're asked a direct question. Accept that whenever something goes wrong it will be all your fault, and don't, whatever you do, leave the lid up on the khazi.'

Dad pulled at his tie, allowing himself a brief interlude.

'The rest you'll have to make up as you go along.' I noticed Mum drain her wine glass and reach for Rick's. 'Given all of the above, I think these two will be just fine.' A small murmur of approval rippled around. 'We already know that Rick makes our Helen very happy.' Rick squeezed my hand. 'And when my wife throws me out tomorrow for getting catastrophically drunk at my daughter's wedding, I know that he'll offer me a comfortable bed for as long as I want it, and that he won't fob me off with the cheap whisky either.'

Dad turned to Rick and me.

'Remember the words you said to each other today,' he said soberly. 'Love and cherish each other, and you won't go too far wrong. Now.' He faced the room. 'Without further ado, I give you . . . the happy couple!'

Everyone stood and chorused the toast, lifting their glasses, breaking into appreciative applause. The master of ceremonies raised a white glove for silence and banged his rod.

'Ladies and gennelmen! Pray silence for the best man!'

A roar of approval went up as the steaming Marcus stood unsteadily in front of the firing squad, smoothing his thinning hair, limbering his shoulders in preparation for his big moment.

'Thank you! Thank you!' Marcus lapped it up. 'No! Please! You're too kind!'

'Oh, just get on with it, you fat git!' Leoni shouted.

'My wife, everybody.' Marcus bowed graciously towards her. 'Do not put water on her or feed her after midnight.'

He took a few prompt-cards from his pocket and

began to shuffle through them, waiting for the throng to quieten.

'Normally, at this stage in the proceedings, the best man would be expected to roll out the obligatory couple of embarrassing stories about the groom, then round off with the usual guff about how he's found the right girl at long last.' Cue the usual bawdy laughter and good-humoured badgering from the crowd. 'Well, in view of the fact that they've already been married for six months, I thought it might do more harm than good to mention Rick's criminal record or the half-dozen prostitutes he hired for the stag do.' Guffaw, guffaw. My mother blanching into her handbag. 'As you probably know, the traditional role of the best man is to marry the bride should the groom decide to do a runner before the ceremony, as I should have done.' A bread roll hit him square in the face. He didn't bat an eyelid. 'Clearly, that was never going to happen today.'

'Boring!' Leoni heckled. 'Get off, you tosser!' Julia silenced her with a hand clamped strategically over the mouth.

'Although I did offer Rick a loaded pistol should he change his mind and need to restore me to bachelor status in order to do the honours. And if the bullets didn't work, I suggested he bludgeon my wife to death with the handle.' Rick let go of my hand and slipped away from the table. Honestly, why couldn't he have gone before the speeches started? Men and their bladders, eh? 'But no such luck, I'm afraid. Not that anyone in their right mind would have had second thoughts about marrying a girl like Helen. She's one in a million. And so is Rick.' A soft relay of *hear, hears* passed around the room. 'So all that's left for me to do is to ask you all to raise your glasses and join me in wishing Mr and Mrs Richard Wilton . . . eternal happiness.' Chairs scraped. Bodies rose. Glasses were waved. *Eternal happiness!* To be honest, I felt a bit daft, really, sitting there on my own, accepting their good wishes while everyone pretended it was perfectly normal for the groom to have disappeared from the top table at such a crucial moment.

'And now!' the MC shouted across the room, his once cool demeanour suddenly bordering on the hysterical, strangling his voice into that of a world-champion darts compère. 'It is my great pleasure to ask you all to show your unbridled appreciation for the groom.' The lights went down and a frisson of anticipation passed from table to table. Rick's seat was still conspicuously empty. 'Mistaaaaaaaaah . . . Richaaaaard . . . WIIIIIIIIIL-TON!!!'

Like a deafening clap of overhead thunder, a band exploded into action, belting out a straight-up twelve-bar blues, every rocking chord tight as a nut, the blaring volume flapping the sides of the marquee. Before anyone could get a handle on what the hell was going on, the stage curtain dropped dramatically from its fixture, and a bright spotlight hit the back of a spangled white Elvis suit.

'Oh my GOD!' My hand flew to my mouth.

The crowd went nuts, scrambling to its feet, screeching and whooping as Rick freed his rhinestoned cape and threw it into the braying audience before blowing me an ostentatious rock-god kiss. 'Thankyaverymush!' He curled his lip and taunted his screaming fans with a couple of pelvic thrusts while the band picked up the pulsating rhythm and worked the drunken rabble into a frenzied, gyrating mass. Marcus quite took leave of his senses, charged at the dance floor and threw himself into a skidding knee slide, ripping his trousers clean in half, instant Bermuda shorts.

'How ya doin' out there, people?' Rick gave it his best Gracelands accent. An ear-splitting cheer of approval went up. 'This one's for ma liddle lady, over there in the white dress with my ring on her finger.' A sea of smiling faces turned to me. I caught sight of Paul a couple of tables away, fists clutched to his burning cheeks, screaming along with the rest of the girls. Leoni was bent double, fingers in her mouth, whistling loud enough to shatter the rhinestones on Rick's spectacular costume. Dad grabbed hold of Mum, pulled her hands from her ringing ears and forced her into a half-forgotten jitterbug, pushing her towards the dance floor. Sally followed suit, wrenching Julia from her seat, spinning her into the seething mass now surging towards the throbbing stage.

Rick grasped the microphone stand, pulled it close to his quivering lips, and launched into a full-throttle rendition, demanding to be my teddy bear. And then I was on my feet, being pulled along, helped up onto the stage by the unlikeliest man in the world as he sang his heart out, brought the house down, then swept me into his arms.

'Hold it!' yelled the photographer.

Flash!

extracts reading groups
competitions books new
discounts extracts
competitions
books
new
events books
extracts
books
new reading groups
interviews
events extracts
discounts
new books events
events new
discounts extracts discounts
www.panmacmillan.com
extracts events reading groups
competitions books extracts new